RAT POISON

RAT POISON

Margaret Duffy

MYSTERY

This first world edition published 2011
in Great Britain and in the USA by
SEVERN HOUSE PUBLISHERS LTD of
9–15 High Street, Sutton, Surrey, England, SM1 1DF.
Trade paperback edition first published
in Great Britain and the USA 2012 by
SEVERN HOUSE PUBLISHERS LTD.

British Library Cataloguing in Publication Data

Duffy, Margaret.
  Rat poison. – (A Patrick Gillard and Ingrid Langley
  mystery)
  1. Gillard, Patrick (Fictitious character) – Fiction.
  2. Langley, Ingrid (Fictitious character) – Fiction.
  3. Gangs – England – Bath – Fiction. 4. Detective and
  mystery stories.
  I. Title II. Series
  823.9'14-dc22

ISBN-13: 978-0-7278-8098-7 (cased)
ISBN-13: 978-1-84751-393-9 (trade paper)

All Severn House titles are printed on acid-free paper.

Severn House Publishers support The Forest Stewardship Council [FSC],
the leading international forest certification organisation. All our titles that
are printed on Greenpeace-approved FSC-certified paper carry the FSC logo.

MIX
Paper from
responsible sources
FSC® C018575

Typeset by Palimpsest Book Production Ltd.,
Falkirk, Stirlingshire, Scotland.
Printed and bound in Great Britain by
MPG Books Ltd., Bodmin, Cornwall.

PROLOGUE

*'Gee, it's amazing when you think this place used to be a
swamp.'*

American tourist overheard in Bath

The man stood quite still in the deep shadow cast by a
bridge that spanned a narrow city lane. Strictly speaking
it was not a proper bridge at all but an old house, part
of which constituted an archway and was situated close to a
crossroads. There were a couple of windows on each side of
it. Not a daydreaming sort of person by any means, the watcher
sometimes thought it would be pleasant to live in such a quaint
abode and could imagine the sloping floors, narrow twisting
staircases and low ceilings within.

Motionless then and actually standing partly within a recessed
doorway, he watched the lane as he had the previous two nights.
There were only a couple of street lights of the 'heritage' variety
and the illumination they provided was quite poor. He had an
idea there was a lamp directly beneath the arch itself but if there
was it was not working. This suited him as here he was invisible.
A church clock struck ten and as it did so a young couple came
around from the road off to the right and walked right past him
without detecting his presence.

The lane was a quiet shortcut away from the traffic in the adjacent main road for residents and visitors alike: theatre- or concert-
goers heading home, to wine bars and restaurants or back to hotels.
One of the terraced buildings in this lane housed a restaurant but
it was closed for refurbishment, which meant that the property was
all in darkness too. This unusual gloom might have been the reason
for the fact that, lately, the area had been the site of several late-
night muggings, and during one such attack five days previously
an American visitor had been stabbed and received serious injuries
after refusing to hand over his gold Rolex watch and wallet.

He was not aware of it but the watcher's mouth twisted wryly as he recollected how a senior police officer based at Avon and Somerset Police HQ in Bristol had appeared on the television news to say that those responsible were reckoned to be local thugs, drug addicts desperate for a fix or low life of that ilk and not part of a large and organized gang being closely monitored that was thought to be moving in from outside the district, probably from London.

The man watching muttered a few choice epithets directed at police personnel in general who sit at desks all day long and shoot their mouths off to tell criminals all they know, admittedly not much, about their underlings' investigations. Again, he carefully surveyed his surroundings, fingering the silver-hafted Italian throwing knife in the pocket of his black leather jacket. More people would be along soon. This was a very good spot to wait for rich pickings and he was surprised that he was alone, or at least, as good as. Not that this was the only place where people had been robbed: another favourite was Riverside Walk. He would head in that direction if there was nothing doing here.

More footsteps approached and a group of three people appeared: a couple and another woman, all of retirement age. The man did not have to be able to see them clearly to know this, building up his picture from the way they were walking and the fact that they were all a little out of breath as it was gently uphill from the theatre. He could have reached out and touched them if he had wanted to. No, not muggers' material – not wealthy enough. The trio went on their way, starting up some kind of minor argument – he could hear their raised voices – before turning right at the end towards the main road.

And now he was no longer alone in the sense that really interested him, two figures moving from the far end of the little street silhouetted briefly against brighter light: bulky, tall outlines, furtive. They merged into deep shadow in a doorway about a third of the way down and stayed there. Then different voices became audible from the opposite direction, speaking loudly with what seemed to be Australian accents.

Prey.

Two men, noisy, slightly drunk, yarning about their schooldays, rolled around the corner by the arch. They went by the watcher in his doorway, oblivious to him, equally oblivious when he followed, catlike, in their wake, keeping in the shadow by the walls of the houses. He stopped when they paused to light cigarettes and waited while they carried on talking, standing in the middle of the road. People are likely to do that in Trim Street as not much traffic risks its wing mirrors in these confines.

They moved off again and the man behind them held his breath for a moment. Then it happened, the two in the doorway springing out as their targets went by. There was a shout of alarm and the glint of steel.

The watcher arrived silently, shoulder-charged the man with the knife who caught his heel on the uneven road surface and went over backwards, then gave the other a resounding clout around the head that floored him, retching. He dragged them by the backs of their sweatshirts until they were neatly side by side on the stone setts and then bent down to speak softly.

'You're both under arrest.'

As he had scooped up the knife from the road that one of them had dropped they did not argue.

In the shadow of an opening that led to the rear of properties on the other side of the archway another figure moved slightly to double-check that he was not being observed and then slipped away, moving as silently as had the other man, and then ran, the blood pounding in his ears, spurred on by a far from name-less dread.

ONE

A couple of weeks after this somewhat unorthodox assistance from the Serious Organized Crime Agency to Bath CID, which I have reconstructed from what Patrick, my husband, told me, gang warfare erupted in this fragrant World Heritage designated city. Predictably, it caused uproar, not least because most of the city centre remained cordoned off getting on for twenty-four hours later. Shops remained closed, traffic was gridlocked, cars abandoned.

The gun battle had started at a little after midnight somewhere near the top of Milsom Street, progressed downhill into Union Street and into Abbey Churchyard. There, two men were cornered having, it was discovered later, run out of ammunition, and killed. Not just shot, but as a presumably hardened paramedic was heard to comment, 'butchered'. With knives. Horribly mutilated. Those victorious then went on a further killing spree in the vicinity of Stall Street and Southgate, chasing and firing at anyone whom they glimpsed as they ran to where the drivers of at least two stolen cars waited for them, having ghosted through a pedestrian precinct in order to stay in contact.

'This was gang warfare,' reported Detective Chief Inspector James Carrick to a voracious media, the information necessary as there had been wild rumours that soldiers at a nearby training camp had got drunk, raided a weapons' store and gone berserk. 'No, we don't know who the gunmen were yet and I'm liaising with my colleagues in Bristol because that's where we think some of them originated. The identities of the three innocent passers-by who were gunned down afterwards, two of whom were fatally injured, will be released when their next of kin have been informed.'

I switched off the TV. I already knew that part of what he had said was not quite true as Carrick had a very good idea who at least three of the dead gunmen out of the nine people killed in total had been and, unlike at least one of his superiors, did not believe in broadcasting police intelligence to the entire country, if not the world. Another two were known to have been wounded in the Stall Street area – a man sleeping rough in a shop doorway had witnessed some of what had occurred and wisely kept his head down – but the only traces of them were bloodstains on the pavement. Enquiries at hospitals had not resulted in anyone being traced who had been admitted with gunshot wounds, so whether these men had been rescued by their accomplices to be treated privately or carted off by the opposition to be held to ransom or killed at leisure was anybody's guess.

I had more than a passing interest in all this. I am an author for most of the time writing under my maiden name Ingrid Langley, and my job description in our contract with SOCA is 'consultant' to Patrick who operates under the title of 'adviser'. The quotation marks are necessary as he goes to work armed with a Glock 17 carried in a shoulder harness. This is not just in connection with his present job: Lieutenant Colonel Gillard and his wife are still on the hit lists of several terrorist organizations after his time in army special services and D12, a department of MI5.

DCI Carrick, a friend of ours, had been grateful for the help supplied by a, let's face it, bored exponent in the art of being invisible who was yearning for a little action, in nabbing the two muggers. As far as any insight into organized crime was concerned it had been a failure, the senior man at HQ having been quite correct with regard to this pair as they had turned out to be local youths seeking to fund their cider-soaked lifestyle. Word had got about though and this, together with increased police patrols, had resulted in cases of muggings ceasing. For the present.

And now a crime war had been fought in the city.

With a distinct feeling of unease about this I tried to concentrate on proofreading. The house was quiet, the children but for Vicky and baby Mark, who were in the care of Carrie, our nanny, at school. When Patrick's brother, Larry, was killed we adopted his two children, Matthew, who is now thirteen, and Katie, eleven. Their mother is still alive but in and out of treatment for alcoholism and wants nothing more to do with them.

We already had two children of our own, Justin, now going on seven and Vicky, nearly three, and since then Mark has been born, a respectable tally for a man who was told after serious injuries when he was in special operations that it would be unlikely he could father children.

We moved from Dartmoor and bought this old rectory at Hinton Littlemoor in Somerset when the diocese was about to sell it off and rehouse his parents, John and Elspeth – John is the incumbent of St Michael's Church – in a cheap and nasty little bungalow at the bottom of the village where the railway station and a couple of sidings used to be. After much work was done to the rectory they now live in a new annex, welcome to join us at any time. It is a perfect arrangement and John has recently, and most generously, given me his study in the main house, which I previously had regarded as sacrosanct, as a writing room.

There was a tap at the door and Patrick put his head around it. He was having a few days' leave.

'Husbands and paramours don't have to knock,' I told him.

He came right in, grinning. 'Well, it's true that you haven't yet actually thrown anything at me when I interrupt you . . . Seriously, I came to tell you that I rang Greenway and he doesn't want us to get involved in the turf war. He's got something else he wants me to do next week.'

Commander Michael Greenway, who came to SOCA from the Metropolitan Police, is Patrick's boss.

'Fair enough. I'm sure James and his team can handle it.'

'We *are* right on the doorstep,' Patrick said.

'Yes, but surely SOCA can't just barge in. Oh, by the way, Matthew's going to ask you to teach him some self-defence moves.'

'It would be better if he went to judo classes.'

'I think he wants to do that too. But James has let it slip that you're pretty good at defending yourself.'

'He's not old enough or strong enough for me to teach him the kind of things I know. The first lesson people have to learn is self-control. That takes maturity – when he's at least eighteen. Why, though? Is he being bullied at school?'

'I asked him that and he said no. It's just that he admires

you hugely and yearns to be just a little bit more like you. Surely you could teach him a few basic moves in case someone tries to mug him.'

'OK, I'll give it some thought.'

He went over to stand by the window for a moment and then turned. There were grass cuttings on his clothes and in his hair which, wavy, black and greying, was, as usual, needing a trim. I never nag about this; I love the way it curls down on to his neck. I love everything about him: his slim grace, the wiriness of his body, the grey mesmeric eyes . . .

'You're looking at me in a funny way,' he said, his mouth twitching with amusement.

'I fancy you, that's all.'

Not being remotely slow in such matters he had, of course, been fully aware of this.

I was just beginning to wonder about the possibilities of locking the door and closing the curtains when my mobile rang.

'We were talking about you not two minutes ago,' I said on hearing a familiar Scottish voice.

'There's an interesting development with my latest case that you might be able to help me with,' James Carrick said. 'I did try to ring Patrick but just got the messaging service.'

'He's been mowing the lawn so wouldn't have heard it,' I said. 'D'you want to come over this evening?'

'Shall I meet you in the Ring o' Bells at eight? I could do with a dram.'

'One good thing,' Carrick began by saying, 'is that you get a hell of a lot of resources thrown at crimes like this that up until now you'd been led to believe didn't exist.'

Patrick placed a tot of the DCI's favourite single malt before him. 'Have you eaten?'

Carrick shook his head. 'No. Joanna's gone to a show and is staying with a friend tonight. I'll fix myself something when I get home.'

'Steak and chips?'

'Look, you mustn't bother to—'

'Man, you look done in.'

'OK. Thanks. But I'll pay.'

'You won't.'

We did not want to badger him with questions until he had refuelled but he told us while he waited for his meal that the identity of one of the dead and presumed innocent pedestrians was proving to be interesting – to the investigating officer, that is.

'He's got form,' Carrick explained. 'GBH, handling stolen goods and fraud in connection with claiming unemployment benefit when he had a job with a false identity. He's from round here, Hinton Littlemoor. I was wondering if you or the rector and his wife knew anything about him – although I realize, Patrick, that your father has to be discreet.'

We were seated in a quiet corner of the village pub so there was no risk of being overheard if we kept our voices down.

'And this man's name?' Patrick asked.

'Adam Trelonic – although, as I said, he's used another.'

'He sells, or should I say sold, logs,' I said. 'Drove a red pick-up. I think we've bought wood from him. I have an idea his wife works as a home help.'

'She does,' Carrick confirmed. 'And quite often behind the bar at this pub, especially when the regular staff are off sick or on holiday. They live at a one-time miner's cottage up the hill at the far end of the village. I really need to know whether he was part of one of these criminal set-ups. His wife's very insistent that he wasn't – apparently she flew right off the handle when the subject was broached but doesn't seem too bothered that he's dead – and is saying she hasn't a clue why he was in the city last night. D'you know anything else about these people?'

We did not.

'Was he armed when found?' Patrick wanted to know.

'No, but if he had been someone might have taken a weapon off him.'

'Where was his body discovered?'

'In the bus station. Which, as you know, is just around the corner from where the final part of the action seems to have taken place.'

'Perhaps he wasn't involved with the shootings and was heading for the last bus – that's at around eleven thirty – missed it and thus got himself killed.'

'It's a possibility,' Carrick said. 'The wounded passer-by, a woman who works in a restaurant and was on her way home, was found near there, in Southgate, and had been going in the direction of the subway under the railway line. She lives in Wells Road and was walking home. She's under guard in hospital and is not seriously hurt so I shall talk to her as soon as the medics say I can. That means we have two potential witnesses when I can find the homeless man who spoke to the crew of the area car who arrived first on the scene.'

'And the other innocent person killed?' I prompted.

'A stage hand at the theatre. He lived in a flat over a shop at Bog Island.'

This is a sort of roundabout that used to have a public convenience in the middle of it not far from the Orange Grove.

Carrick added, a hard edge to his voice, 'His body had been thrown into a skip outside a hotel that's being renovated, again close to the railway station.'

'So you have three deceased known local-ish hoodlums, plus two missing wounded and two who so far have not been identified,' Patrick said.

'That's right. And by local, we mean Bristol. Then there's the additional two found in Abbey Churchyard who are unknown to us at present. That might be because they've never been in trouble before.'

'No means of identification on the bodies?'

'Not on those two. They were the ones who had been mutilated.'

'Are you thinking then they were probably members of the gang trying to move into the area?'

'Yes, I am. And also that the Bristol lot are planning to extend their manor to Bath too. Hence the war. There have been rumours going around for a while along the lines of a London mob joining forces with a Bath outfit to see off a Bristol gang. Nothing concrete, but now it's happened.'

'Would you like me to run the physical details of these unknown bods through SOCA's database?' Patrick offered.

'No, it's OK. I'm sure I can get all the info I need.'

When the DCI had eaten we invited him home.

'Lovely to see you, James,' exclaimed Elspeth, Patrick's

mother. I think she is very much taken with his blond hair and blue eyes. 'Are you staying for coffee or is Patrick planning to cart you off and ply you with whisky?'

He shook his head. 'Thank you, Mrs Gillard but no, I dare not drink alcohol as I have to keep my head on my shoulders for tomorrow. Coffee would be most welcome, though.'

'Is it local intelligence you might be after?' John queried when we had all settled in the main living room of the rectory to give everyone more room.

'You might be able to help me in connection with one of the deaths last night, sir.'

'Adam Trelonic?'

The DCI's eyebrows rose.

'The village grapevine's hot with it,' John said. 'But my assistance has to be limited as I didn't know the man personally – he never came to church.'

'Does his wife?'

'Yes, sometimes.'

'What does the grapevine have to say about him?'

The rector hesitated, then said, 'I gather that he was a bad sort and tried to make up for his lack of wits by being a foul-mouthed bully. This is information given to me by people I know and respect, not gossip.'

'The sort of man then who might have been involved in serious organized crime?'

'Possibly, but I should imagine only as some kind of paid bruiser. But as I said, I hardly knew the man. I have an idea we bought logs off him a few times. He'd do that during the winter months and odd jobs for people during the rest of the year.'

Elspeth said, 'It's been rumoured that he did work for people, eyed up their houses and sold any interesting information to cronies who were in the burglary business, especially if the householders were old, frail and had some nice antiques.'

'That *is* gossip,' her husband remonstrated.

'But a couple of houses where he'd worked *were* broken into,' she insisted.

'There's no proof he was connected with it though, my dear.'

'It's nevertheless a good idea for me to keep it in mind,' Carrick observed.

'His wife's a lot younger than him.' Elspeth went on stubbornly. 'One of those women who set my teeth on edge.'

'Why's that?' Carrick asked.

But she shook her head, refusing to be drawn.

I knew that Patrick was desperate to get involved with the case but authority in the shape of Commander Greenway decreed otherwise and the one-time member of MI5 dutifully caught an early train for London on Monday morning. What he might do on his weekends off if Carrick needed help – and that proud Scot would need to be even more desperate before he would ask, a little night-time undercover assistance notwithstanding – was another matter. I decided to concentrate on family matters and finishing the proofreading.

I have often wondered if other writers feel as I do: a kind of loss when they have completed a novel and then drift in a state of limbo even when involved with the editorial aftermath. There is a large full stop at the end of the previous work and any future story merely a few vague ideas floating around in the imagination. What if . . . *nothing happens*? No ideas. No story. No bloody nothing.

Horrors.

It is hard work with such a large family to keep closely in touch with them all even though I'm only involved part-time with SOCA and usually at home, writing, for weeks on end. Carrie is only directly responsible for the three youngest children so I have to ensure that Matthew and Katie are well looked after and do not feel out of things and here, of course, their grandparents are invaluable.

'Those two seem to spend a lot of time rummaging around the district and don't seem prepared to tell you what they're up to,' Elspeth said that same Monday morning when they had left to catch the school bus. 'I get a bit worried when children become secretive.'

'They have a mystery-solving enterprise,' I told her. 'Perhaps it's in connection with that.'

A successful one too. Not all that long ago they traced a fly-tipper by carefully going through rubbish dumped in a lane and found the same name and address, someone local, on several old letters and junk mail. This resulted in their uncle taking it all back and leaving it on the culprit's doorstep with a terse note, adding some other stuff, tyres and bits of carpet, he had found in the vicinity for good measure. At around the same time they had taken the registration of a car and noted the description of the driver who had parked at the top of the village on several occasions and appeared to be undertaking covert surveillance. This had had a direct bearing on something we had been working on for SOCA at the time. There were other 'cases', I gathered, in the pipeline.

'You might need to have a word with them,' Elspeth persevered. 'They could be up to something that'll get them into trouble.'

'You're really concerned then.'

'Yes, I am.'

I knew Elspeth also disapproved of the time Matthew spent with his beloved computer, thinking he ought to be out in the fresh air more, and was inclined to agree with her. But this time I thought she was worrying about nothing.

TWO

I f DS Lynn Outhwaite, Carrick's assistant, had not shortly
afterwards been taken out to dinner to the most highly
regarded restaurant in Bath by her boyfriend as a surprise
birthday treat, then SOCA might never have become involved
in the investigation, or at least, not until things had become
very much worse. As it was she recognized another diner,
somehow restrained her burning desire to arrest him on the spot
and, when she and her boyfriend were leaving, the other party
having already departed, produced her warrant card and
demanded to know if there were any contact phone numbers.
She was given two.

'You even carry your warrant card in your evening bag?'
asked her boss the next morning, in receipt of the
information.

'Yes, I do,' Lynn, petite, dark-haired and clever, replied.

'And if I say something like "Attagirl!" right now I suppose
I'll be branded non-politically correct and sexist.'

'No, not at all, sir. As long as it's OK for me to say,
"Attabloke!" when you do something that shows initiative.'

'She's a real star,' Carrick said fervently, relaying this conversation to us a few days later, a Saturday morning, when we met
in the street in Bath. 'And she saw – if she's right, and why
shouldn't she be? – one of the most serious organized criminals
in Britain, the man the London criminal underworld refers to
with the blackest of humour as "Uncle".'

'I know *of* him,' Patrick mused. 'They're right, he's far from
avuncular, more the murdering bastard.'

I said, 'So was this just a weekend trip for him or is he
controlling the gang trying to move into the area?'

'You can be sure that it's my first priority to find that out,'
Carrick answered. 'Lynn did absolutely the right thing in not
trying to arrest him or call for assistance. He was with several
other people who will now be of extreme interest to me as well.'

'Did she recognize any of them too?'

'Yes, there was a local bad boy by the name of Charlie Gill; at least, that's one of the identities he's been known to use. Another was a Cardiff-based mobster who once killed a girl-friend he thought was cheating on him by mowing her down with his car, and there was a woman whose name escapes me for the moment who has more convictions for soliciting and being drunk and disorderly than you'd believe possible. She was with a man with red hair who I don't recognize from Lynn's description. The other member of the party was the woman with Uncle and until I find out who she is I'm going to refer to her as Auntie.'

'What about the contact phone numbers?' Patrick enquired.

'Phoney. Lynn's furious, saying she wished she'd grabbed him, until I told her that she would probably be on a mortuary table right now if she'd tried.'

'So you're working weekends because of all this?' Patrick enquired casually.

'At the moment,' the DCI replied shortly, adding: 'It's not the only case ongoing. You're obviously not.'

'No, it doesn't happen very often. I'm probably going to be sent up to Manchester next week. Someone we investigated at MI5 has retired from trying to blackmail MPs and gone into extortion and money laundering for drug dealers instead.'

'And Greenway's hoping that when he catches sight of you again he'll head straight back to the hills?' Carrick said with a big smile.

'No, when we locate him this time we're going to heave him straight back in the slammer.'

Meanwhile, SOCA, in receipt of an official request from someone at Avon and Somerset Police HQ, a new man who Carrick had never heard of, sent me to liaise between the Met and his team on what had become known, hardly surprisingly, as the Bath Turf War Case.

This had not happened before as, officially, Patrick and I work together. But the job up north was mostly routine and involved, initially, his investigating the present whereabouts of known contacts of the person in question that MI5 still had on file.

Gaining access to this information was not difficult as Patrick's old boss at D12, Richard Daws, was now inhabiting the rarefied air at the summit of SOCA, and it was for this reason and the former's familiarity with the past cases that he was being sent to Manchester. It was not thought that he would be there for very long.

Patrick, on hearing of my new assignment, was not happy for at least two reasons.

'Look, I shall just be on the end of phones and computers collating information,' I told him, endeavouring to deal with one of his reservations. '*Not* packing hardware at stake-outs and other wildly exciting things that cops love doing. Besides which, it'll mean I can keep my finger on the pulse of events at home.'

Grimly, as he does not like it if we are on duty apart either, my husband left even earlier than normal on Monday morning, taking the car as I did not really need it in the short term. He had made me promise that I would contact him, *immediately,* if I became embroiled in anything with which I could not cope. Slightly shaken by his apparent conviction that this would happen, I took the short-barrelled Smith and Wesson that he had never returned to MI5 from the wall safe pronto, loaded it and put it in my handbag. Most of my bags, even the Gucci one, smell of gun oil.

I settled into a routine of spending the mornings at Bath's Manvers Street police station where I was given a cubbyhole with a desk in it just off the general office. A DI Black from Bristol came and went and I liaised with him as he knew about the Bristol-based mobsters. Together with Black, Carrick invited me to attend all briefings, whether they were pertinent to the case I was working on or not, which was kind of him although I had an idea he secretly hoped I would come up with a Big Idea breakthrough. Sadly, this did not happen.

As Carrick had said, most available resources were being allocated to the shootings. As was normal in such serious cases one wall of the general office, deliberately kept bare for this specific purpose, was host to maps, diagrams, information that had been gleaned, including photographs, where available, of the dead – those known to have taken part in the 'war' and their victims. Where these people had fallen was marked on a large and detailed map of the city centre. Also, arrows marked the assumed, assisted by the homeless man's brief account, movement through the streets of the skirmish and the murders which followed afterwards. This man had so far not been traced.

A week went by during which slow progress, mostly of the eliminating from enquiries variety, was made. Then the woman in hospital had a setback to her recovery and had to undergo more surgery which meant that she could still not be interviewed. I knew that Carrick was extremely frustrated by this as he had been hoping she would be able to give him valuable information.

Regular communications with Manchester had been established. Patrick seemed to have got his teeth into what he was working on, fuelled, I was sure, by his extreme distaste of the man he was investigating, who had a nasty penchant for drug-fuelled violence. There was no point in his coming home at weekends as he was working Saturdays to get the job done quickly.

Then DS Lynn Outhwaite went horse riding on a day's leave, fell off and broke her right leg in two places.

I was first made aware of this when Carrick marched past where I was working – it was just after nine thirty in the morning – and slammed into the large room, the general office, next door. He emerged almost immediately, went back the way he had come, having given me the merest of glances on the way by, and then reappeared framed in the entrance to where I was working.

'It's a complete disaster!' he declared, having given me the news. 'She can't work with her leg in plaster even if she hadn't hurt her face as well and suffered a black eye and grazes.'

'Is she still in hospital?' I asked.

'No, at home, or at least, at her mother's.'

'You have that address?'

He seemed a bit thrown by the question. 'Yes . . . of course.'

'Flowers then. Shall I organize them for you?'

'Er – yes . . . please.'

'Who will take over her job?'

'There isn't anyone spare or with the seniority. Some of the

team are going flat out on other stuff. But I might be able to
get someone on loan from HQ in a couple of days' time.'

'Then I could give you a hand until it happens – that's if you
want me to.'

Never one to rush headlong into decisions, he thought about
it for a few moments. 'I'd have to get the OK from Greenway.'

So would I.

I decided, after this had been immediately forthcoming – the
commander seemed really keen so perhaps was hoping for some
kind of inside intelligence, although I could not imagine what
– that my change of role represented demotion so I would have
to watch what I said, especially in front of others. Carrick, to
his credit, made no comment on the matter. As far as the Smith
and Wesson was concerned I regarded that as part of the package
he was getting.

The DCI was still trying to establish the identities of the
remaining two out of the five men who had been shot and killed
during the gun battle, not the pair who had been found mutilated,
also still unidentified. One theory regarding these latter two was
that they might have been illegal immigrants and, as Carrick
had already surmised, part of the 'invading' gang, hence the
horrible retribution.

'So who won?' I asked when we were on our way, in Carrick's
car, to an address in Southdown St Peter, the village locally
regarded by everyone who did not live there as being the home
of all iniquity, past, present and no doubt future. 'If this Uncle
character was in a five-star restaurant was he celebrating
victory?'

'He might have been if most of the dead were on the opposing
side. Lynn said there was plenty of champagne drunk. If so you
almost have to admire the man's nerve.'

'You still don't have any evidence that he's involved, though.'

'No, not yet.'

'Am I correct in guessing that we're on our way to visit the
Huggins clan?'

'We are,' Carrick agreed succinctly. 'They might just know
something about this Trelonic character.'

I was wondering if a little backup might be required when
he added, 'We went in with a search warrant yesterday and

took the whole place apart, picking up two of the lads on account of finding half a shedful of stolen property. It pays to turn the place over occasionally, especially when there's been a robbery. They're all as thick as two short planks and haven't quite worked out that to keep the stuff at home, even for just one night, is a very bad idea.'

'I met some of these people not so long ago – Patrick and I helped you arrest them.'

'Oh, yes, the antiques job. That was Carlton Huggins and two of his sons, Ricky and Riley. They're still on remand. Yesterday I pulled in Darrell and Shane, Carlton's brothers. That leaves sundry weans and womenfolk – common-law wives, hangers-on, girlfriends, call them what you will – and Clem, Carlton's youngest son who will have probably bunked off school, again, and will see the inside of a young offenders' establishment soon if he doesn't change his ways. It's inevitable.'

'It's sad though, isn't it?'

'I suppose so, but it's in their genes – the whole boiling lot are descended from tinkers and horse thieves who were bothering Somerset over a hundred years ago. One of them was the last man to be hanged at a crossroads, nationally. The attitude seems to be that it's what they do. How else do you get money when the social security scams have all been found out? When they start thieving, handling stolen goods and threatening people it's my job to lock them up.'

Carrick was still distinctly put out, a bit adrift even, by the loss of his assistant but here was the usual pragmatic policeman talking: I had an idea Patrick would have the same attitude. Clem was in Matthew's class at school.

Where the Hugginses lived was like a small colony: caravans, huts and trailers of various sizes clustered around what had once been a council house on a corner site with a large garden. None-too-clean washing was hanging out on several lines which were tied to trees or leaning poles. A couple of dogs, snarling and barking at us, were tied up too; mostly, Carrick told me afterwards, on account of the likelihood that they would kill one another otherwise.

'I'm going to ask whoever's here if they know anything about this shoot-out too,' the DCI was saying. 'They may not as it's not quite their scene. But the grapevine might be alive and well in this rats' nest.'

'And give the impression that cooperation will result in you taking a more favourable attitude to their menfolk's present difficulties?' I ventured.

'Yes, something like that.'

'And will you?'

He paused in walking up what could not really be described as a path that meandered between general rubbish towards the house and gave me a straight look.

That had to be a 'no' then.

Already this venture of mine into coalface policing was proving to be an eye-opener. Previously my involvement with preserving Her Majesty's peace and law enforcement, MI5 and SOCA, had been concerned with what I can only describe as the 'exotic' variety where I had been dealing with mostly sophisticated and clever criminals, albeit ruthless and vicious ones, who were often also wealthy and influential people in their spare time. Here was 'subsistence' crime, those brazenly and illegally fighting for survival.

'The whole place reeks of poverty,' I muttered, glimpsing the worried faces of a couple of women as they peeped fleetingly from caravan windows.

'It's deliberate,' Carrick said with relish. 'So social services don't get an inkling of how much money they've really got stashed away.'

He picked up a stone from the path and rapped on the battered front door with it, sending the dogs into a frenzy. I expected the knock to be ignored but, moments later, the door was flung open by an enormously fat, middle-aged woman. She looked us up and down in utter disgust.

'Come for the little kids this time, have yer?' she bawled at Carrick.

'No, I'd like to talk to you about the turf war we've had in the city.'

Her eyes screwed up in amazement. 'And what the bloody 'ell d'you reckon I know about that?'

'Your sons Ricky and Riley seem to know something about it.'

I busied myself taking a notebook and pen from my bag, not looking in Carrick's direction. He had said nothing about this to me. Was it true? I had an idea it was not.

'My sons are too clever to get involved in anything like that,' the woman protested.

No, sorry ducky, too stupid.

'I'd like you to give me the names of their friends.'

Slowly, she shook her head. 'I don't know who their friends are.'

'Did they knock around with Adam Trelonic?'

'Him! The one what got done in? I should say not! He owed my husband a packet of money. Sold a car for him and kept all the dosh.'

'A stolen car?' Carrick asked silkily.

The ensuing silence was broken by a baby starting to cry somewhere within.

'May we come in?' Carrick asked.

'No, I'm busy.'

'I can get another warrant and search the place again.'

'Look, we don't get involved with the big gangs and have guns and stuff like that. You know we don't. Go away and stop pesterin' me. You've got all the blokes in custody for one daft reason or another so why the 'ell don't you ask *them*?' She began to close the door.

Carrick put his foot against it. 'I have and—'

She cut him short with a salvo of obscenities designed to blast him right off her doorstep.

'Would you like me to have a word with Mrs Huggins while you talk to some of the others?' I suggested brightly to Carrick when she paused for breath and before she could deliver the second volley I was convinced she was composing.

A whistling kettle started to shriek and the woman swore and waddled away. I gave Carrick the thumbs-up, went inside and shut the door on him. The baby's cries went up several notches to screaming level, only oddly muffled now and I discovered it in a pram in a mind-blowingly untidy front room. The child had pulled a blanket over its face which I duly whipped off. A snotty, pig-faced little being in dire need of a nappy change glared up at me.

The kettle was silenced.

'Oh, thanks,' said Mrs Huggins when she reappeared and I had explained.

'Your grandchild?' I queried.

'Yes, she's Maxine's, our eldest. God knows who the father is. Maxine works at the meat-packing place at Trowbridge now. I told her I was damned if she was paying me to look after this child full time by staying on the game and she'd better get a decent job. I mean, she'll be thirty next month; fifteen years a tart. She disgusts me actually.' She stared at me. 'You're not his usual helper. God, his snooty Scottish way of looking at you as though you're something he's just trodden in really gets up my nose.'

'No, DS Outhwaite's broken her leg.'

Mrs Huggins chuckled. 'That's one less for a bit then.'

'Look, I know the police must really make your life a misery sometimes but some perfectly innocent passers-by were murdered during this gang war in Bath. They just went round shooting people for the fun of it. If you know anything or have heard anything, please tell me.'

'I've already told you, my family don't get mixed up in big crime.'

'I believe you. But they must hear gossip. In the pubs, places like that . . .'

'No one knows who these folk are. No one wants to know. These mobsters are almost all outsiders. Foreigners, some of 'em. Them what sneak over hidin' in lorries.'

'We thought it was people from outside trying to take over from the local gangs. Three of the dead men were from Bristol. But as for the others . . .'

'The local mob hired 'em in, didn't they?' Mrs Huggins said triumphantly, as though speaking to an idiot.

'How do you know that?'

'Because—' She shut her mouth tightly and then turned away from me.

'Because?' I whispered.

She was silent for around a quarter of a minute and then said, 'Someone was goin' round pubs quietly offerin' . . . work.'

'Hiring gunmen?'

'Them an' heavies.'

'He asked your husband if he wanted a job?'

'No, a mate of 'is.'

'From round here then.'

'Frome. I'm not sayin' no more. I've said too much already.'

'Can't you give me the friend's name?'

'Derek someone. Now go away and leave me alone. My boys 'ad nothin' to do with it.'

I made my way towards the door.

'D'you want a kitten?' she called after me. 'They'll only get drowned and I hate that.'

Pirate, our very, very old cat, had recently failed to wake from sleep and had been buried, with tears all round, in the garden. Which one of the three playing with a ragged piece of string under a hedge did I want? The ginger, the tortoiseshell or the fluffy black and white one? Which two to condemn to an early and not at all merciful death?

The tortie was a must, exactly the same colour as Pirate had been. But . . .

'What have you got there?' Carrick asked when he got back to the car, eyeing my battered cardboard box.

'D'you mind dropping me off at home for a few minutes?' I asked winningly. 'It's not really out of our way and we could have coffee.'

'Oh . . . all right.'

'Did you learn anything at the caravans?'

'No,' he answered shortly.

Three flea-ridden, gummy-eyed kittens?

'A mate of Carlton Huggins called Derek who lives in Frome?' Carrick mused, frowning. 'That must be Derek Jessop. A real rough 'un. He works at a quarry not all that far from here so I think I'll go and have a word with him.' Pensively stirring his mug of coffee he went into a reverie, no doubt planning interrogation tactics. Plus still grieving the more than temporary loss of his assistant.

Elspeth had taken immediate charge of the kittens, saying that she knew exactly the right home for at least one, and then disappeared off to the vet with them. Always discreet, she had not questioned why I was accompanying Carrick. Patrick and I have never told his parents of my close involvement with his job but I know Elspeth has a good idea that, for some of the time, we work together.

After making a routine call in connection with another case we drove to the quarry where we discovered that Derek Jessop had not turned up for work for a while.

'But we were thinking of giving him the boot anyway,' said the covered-in-white-dust man in charge. 'So I'm not too bothered.'

'For what reason are you sacking him?' Carrick wanted to know.

'Bad timekeeping, turning up still canned from the night before. You can't have that with dangerous machinery around. He's a troublemaker too – none of the other men like him.'

'So I assume there's no point in my asking them if they know anything about his private life.'

'I wouldn't have thought so. But ask away, they'll be having their lunch break in five minutes or so.'

We were told nothing of value, other than in one man's view there was a shortage of soap in Jessop's house as he smelt so bad. The only useful information was his address, given to us by the foreman and different to the one Carrick had in his records so presumably the man had moved house. This was close to Radstock in a little hamlet by the name of Spinner's Grave. There is a very old story that someone, no doubt on a dark and stormy night, had been murdered there and buried under the threshold of the pub. Patrick, who seemingly has been in every hostelry west of Chatham, once commented that the beer they serve, whatever the brew, tastes as though there's a corpse in it.

It was a dreary village with a few terraces of grey little cottages, a couple of larger houses, a filling station, a small modern estate and the pub. No one who had any money had ever lived here and probably never would unless someone took a bulldozer to the place and started afresh. Set high up on a ridge of hills with far-reaching views to the Mendips and beyond the location was magnificent, if breezy. Today, with a north-wester blowing from the direction of the Bristol Channel, it was decidedly chilly.

We parked and made our way along the village street, which was mainly deserted with only a little light traffic. Carrick was still quiet, dour even; perhaps this was his normal working persona. It was obvious that he was a very hands-on policeman, preferring to be out and part of the investigation, not just sitting behind a desk issuing orders. Although he has worked with Patrick and me on assignments I had never seen this side of him before: the everyday, Monday to Friday man. I went on to wonder if his moroseness was due to the fact that he was missing Lynn Outhwaite more than I had thought. Or was he still smarting from the broadside he had received from the Huggins woman? Whatever the reason he needed shaking out of it.

'I'm not quite sure what my role is,' I murmured.

He broke off from trying to read the carved in stone, time-worn names on the individual terraces of cottages to give me a quick glance. 'Just to make a few notes and undertake any little jobs I ask you to do.'

'That's what Lynn does then.'

'No, not really but—'

I interrupted with, 'Or would you really like to get your money's worth and have me work the way I do for SOCA?'

'That's different.'

'Yes, I know but normally not *that* much. The jobs you've helped us with have tended to be at the go-in-there-and-grab-them stage, not normal routine.'

'Yes, but it's still not relevant to what we're doing now.'

'So you don't want me to say the kind of things I would if I was working with Patrick right now, use what my Dad used to call my cat's whiskers?'

Patrick thinks of me as his oracle, voluntarily consulted or not. I read recently that crime writers should never, ever have their detectives using intuition to solve crimes as it's cheating and very bad practice. In real life, however . . .

'No . . . but, thank you.'

'Fine,' I said lightly.

We carried on walking, Carrick frowning at his piece of paper with the address written on it. Then he stopped dead. '*What* kind of things?'

'You have two missing wounded gangsters. I've just been

told that someone was going round pubs recruiting potential mobsters and Jessop could have been one of those approached. He's not reported for work for a while. Are we just going to knock politely on his door?'

'He's never been known to carry firearms,' Carrick said dismissively.

'Fine,' I said again.

We arrived at our destination. All the curtains at the front were drawn and this, plus the sodden bags of rubbish in the concreted-over front garden gave every impression that the house had been unoccupied for months. In such a situation as this Patrick and I would have immediately gone down the side way to the back door with a view to taking by surprise any possible occupants who were trying to lie low.

Carrick pressed the bell-push and, on hearing nothing, rapped on the frosted glass panel with his knuckles. We waited but nothing happened.

'Let's go round the back,' I suggested in a whisper.

He gave no sign of having heard me but then did indeed move towards the narrow passage that ran down the side of the house. It was difficult to squeeze past the rusting bikes, rotting vehicle tyres and other rubbish without dislodging anything by getting it hooked up on our clothing, but we eventually arrived at a small area at the rear also utilized as a junk yard. A rear door was slightly ajar.

I knew that he was about to bellow through the opening and announce the arrival of the strong arm of the law. My cat and all its whiskers were screaming caution.

'Be careful!' I exhorted quietly. 'We don't know who the hell's in there.'

Ye gods, Patrick would have pushed the door back as silently as possible and then—

'Police!' Carrick shouted, following this up with battering of his fist on the door. It swung open a little more to reveal one corner of a dingy kitchen.

Moments later there was the thump of running feet within and a man burst into view. I registered the fact that he was carrying a gun at around the same second that he fired it at almost point-blank range. I flung myself to one side, tripped and fell flat, landing on a large cardboard box as he dashed by me.

'Stop!' I heard Carrick shout, seeing him out of the corner of my eye picking himself up.

The man did stop in his headlong flight, then turned and took aim.

There was no time to utter a warning.

THREE

For some reason I had noticed the twisted grin on his face as he prepared to shoot the DCI. This was now a grimace of pain but he did not seem to be in any immediate danger of dying. I retrieved the gun from where it had been dropped, aware that Carrick had found his mobile, then entered the kitchen far enough to grab a grubby tea towel. With it I made a rough tourniquet to help stop the bleeding in the man's leg. I was not feeling at all pleased with myself as he was already injured, blood seeping through a smelly makeshift dressing on his upper arm. But what else could I have done?

Carrick, sensibly, and having called up reinforcements and an ambulance, stayed right where he was. Checking the tourniquet and keeping a weather eye on my patient – whose face was wearing a snarl for me alone now – for signs of imminent collapse brought on by shock or a heart attack, I felt Carrick's gaze on me but he made no comment just then.

'Were you alone in the house, Jessop?' he enquired.

Jessop, short, very thin, supporting himself on one elbow, found the energy to spit in his direction.

'Who else was hurt?' I asked him. 'Run out of slobber?' I continued when he remained silent. 'Just think, if his wound's as bad as yours appears to be, judging by the way it stinks, he might end up having something off too. So at least you could—'

'What?' Jessop gasped. 'Have my arm off? No, surely not! For God's sake—'

I interrupted him with, 'Unless you smell that bad normally. Someone at the quarry said you were a stranger to soap and water so with a bit of luck it might only be your hand or some fingers that have to be amputated.'

By this time Jessop had gone seriously pale, staring up at me with bloodshot eyes.

'So do your chum a favour,' I cajoled. 'You'll probably save his life. We know he's not in hospital so just think of him lying somewhere like you with the gangrene creeping through him, bits of him slowly turning black . . .'

'It's my brother, Billy,' Jessop choked out after a short silence.

'But he's never been in real trouble!' Carrick exclaimed.

'He needed the bloody money as well, didn't he?' Jessop yelled at him.

'Where is he?' I asked.

'At his girlfriend's place.' He flopped down on to his back and when he spoke it was in a whisper, barely audible. 'Oh, God. God. D'you really think I might have to have my arm off?'

'Tell me where she lives before I answer.'

'In Bath. In a flat over the dry cleaners on Wellsway.'

'No, you won't,' I said.

'You should have told me you were armed,' Carrick reproached a while later.

'What difference would it have made?' I retorted.

I think he was taken aback by the vehemence of my reply for he said nothing for a moment. Then, 'Does Commander Greenway know you carry it around with you?'

'Yes.'

Awkwardly, he then said, 'I'm sure you saved my life.'

'In such a blind panic he would probably have missed again. My regret is that I had no time to warn him.'

'*That* would have made no difference,' he pointed out.

We dealt with the immediate aftermath, DI Black arriving to volunteer to take charge so Carrick would be free to carry on with the main investigation. The house was searched but no one else was found. Jessop and his brother – who someone, with suitable backup, had already gone to arrest – were known to Bristol CID for committing football hooliganism offences. Billy was found having a blazing row with his girlfriend, who wanted to call an ambulance, and was duly taken to hospital, where his neglected wound led to septicaemia from which he almost died. It went without saying that neither of the Jessops was fit for police questioning.

I had an idea Carrick would have a problem explaining why

I was carrying a firearm as, strictly speaking, Patrick is the only one of us permitted to do so for personal protection reasons, as explained already. What was supposed to happen when his wife was on her own had never been addressed.

As usual, he rang that evening.

'Oh, you know, the usual routine stuff,' I said in answer to his query about my day. 'Armed raids on suspects, that kind of thing. I shot a bloke and saved James's life.'

Patrick laughed.

No one laughed when, the following Saturday morning, Matthew and Katie were caught breaking into the Ring o' Bells. It was not the manager who phoned to tell me what had happened but Jenny, who works in the kitchen at weekends. Needless to say I went straight over there.

The manager, whose name I seemed to remember was Colin Andrews, a tall, lanky and quite smartly dressed individual, was standing outside. 'I caught them red-handed!' he called in his rather high-pitched voice as I approached. 'They were probably after alcopops and crisps. I've called the police and insisted they're dealt with.'

'Where are they now?' I asked.

'In my office. And they'll stay there until the police come.'

'There's no need to involve the police. It can be dealt with between us.'

'Not a chance. I want this to be a lesson to all the other kids in the village who fancy free booze.'

'My children don't drink, Mr Andrews. You have no power of arrest. Kindly let me see them.'

'Sorry, they're staying right here.'

I began to lose my temper. 'You have no right to lock up children on your premises, no matter what you think they've done.'

It is doubtful whether this would have ended without everything going on to a war footing had the police not then arrived.

'What's going on?' James Carrick demanded to know, adding, 'I was on my way home and heard the call.'

'You a cop then?' Andrews said.

Carrick showed him his warrant card.

'Oh, splendid,' Andrews chortled. 'A Detective Chief Inspector, no less. That'll please them.' He turned and went towards the back entrance, the establishment being at present closed. He had an odd, floppy way of moving, like a puppet whose strings are not quite right.

'He didn't recognize me as one of his customers,' Carrick said out of the corner of his mouth as we followed.

'He hasn't been here all that long and doesn't normally serve behind the bar,' I whispered back.

There was no time for any more exchanges. We went in, Carrick having to lower his head as the doorway is at least three hundred years old and people were smaller then. We caught up with Andrews after taking a right turn in a dark passageway as he was unlocking another door. With a flourish he flung it open and went in. I was right behind him.

Matthew and Katie were standing, almost to attention, in a far corner of the room, which was not large, the pair of them pale but defiant. I expected a dash towards me and floods of tears from the latter but she just stood there, at Matthew's side. It was I who almost wept.

'Found them in the storeroom,' Andrews was saying. 'As I said just now, after the alcopops and crisps.'

'They were holding some then?' Carrick said.

'No, but—'

'So how do you know they were out to steal?'

'Well, what the hell else could they have been in there for?'

Carrick turned to the children. 'What *were* you doing in there?'

'Nothing,' Matthew said. 'The door was open so we just took a look inside.'

'I'm not sure what you were doing being anywhere near this place,' was the DCI's not at all friendly response.

'Tell the truth!' Katie said to Matthew, giving him a hard nudge.

He said nothing for a moment and then blurted out wildly, 'Well, we were a bit hungry and thought there might be something sort of lying around. Perhaps a few leftover chips. But there wasn't.'

To Andrews, Carrick said, 'I shall deal with this. Is that satisfactory to you?'

'I want them charged,' Andrews said. 'To set an example.'

'They're only guilty of trespass and that's a civil not a criminal offence – which doesn't mean they won't get into trouble, though. They don't appear to have actually broken in. Was the outside door unlocked?'

'Er – yes.'

'Can you confirm that nothing's been stolen?'

'I haven't checked.'

'Then check. I'll come with you.'

The pair went. Still the children stood there, defiant.

Then Matthew whispered, 'Dad'll kill me.'

They have only recently asked to call us Mum and Dad: they had loved their real father dearly.

'Of course he won't,' I said, my tears ready and waiting. 'But you will get a real talking-to.'

'The soon-to-be horribly stroppy teenager,' Matthew said, shocking me with the bitterness of his tone. 'That's what it'll be and a criminal record before I've even left school. I mean, it's normal these days, isn't it?' He lapsed into silence and I was further shaken when it appeared that it was he who was about to cry.

A few minutes later we left, Andrews having refused to withdraw his complaint in lieu of a police reprimand from Carrick, and it was a sad little procession that wended its way across the village green towards the rectory, Katie crying now, my arm around her shoulders. I had expected James to leave the problem with us but his car turned up in the drive a couple of minutes after we got home.

'Can we talk with them somewhere private?' he asked when I had let him in.

'You'll have to come upstairs,' I said on a sigh. 'They bolted for their rooms.'

'If you'd rather I left it for—' he began.

'No, please. Let's do it. Then at least I shall know what to tell Patrick.'

I knocked on Matthew's door. 'May James and I come in, please?'

It was opened by a wan, red-eyed Katie who went to perch on the window seat. Matthew was sitting at his computer but

closed it down at our entry. My heart turned over: his face had
an expression on it that made him look exactly like Patrick
when in a tight corner.

'So,' Carrick said, seating himself on the bed. 'What's the
real story?'

The two exchanged glances.

'Look,' Carrick went on, 'I've known you two for a long
time now and you don't go in for pinching things, not even
cold chips. What's the real story?'

'You won't believe us,' Matthew said.

'Try me.'

'Mum didn't.'

'What didn't I believe?' I said.

'That there's a fiddle going on over there. Only it's worse
now.'

'They have an investigation enterprise,' I explained to Carrick.
His brow cleared. 'Oh, I see.'

'We told you *ages* ago,' Katie said to me. 'The wholesale
butcher's delivery man goes in the pub with a load of meat and
comes out with bottles of whisky and stuff like that. It's a racket
going on. He's pinching the meat from his employer and swap-
ping it for drink at the pub. And now—'

'This is a new angle,' Matthew broke in with.

'And now there's another man taking in stuff from a van in
boxes and coming out with drink,' Katie continued after giving
her brother a withering look. 'And it's far too much for one
person to drink. That's what we were looking for
– evidence.'

'All this must have a perfectly logical explanation,' Carrick
said when she had finished speaking.

'That's exactly what Mum said.' Katie sighed.

Carrick leaned forward and spoke earnestly. 'Look. Even *I*
have to get a warrant if I want to search someone's private
property. You mustn't do it. It's trespassing. Not only that, if
there had been a guard dog there you could have been badly
bitten.'

Silence but for Katie sniffing.

'I thought *you'd* believe us,' Matthew said.

'What I do believe is that these things are happening exactly as you describe but for different reasons to the ones you've read into them. And please take my advice when I tell you that if you go in there again you'll be in real trouble.'

He got up and left the room.

I followed him down the stairs to let him out.

'You might tell them that the police are far too busy to haul kids in front of them for playing detectives,' he said over his shoulder. 'I just thought I'd let them sweat for a bit. By the way, we can now interview the woman who was injured in the shootings. But I might have a helper by then – I'll let you know.'

Whether the stubborn Gillard genes really kicked in then I do not know but the result was that Matthew climbed out of his bedroom window at around ten fifteen that night, shinned down the wisteria and carried out some more surveillance at the pub. Someone did have a dog, which discovered him, and in the resulting scramble to escape the young intruder caught Andrews with a flying fist, blacking his eye. This time it took three of them to lock Matthew in the office and when the police arrived after what must have been a longish wait he was removed, beside himself by now, and taken to Bath's police station where he was put in a cell to cool off. Andrews had been livid and Matthew was to be charged with assault.

When someone rang to tell me about it, belatedly, just before midnight, I felt I had definitely become embroiled in something with which I could not cope and called Patrick. He promptly got in his car and drove home, breaking every speed limit to arrive at around three. Extremely tired, worried, and worse, coming up to some kind of boil of his own, he found me in the kitchen where I was making myself a mug of stay-awake coffee.

'I've just come back from Manvers Street,' I told him.

'They're not keeping him there, surely.'

'They're worried he might run off again and would prefer to release him into the care of both parents.'

Patrick turned to go. 'Then let's get back there.'

'You'll have to be very careful – not blow your top.'

'He's behaved abominably.'

None of the children, thankfully, has ever seen Patrick really lose his temper. I went, dreading what might happen.

*   *   *

Matthew was sitting hunched up on the bunk bed, clutching his knees. He looked up when Patrick and I entered and then jumped to his feet as if poised to flee.

'I knew you'd be mad at me,' he said tautly to Patrick.

'You've deliberately disobeyed just about everyone and injured a man,' Patrick replied quietly. 'Do you expect me not to be?'

'No.'

'I've driven all the way back from Manchester to deal with this.'

'Thank you,' was Matthew's surprising whispered reaction, meeting what I knew to be a look of seething suppressed fury, something not many people succeed in doing.

Patrick let out a gusty sigh and subsided on to the bunk. 'Please sit down so we can talk about it.'

Matthew stayed where he was. 'There's nothing to talk about, end of story. No one believes me – us. I really thought James would. He said he's going to coach me when I start playing rugby at school and yet he doesn't believe what I'm telling him. People think I'm just a stupid interfering kid so I went there to try to prove that I'm not. That man at the pub came at me as though he was going to kill me tonight and I hit out in a bit of a panic. His chums rammed their fists in my ribs to get me into that room. But no one will believe me, they'll believe *them.* I've got a criminal record now and it'll be with me for always.' His voice had broken recently and as he uttered the last words it slid up into the childish treble.

It appeared that he was really was going to cry now, from sheer mortification.

Patrick said, 'I understand you want to learn a few self-defence moves.'

Matthew blinked quickly a few times and then stared at him. 'Er – yes, please.'

'And you rather fancy the job I do and one day would like to do the same kind of thing.'

The boy's chin came up. 'Yes.'

'To the extent of following me to Bath a couple of times, having presumably overheard a conversation as to where I proposed to hang out to give James a hand.'

'I wasn't eavesdropping,' Matthew hastened to say, going pink. 'I – I just happened to hear as I walked past an open door. Why, did you—?'

'Yes, I knew you were there. I saw you the first night as you trotted off back towards the bus station and had an idea you were somewhere around on the third when I nabbed those two muggers. I could smell the kind of stuff someone had put on a cut on your wrist. Never be upwind of anyone you're watching. Now please come and sit down.'

Matthew sat alongside him on the bunk and then murmured, 'Please help me. I don't want to have a criminal record.'

'Don't worry, you won't.'

'But that man—'

'I believe you.'

'But—'

'Anyone who comes at a lad as though he's going to kill him is a crook. I'll work on it. Shall we go home?'

'You should have told me that Matthew had followed you to Bath,' I said when we had had a couple of hours sleep and, weary-eyed, were drinking tea in the kitchen.

'You would only have freaked out.'

'That's what women do.'

Patrick smiled. 'Only a short while ago you were worried because he was still nervous of the dark.'

'But he could have been attacked by yobs in the bus station!'

'I know. I thought about it. But there are usually plenty of people around at that time of night. And, sometimes . . . you have to let go a bit. Besides which, he can run like a stag and knew exactly where I was likely to be.'

'It would look very bad if you went and spoke to Andrews about what happened.'

'Give me credit for some sense. Any more nags right now?'

'Sorry,' I said, blowing him a kiss.

'Andrews might leave it for a couple of days and then contact Carrick and, all smiles, say he's going to forget all about it.'

'Why should he do that?'

'Because even if he isn't involved with anything iffy he has a business to run and must know that the rector and his family are respected around here.'

'Do you really believe that Matthew and Katie have found out something important?'

'What they've seen doesn't *necessarily* mean they're right on target about dodgy goings-on at the pub. But as I said to him, I'll work on it. Frankly, if Carrick had said something similar we probably wouldn't be where we are now. But he's overstretched and having to work on the shootings case so one can hardly blame him.'

I had felt somewhat sidelined in all this but my feelings did not matter, for this affair was primarily a man and boy situation. I knew that Patrick and Matthew had had another heart-to-heart discussion later when a promise had been extracted from Matthew that he would not, under any circumstances, go near the Ring o' Bells again and that he and Katie would file this particular case under 'pending'. I knew, though, that deep down Patrick was extremely proud of the way he had behaved under pressure.

But Andrews made no contact with Avon and Somerset Police and the charges against Matthew remained. We received a letter to the effect that an appointment would be made for us at the offices of the local Youth Offending Team. It seemed likely that, because of his age, he would get an official police reprimand, noted down, that would lead to a final warning if he got into trouble again. After that it would be a matter for the courts.

FOUR

'Mrs Stonelake?' Carrick said quietly.

The woman in the hospital bed opened her eyes and looked surprised. 'Oh . . . hello.'

'I'm Detective Chief Inspector Carrick and this is my assistant, Miss Langley. I'd like to ask you a few questions if you're feeling well enough.'

It appeared that I would be riding shotgun for him, literally or not, for the next few days at least, the force not being remotely with him, having gone down in droves with some mystery stomach bug. HQ was reported to be like a ghost town.

'Yes, I – I think so,' stammered the lady, slightly overwhelmed.

Well, the Scot was once described to me by a friend as 'wall-to-wall crumpet'.

'Miss Langley will take a few notes if that's all right.'

She flashed a wan smile at me and, when we had drawn up a couple of chairs, said, 'Not that I can really remember very much. And it all happened so quickly.'

She was around fifty years of age, from what I could see of her of slight build, fair and with pale blue eyes. Her head was bandaged, an injury resulting from her fall, hitting the kerb, a bullet having taken her in the left leg, breaking the tibia.

'I understand that you were on your way home after work,' Carrick began by saying.

'Yes, it was later than usual as there'd been a big party. Lots of clearing up to do.'

'Please tell me as much as you can recollect.'

She thought for a few moments. 'Well, I did hear bangs in the distance but not for a minute did I think it was guns. Fireworks, perhaps, or a car. Even when the noise came closer I still didn't get really worried although I don't like it at the best of times when stupid boys mess around with fireworks.'

'The restaurant's in Nash Square. Where were you by this time?'

'Just coming from Hot Bath Street and crossing the road where Macfisheries was years ago. All the shops seem to sell gifts for visitors now, you know, no real shops at all. My husband used to say that you couldn't even buy a bag of nails.'

'Then what happened?'

Her eyes narrowed. 'These men came running down the hill from Milsom Street, first two and then more a little way behind. The front two were looking absolutely terrified. Then there was another bang from somewhere behind them and the two turned round and fired their guns. I hadn't noticed until then that they were carrying them. I ran myself then, I promise you.'

'Can you describe them at all?'

'The first ones looked a bit sort of foreign, but street lights make people look different, don't they? I didn't see the faces of the ones behind them.'

'Foreign in what way?'

'Well, sort of quite short and dark-haired. Curly hair. I don't mean they were black, mind. More like gypsies really.'

I wrote HUGGINS followed by a question mark in my notebook.

'That's all really,' Mrs Stonelake said. 'Only that I ran and ran and at least two of them were behind me all the way down Stall Street into Southgate. A couple might have gone somewhere else. Someone was laughing. Then they must have fired at me for I fell down. I didn't feel anything straight away so I thought I'd just tripped. I played dead and that's all I remember until I woke up here. They won't come after me again if they find out I've talked to you, will they?' Her lips quivered.

Carrick put a hand on her shoulder. 'No, no chance. There's an armed police officer just outside the ward at all times. Is there anything at all that you want to add – even if it seems unimportant to you?'

'No, I don't think so.'

'Was there any traffic?' I asked. 'Cars whose drivers were trying to get out of the way, for example?'

'No, at least . . . Yes, that's right, I remember now. I did glimpse some cars but they'd stopped at the top of the road, from where the men had come. They were too far away to see exactly what they were, though.'

'And of course lower down it's a pedestrian precinct,' Carrick said.

'Yes, but they drove down that,' I reminded him.

'So they did.'

'Oh, yes!' Mrs Stonelake exclaimed. 'That's right, I did see some cars around Southgate. And there was a big car parked without lights.'

'Something like a Rolls-Royce?'

'Not quite as big and posh as those.'

'Where was it exactly? Can you remember?'

'Near the bottom where I was hit.'

'Was anyone sitting in it?'

'I didn't notice.'

'What colour was it?'

'Very dark. Black, probably. Yes, that's right, the windows looked dark too – dark glass so I don't suppose I would have been able to see anyone in it. Now you've reminded me I remember thinking it might be the mayor's or somebody like that, waiting to pick him up from a do.'

'And it's silly to ask if you noticed any of the registration.'

Another wan smile. 'No, sorry, I didn't.'

Carrick said, 'Do you think you might be able to recognize any of the men if, when you're better, you looked at some photographs?' He did not add that included those of the dead, the bodies carefully made more or less presentable by the mortuary assistants.

'I wouldn't have thought so,' Mrs Stonelake said dubiously. 'I suppose I could always try. But I'd be worried I'd get people into trouble if I picked out the wrong ones.'

'That's my responsibility,' Carrick assured her. 'And we don't arrest people without good reason.'

Well, not for most of the time, I thought.

We left, Carrick giving her his card should she recollect anything further.

That afternoon there was a meeting designed to create a progress report. It proved to be a depressing experience. The first thing to emerge was that no evidence had been found to connect Adam Trelonic with the shootings even though there was no satisfactory explanation as to why he was in the city centre at that time of night. His wife still maintained that she had no idea why he had been there – but surely, I thought, a woman would know if her husband had gone out for a beer – and it had become obvious that the couple's marriage had not been healthy. She had finally refused to cooperate any further. With reluctance on Carrick's part the man was now being regarded as an innocent passer-by either caught in crossfire or singled out later by those who had 'won' or, at least, survived.

The two mutilated bodies were still unidentified but due to their appearance and blood group types were being tentatively labelled as belonging to men of mid-European extraction. Their fingerprints and, when available, DNA details would be circulated to all relevant authorities. It would all take time. And, adding to the DCI's gloom, the people who Lynn Outhwaite had spotted in the restaurant were proving impossible to trace.

On the positive side, the man living rough who had witnessed some of what had happened had been located at a Salvation Army hostel. He had been sufficiently close to the injured to be able to positively identify the Jessops from mugshots and was emphatic that they had been carrying weapons, at least one of which had been swiftly grabbed by someone although it had been impossible to tell whether whoever it was had been one of those who had shot them. This was valuable, pre-empting any claim by the brothers that they had merely been passing.

DI Black could not be present at the meeting but I was able to stand in for him and update those not in the know with regard to the Bristol-based mobsters. Three of the dead had been identified almost right at the start with another two, at the time, unknown. One of these had been found to be listed as a missing person; the other had assumed a stolen identity. Both had been known to the police at one time and all five had been connected to a crime boss who called himself Mick the Kick on account of his enthusiasm for kick-boxing. This individual was being sought to help with enquiries.

That left finding out who was running the other gang. Someone had gone round recruiting men fairly local to Bath.

It was vital to discover what part, if any, the London crime lord referred to as Uncle had played in all this. More might be learned when Derek Jessop was deemed fit enough to be questioned, soon it was hoped. His brother Billy was still dangerously ill.

'You need to get SOCA involved,' I finished by saying.

'You think that would be useful?' Carrick asked, his tone light and neutral.

'There's a possibility the pair who are thought to have been of mid-European extraction could have broken away or were fugitives from gangs from Romania and the Czech Republic that have moved to the UK and SOCA are trying to smash. We might be able to discover who they were from cases that are being currently worked on.'

'All details *were* sent to the Met,' he responded.

'May I send them to Commander Greenway?' A breakdown in communications would be nothing new.

He pondered for a few moments and then said, 'Yes, that's fine by me.'

Patrick set off from Manchester to drive to London that evening.

'I've briefed someone and handed over the job to her,' Patrick said when he rang me before starting his journey. 'There's actually very little left to do as thanks to old intelligence from Richard Daws we've located most of this guy's chums – he originally came from the Midlands – and there'll soon be a few dawn raids. Hopefully that'll lead to info as to where he's hiding out.'

'I take it you've been recalled by Greenway for another job,' I said.

'Didn't you suggest I was brought in to help with the turf war?'

'I did, but was being careful as I wasn't sure what had been said – and you might not have been.'

'Are you coming up?'

'What, to London? Do you need me right away?'

'For several reasons,' he replied before uttering a dirty chuckle. Then, 'What's that faint rumbling noise I can hear?'

'Pirate's successor and her brother,' I answered. 'They're on my lap, purring.'

Michael Greenway had suffered a gunshot wound to his left shoulder not all that long ago and was still moving a little stiffly. I knew it must be causing him huge annoyance as he has a large garden in the Ascot area and unwinds by getting it into shape with various powerful implements.

'I understand you winged some bloke who took a pot shot at Jim Carrick,' was his opening remark to me. He and the DCI have met several times.

'Derek Jessop,' I said. 'With his brother Billy he was involved in the Bath shoot-out.'

'I thought you were joking!' Patrick exclaimed.

'I rather hoped you thought I was joking,' I told him.

It was mid-morning the following day and we were in Greenway's spacious office. On the way up to London on the train I had been wondering about the wisdom of my impetuous suggestion to involve SOCA. While it was true that Patrick had wanted to be involved with the case right from the beginning, the people we would be dealing with were highly dangerous and organized criminals. I had cheered up slightly when I remembered that Patrick is a highly dangerous and organized investigator.

'I've been following this carefully,' Greenway said, seating himself in the revolving leather chair behind his desk with more care than usual. 'Even more so when Uncle's name was mentioned.'

'Why is he referred to as that?' I enquired.

'I understand it stems from when he shot and killed his nephew on account of the young upstart thinking it was about time he took over the old man's business.'

'Do we know his real identity?' Patrick said.

'Do these people ever have real identities? Once upon a time he was a man from East Ham by the name of Fred Gibbons who used to be a hairy yob with tattoos. This character disappeared for a couple of years after he came out of prison for robbery with violence and then a man with a shaven head came on the scene in the same area calling himself Dobson. So there was a bald yob with the same kind of tattoos getting up to the same kind of criminal activity. He went down for six years for the nephew's murder, the sentence reduced because he dropped any number of his seriously wanted so-called buddies in it and at the time the nephew was armed to the teeth and tried to shoot him first – you realize we're talking gang warfare here too. He went from sight again after release and then a man we're convinced is the same villain has popped up in Hammersmith with money to burn and, according to a reliable grapevine, is running a crime ring involving some of the same mobsters. This bloke has blond hair and the same kind of tattoos, although some of them seem to have been removed. Like Carrick, I've seen covertly taken pictures and agree with him that it's the same man: Uncle. This is the description that's been circulated to all police forces. The house he's living in is rented in the name of Brad Northwood.'

'Were you sent the descriptions of the other people DS Outhwaite saw in the restaurant in Bath?' I asked.

'I was, and quietly as I'm not up to full ops yet, I've been working on it. The woman with Uncle that night sounds like Joy Murphy. She's not his current squeeze – he usually has a few cast-off footballers' wives for that – more like an in-house harpy who acts as his bodyguard. Apparently she likes nothing better than to be let loose on someone Uncle's got a grudge against. She was probably involved in the mob war in Bath. I get the impression the rest of those present at the restaurant were locals known to Carrick.'

'Someone called Charlie Gill,' I recollected. 'And a Cardiff-based crook Carrick also knew about.'

'He's probably aware by now that the latter mobster's very recently been picked up by the eastern division of South Wales Police to help with enquiries into a warehouse raid in which a security guard was shot and seriously injured.'

'He also mentioned a woman who had more convictions for being drunk and disorderly than seemed possible but couldn't remember her name. She was with a man with ginger hair. He didn't recognize him from Lynn Outhwaite's description.'

'I emailed Carrick about them,' Greenway said. 'Just to get as much info as possible. She's one Gilly Darke, a local petty criminal. The man hasn't appeared on anyone's radar so might be perfectly innocent.'

'Going out to dinner with a crime lord like Uncle must have been a bit of a culture shock then – if he even knew who he was,' Patrick drawled. 'But why was a petty crook and her boyfriend there?'

'Recruits?' I suggested. 'Someone's been going around the pubs in the area looking for potential gang members. Were they brought along as they might know the set-up at Bath nick and/ or CID? And you could ask Carrick how many male coppers there are in the area, past and present, with ginger hair.'

You are on dangerous territory when you say things like this to policemen. But as Greenway knows perfectly well, to bring in ideas from new angles is exactly my role. He gave me a straight look and then muttered, 'Yes, all right, I'll get on to him.'

'So what would you like us to do, sir?' Patrick asked.

There was a little silence and then Greenway answered with, 'This is a brainstorming session.' He sat back in his chair with a tight smile and regarded us steadily. 'Ideas, please, from my adviser and his consultant. I want to put together a list of proposals that you can take to Carrick with a view to getting quick results with this. And don't call me sir – you used to be a lieutenant colonel, for God's sake.'

'You don't need anyone to search out Uncle as it's known exactly where he is – if indeed it is the right bloke,' Patrick immediately said, having chuckled at the final remark. 'But you do need to build a copper-bottomed case against him before he's picked up and find out how far his empire stretches. Not only that, you need to know whether he really has got as far as Bath or if that was just him and a few cronies having a weekend off and living it up on their ill-gotten gains. I reckon he's had enough of being inside and is going upmarket having found rather a lot of emergency loot somewhere. He'll get his dirty work done for him from now on and if the hirelings are arrested that's tough on them. If we're not careful he'll be virtually untouchable, on the face of it living a respectable life. I'm prepared to go undercover with a view to infiltrating his set-up.'

'Thank you but I don't think that needs to be our number one move.'

'The interesting bit is the presence of the petty crook, Darke. Is she stunningly beautiful and possibly in line to decorate his bed, by the way? I haven't seen her description.'

Greenway consulted his computer. 'Tall, medium build, brown hair, brown eyes, no other distinguishing marks. That doesn't tell us much.'

'I'll ring Lynn,' I said. 'She's at her mother's with a broken leg but will probably still answer her mobile.'

Lynn had a few choice words to say about Darke and in response to my query as to her own well-being grunted and then said that she would rather be at work and was planning to shoot the horse.

'Grumpy as hell,' I reported. 'In which case it might be wise to slightly temper her pronouncement that Darke resembles a pig's arse.'

'I think it answers your question, though,' the commander said to Patrick. 'And I can understand why Carrick doesn't want to pull her in at the moment. It's best to proceed with caution or they'll go to ground.'

I had an idea Carrick could not even find her but said nothing.

'This Charlie Gill . . .' I ventured.

'James'll be able to fill us in on him,' Patrick said.

'Yes, I know but he's someone you might expect to be involved if this man is trying to extend his criminal interests. Uncle might be offering him some kind of partnership with whatever he controls and then when he's got what he wants quietly have him dropped into Bristol docks one night in a weighted sack.'

'And?' Patrick said.

'Charlie might not be very bright and doesn't know who he's up against. So a friendly warning might not come amiss – hoping that he'll then be scared into coming up with some really useful info.'

'It's too risky,' Greenway said. 'Patrick's a local too – he'd be recognized.'

'While it's no secret in Hinton Littlemoor that Patrick's working for SOCA I'm not sure about the wider area. But this doesn't have to be done undercover. I'm sure he could portray himself as a bit of a maverick – one of those cops who hover on the edge of the criminal fraternity.' I gave Patrick a big smile. 'Sorry, I'm talking about you as though you weren't here.'

Smiling back, Patrick said, 'But if Gill really is in this man's pocket and thinks he's got a good deal it would be risking the investigation – they would know they'd been spotted together.'

'Then arrange for Gill to have a little encounter that would unnerve him so he'd be more likely to believe you.'

'Bloody hell!' the commander burst out with. 'This isn't one of your books, you know!' He was silent for a few moments and then said, 'What sort of encounter?'

'Oh, just being pushed around a bit by someone hooded and scary should do it. Does he have any minders?' I asked.

They did not know.

'Shall I ask James?' I offered, picking up my mobile again. Words seemed to have failed them just then so I hit buttons.

'He's grumpy too,' I said, after a couple of minutes' conversation. 'There's a bloke Gill knocks around with who James describes as being a spavined idiot who he really, really wants to get his hands on to help with several inquiries, but like nearly everyone else he needs to find in connection with this case he's gone to ground. He sometimes drives the car as Gill's banned.'

Silence.

'I suppose . . .' Greenway began and then stopped speaking.

'I'd have to get Carrick on board,' Patrick observed.

'Yes, you can't act behind his back,' I said.

'That could be our first move then,' Greenway murmured. 'Then what? Surely at least one of the Jessop brothers should be fit for interview soon.' He gave me a Patrick shark-style grin. 'Perhaps we ought to have you in on that, Ingrid, to help sharpen up Derek Jessop's memory.'

'Well, officially, I'm still standing in for Carrick's sergeant,' I said. 'So if I haven't been replaced that will be normal case-work progress.'

'Good. Now, one bit of intelligence you might not be aware of is that Uncle and co. have adopted various Mafia practices, one of which is a kind of money laundering-cum-protection racket – it can only be described as a small offshoot – that involves a lot of small businesses. It's how they deal with some of the loot from drug dealing and robberies and at the same time drag people, by intimidation or brute force, into their sphere of operations. Outfits like independent cafés, bistros, bars, independent drug stores and upmarket fashion boutiques are the favourite targets: not places you'd first look for involvement in crime.'

'Cooperate or your premises will be firebombed?' Patrick said.

'Yes, apparently that's the most common initial approach. But, far more difficult to trace, they also barter stuff – force the proprietors to accept goods, originally bought from cash and carries by people who appear to be running a perfectly normal business and then head for their prey and demand in exchange stuff like food, wine, pharmaceuticals and clothing. They always choose what they want and take better goods than they're leaving behind. So the money goes round and round – some of the stuff they consume themselves – and they finally sell top-of-the-range stuff for a profit. Then it starts all over again.'

'Using vans with bogus company names on them?' Patrick hazarded.

'That's right. It's also used as a method of getting rid of stolen property that's not particularly valuable, in other words stuff that's perishable, like food, or not sufficiently interesting to a fence. This might sound as though it's only peanuts' – he smiled at his own pun – 'but multiplied by over a hundred businesses that are thought to be involved, mostly in the south of England, it adds up to a lot of money. And of course it's only one small layer in their scheme of dealing with illegal funds.'

'And I suppose with regard to slightly larger concerns which would be difficult or impossible to take over, gang members could apply for jobs such as managers or supervisors and operate a scam on the inside.'

'I hadn't thought of that angle in connection with this case,' Greenway admitted. 'But, yes, I'm sure you're right.' He made a note on a jotter pad, threw down the pen and continued,

'Another thing is that in my view small sometimes means weak. The not-so-bright guys get given this job and that might be a way to get to those at the top. So that's two avenues of investigation you can put to Carrick.'

We duly brainstormed for another hour or so and failed to come up with any more useful ideas. It was reluctantly concluded that further lines of inquiry might be opened up after Derek Jessop, and possibly his brother, were questioned but until that happened nothing would be gained by sitting around talking.

Patrick phoned Carrick, who immediately vetoed my idea of approaching Charlie Gill on the grounds that the man was hard-headed, by no means stupid, had originated in London and would go into any business agreement with both eyes wide open. He was fairly dismissive about making discreet enquiries at small businesses in the area too.

Stalemate?

FIVE

We went home for the weekend, Patrick with the avowed intention of making Carrick change his mind, starting by cunningly inviting him and his wife Joanna to dinner on Saturday night. But the pair had already accepted another invitation so regretfully had to refuse. This meant that Patrick focused on activities with the children in between lone brainstorming while, in the afternoon, I helped Elspeth with a village jumble sale. Predictably, I always get landed with the book stall.

At some stage in the minor warfare being conducted over bargains Elspeth brought me a cup of tea and a cake.

'That's her,' she said, jerking her head over to her left. 'Carol Trelonic, Adam Trelonic's widow. Betty Williams has just told me that the woman brought in what must have been most of her husband's clothes this morning. I call that a bit soon, don't you? I mean, the funeral hasn't taken place yet.'

I happened to know that the delay had been caused by the body having not yet been released by the police.

'How can I get to talk to her?' I asked.

'I'll introduce you – that's a perfectly normal thing to do.' She gave me a very straight look and said quietly, 'You and Patrick do work together sometimes, don't you?'

I nodded.

She patted my arm. 'John thinks so too. But if anyone asks of course we know nothing about it.' Again I was subjected to her searching gaze. 'Guns too?'

'I'm a pretty good shot,' I told her. 'We watch each other's backs.'

'Good . . . lovely,' she said, gazing around a little distractedly as though we were discussing the time of the next Mothers' Union meeting. 'Let's grab her before she scuttles off.'

Finding the choice of words fascinating I put my tea and cake on a window ledge and followed her through the throng

to where a woman was ferreting around with others on one end
of the bric-a-brac stall. A certain amount of elbowing and dirty
looks exchanging seemed to be taking place.

'Mrs Trelonic, I'd like you to meet my daughter-in-law,
Ingrid,' Elspeth said quite loudly on account of the hubbub. 'As
you probably know she and my son bought the rectory when
the diocese was going to sell it.'

'Scuttles' suddenly made sense when the woman turned
towards me. Her tongue flickered across thin lips nervously and
she gave me a brief and wary smile. She was younger than I
had for some reason imagined and I could not picture her
partnered with the unshaven and taciturn individual who had
delivered our logs.

'I'm very sorry about your husband,' I said.

Her face became expressionless and, woodenly, she thanked
me.

'Ghastly to be caught in crossfire like that,' I went on. 'Just
an innocent passer-by.'

'He was always a loser,' she snapped and turned away from
us.

'Well, that was a waste of time,' Elspeth said when we had
returned to the bookstall.

'You told James that she set your teeth on edge. Why?'

'There was a time . . .'

I waited.

'When I thought she'd set her sights on John.'

'Surely not!'

'All smiles and volunteering to do things. Staying behind
after the services, sort of . . . hovering.' Determinedly, she
added, 'Yes, I know the man's in his early seventies but he
doesn't look it since he had his heart op; he's quite charismatic
really.'

Like his son.

I sold a couple of books and then said, 'Look, you don't
have anything to worry about. John loves you to bits.'

'I suppose she's quite attractive in a funny sort of way and
there *have* been rumours that she's had affairs with several men
in the village. But . . .'

'Is this still going on as far as John's concerned?'

'I thought not, but now I come to think of it . . .' She shook her head. 'I must go and help with the teas. See you later.'

Patrick appeared carrying Vicky and with Justin, and the trio went over to the toys where the latter immediately pounced on a large plastic water pistol. No, I willed his father to tell him, you already have a large water pistol. They bought it. Then parental control had immediately to be exercised when Justin wanted it filled right there and then. He was safely diverted by a rather flabby football that I knew would go straight in the bin that night by which time it would have fully deflated.

'Busy?' Patrick asked when they arrived, Justin with his armful, and I had presented Vicky with a couple of little picture books I had chosen for her. 'Any of yours here?' he went on to ask before I could reply, peering at the titles.

'No,' I replied evenly.

'Just trying to wind you up.'

'I know. That woman over there in the queue for teas wearing the red jacket is Mrs Trelonic. I tried to talk to her but she was having none of it.'

'What did you make of her, though?'

'Furtive.'

'She could have been involved if he was.'

'All she said was that her husband had always been a loser.'

'I wonder if he took up the offer of that recruiting officer. I really need to find out who that was.'

'Then question her. You have the authority.'

'She's refused to talk to the police any more.'

'You could try charm.'

My advice has never actually been catastrophic before.

He went later that afternoon on his own, as I knew my presence would not be remotely useful. When he returned I was in the garden carrying Mark, who seems to love looking at trees waving in the breeze. I walked over to where Patrick was parking the car.

'I take it you didn't hoist in the fact that she was a grade one troublemaker,' was Patrick's opening remark as he slammed the driver's door with more force than was necessary.

'I only spoke to her for a matter of seconds,' I said.

'Pity.'

'Why? What happened?'

'She said she'd already put in a formal complaint to the police about what she called "continuous harassment" – Carrick didn't quite mention that, did he? – and then told me that she'd sort me out by telling the village that she and Dad are having an affair.'

I swore under my breath. Then I said, 'Sorry, Elspeth did say that she thought the woman had been giving him sheep's eyes.'

'Ingrid, you should have told me that before I went!'

He strode away towards the house and I hurried to catch up. Patrick rounded on me. 'For God's sake don't run with him!'

'Look, I'm sorry. I've apologized, haven't I? I can't always get everything right!'

But he went off without another word.

If oracles had boxes I had definitely been shoved back in mine. For when you do something, wittingly or not, to threaten the stability of a man's family, in his eyes it is unforgivable. I could hardly tell Elspeth and John what the problem was although I knew the former, although upset, would probably inform her son that he deserved to be shaken until his teeth rattled for blaming me.

On Sunday Patrick helped his father with the morning communion service, singing in the choir and acting as server, and then retired to the dining room in the afternoon to catch up on household accounts and more work-related brainstorming. I never write on Sundays unless I have a rapidly approaching publisher's deadline so I carried on devoting my time to the children, having given Carrie the day off. Early on Monday Patrick left, in the car and presumably for London, without telling me what he intended to do. This was against our working rules but hardly surprising as we had barely spoken for twenty-four hours.

Would this wretched Trelonic woman carry out her threat? In my view the fact that she had made it proved not only that she was a complete bitch but had something to hide. I borrowed Elspeth's car and drove into Bath.

'I'm not sure who I'm working for this morning,' I said, putting my head around James Carrick's office door.

'For me until tomorrow unless you've pressing SOCA stuff,' he answered. 'I'm getting one DS Keen. I just hope he is.' A file he had been reading was tossed into a wire tray on his desk. 'We can go and talk to Derek Jessop. Coming?'

'Of course.'

We were making our way across the car park when Carrick said, 'I was expecting to be given the full treatment by that man of yours to make me change my mind about the best way to carry the case forward.'

'He would have tried,' I said.

'Is he not around?'

'No. He went off to London this morning. I don't know why. We had words over the weekend.' As I felt it affected the case with which we were all involved I related what had happened.

'She's done nothing of the kind!' the DCI said, referring to the complaint. 'Or, at least, hadn't done at the end of last week. And nobody's been harassing the woman. You know, all she's succeeded in doing is making me suspicious that she was involved in some kind of scam her husband was in, mobsters or whatever.'

'Patrick's livid with me for not warning him about her apparent attraction to his father.'

'Och, why would you normally bother him with it? It's exactly the kind of thing that men dismiss as women's gossip.'

Coming from a man, I reckoned this to be a noble remark.

'But Mrs Trelonic could do damage if she put a rumour about,' he added. 'This is nothing to do with me really but you might have to warn your in-laws.'

When we moved to Somerset I really thought everything would settle down into an interesting but fairly quiet routine.

Billy Jessop was still very ill, although improving. His elder brother was due to be discharged the following day, freeing him from his police 'minders' and into the care of a remand centre.

'I don't know how you have the brass neck to come here,' he shouted at me when he saw me.

'You're disturbing the peace again,' I admonished, not in a

mood to take any nonsense from him. 'And I would like to remind you that but for me you might be on a murder, rather than attempted murder, charge right now.'

We drew up chairs around where he was sitting, his shoulder bandaged, arm in a sling, in a patients' lounge. A television in one corner was being gloomily watched by three elderly men, the programme some kind of shopping channel.

'You're not being interviewed under caution as the docs don't think you're well enough,' Carrick began by saying in conversational tones. 'We're just here for a chat.'

Jessop grunted.

'You don't normally carry firearms,' the DCI continued. 'How did that come about?'

'I found it,' Jessop replied, picking up a newspaper and pretending to read it.

'Was that before or after it was used in the shoot-out in Bath?'

'I don't know what you're talking about.'

'You deny you were wounded during the night when rival gangs clashed in the city centre?'

'Billy and I were just coming back from a bar and we got caught up in it. We're victims.'

Carrick snatched the paper away from him. 'I have a reliable witness who *saw* you and your brother, has identified the pair of you from mugshots and is prepared to swear on oath that he saw you firing weapons. At least one of these was removed by other people when you were injured. Who were the others, Derek?'

'Sod off.'

'Who was the person who recruited you? We know someone went round pubs hiring men like you.'

'Like me?' Jessop said angrily. 'You mean thick, I suppose.'

'No, expendable,' I said before Carrick could reply. 'You know, cannon fodder, people they regard as nobodies hired for no money to make the crime bosses look big – what law enforcement agencies refer to as disposable associates. But it all went wrong, didn't it? And two of those involved were literally gutted. That wasn't quite the plan, was it?'

'Gutted?' Jessop repeated.

'Yes, they were shot and then knifed around, mutilated.'

'I don't know anything about that.'

'We don't actually know yet whose side they were on. Eastern European sort of men; Romanians probably. They might have had quite thick accents or not spoken much English at all. Ring any bells with you?'

He shook his head. 'No.'

'Men like that weren't working with you?'

'No.'

'You know what that means, don't you? It was people from your lot who did it. That makes you some kind of accessory to disembowelling. I understand their guts were strewn all over the pavement.' Actually, I understood no such thing but as our American friends say, it figured.

'I didn't do it!' Jessop bawled, making the old men in the corner almost jump out of their pyjamas.

'If you were drunk you might have done. Was a man called Adam Trelonic hired as well?'

'I don't know the name.'

'Tell us who paid you rubbish money to spend most of the rest of your life in prison.'

Jessop, white-faced, carried on shaking his head.

'How much?' I persevered. 'Fifty quid? A hundred? How he must have laughed telling the boss man how cheaply idiots in the sticks could be hired. Yes, I've changed my mind now. The DCI's right: he was looking for the really stupid. He was there, you know, one of the chief mobsters. Sitting in his big car down near the station watching it all happen. Seeing you writhing around in agony with young Billy and—'

'The bastard sent someone over to take our money off us!'

Jessop then looked as though he wished he could bite his tongue off.

'Who? The man you were working for?'

After a long silence Jessop muttered, 'Him.'

'You've no proof, though.'

'Billy's gun and both our wallets was grabbed.'

'Yet you're protecting this man,' Carrick observed.

'I'm not saying nothing more.'

'You've no proof it was *him*!' I repeated.

'Well, I saw who done it, didn't I!' Jessop yelled.

The ancients in the corner turned round to stare at him.

'You recognized whoever it was? The boss man's right-hand honcho?'

'I'm not saying nothing more.'

Turning to Carrick, I said, 'It was almost certainly the one who did the hiring. He was safe and sound in the car no doubt or he couldn't have been given the nod to retrieve the weapons and get their money back. You know, the more I think about this the more I'm coming round to believing that—'

Well . . . no.

To Jessop, I said, 'Was it a woman who took your money and the gun? Who hired you promising riches unlimited? A hooked-on violence woman who's as rough as rats, behaves more like a man and scares the bejesus out of everyone?'

Jessop stared at me, his eyes like holes in his head, and I knew I was right.

'*She* was safely in the car, possibly with others, helping direct what was going on,' I said to Carrick. 'Then joined in and was probably the one who did a bit of fancy knife-work on two of the opposition. I'd put money on her gunning down the innocent people who just happened to get in her way too.'

The DCI nodded sagely, letting me have my head.

'And you're the poor sap who's going to prison for a long time,' I said to Jessop. 'Yes or no: was it a woman?'

'Yes,' he whispered. 'Some London bloke's loony minder. He fancies having a bigger manor.'

'Didn't he have enough of his own heavies to call on?'

'She said he believed in having local talent. Was all charm then.'

I almost felt sorry for him. 'What did this woman look like?'

'Oh, I dunno. Short dark hair, tough-looking. She liked wearing combats and desert boots. Deep sort of voice.'

'So her boss is joining up with Charlie Gill,' Carrick said.

'God knows. I don't know the ins and outs of it.'

'Rumour has it that Mick the Kick was going to try his hand at getting into the Bath scene as well,' Carrick continued. 'War then: the London mobster joining up with Charlie to teach

Micky a lesson and kick him out for good with a view to taking the whole prize.'

'Micky's a real bad sort,' Jessop muttered.

'Get the feeling your new friends are far worse?' the DCI said in disgust.

'Do – do I . . .' Jessop floundered into silence. It had become obvious that he was still very weak with, I could swear, the hint of tears in his eyes. 'Sorry, I feel a bit strange.'

'What?' Carrick said.

The man actually swayed a little in his chair. 'Do I get – well – a deal if I tell you what I know?' he asked faintly. 'You know, make a statement.'

'I'll think about it.'

I endeavoured to beam into James's head that this was not the time to play cat and mouse and that he really, really needed this information, even if it did not amount to much. I must have been staring at him rather hard for he suddenly stood up and snapped, 'OK. I'll interview you again in a couple of days when you're feeling stronger. You'll be brought to Bath nick and it had better be worth my trouble so use the time to have a damned good think.'

'Good,' Carrick said crisply when we were outside. 'Thank you. You're getting as good as Patrick.'

But he and I would never achieve the alchemy that Patrick and I do.

'What were you going to say before you thought it might be Joy Murphy?' Carrick wanted to know.

'Oh, I was working on the theory that Uncle had masterminded the Bristol lot too to give Gill a fright in order to persuade him to join up with him.'

'He has Mick on his payroll already, you mean?'

'Yes – and a little thing like collateral damage in the form of spilled guts and the murder of the innocent wouldn't have bothered him.'

'Expensive cash-wise, though. What's the special interest?'

'Perhaps it's just a case of divide and rule by causing as much confusion as possible. He might even be hoping that all the opposition will kill one another, leaving him with a clear field. I don't know. You tell me: it's your manor.'

Reminding him that this might be a personal issue struck home and the DCI, deep in thought, did not speak again until we were in the car.

'Can you let me have that typed up?' he requested, gesturing towards my notebook.

'Give me around a quarter of an hour when we get back,' I said.

'You know, I think you might be right. We need someone to get Gill by the ears and tell him the way it is.'

'I thought you said he was a hard-headed businessman who knew his way around people like Uncle because of his London origins.'

'I know, but I've spoken to the man and he didn't give me the impression that he was the sort who'd be overjoyed at the bloody outcome of that night. He might be thinking that the Murphy woman had overdone it. And, as you say, what's Uncle after? I would have thought that Bath was small beer for a man who no doubt thinks of himself as a top crime lord.'

'I take it Gill runs the drug dealing in the city.'

'Mostly, yes. But would that alone attract the likes of Uncle?'

'Can't you touch Gill?'

'We're building a case against the man but as you know it'll have to be solid as people like him can afford the best briefs. I think I shall have to concentrate on working out what Bath's attraction is for Uncle and try to be one step ahead of him.'

'It might be nothing more than the Met making life too difficult for him where he is.'

'That's quite possible. You might get hold of Patrick and tell him that I've reconsidered. Meanwhile, all the routine enquiries into the gang war will continue.'

'Have you written the Huggins clan out of this investigation?'

'Reluctantly, yes. Oh, by the way, Mrs Stonelake was shown some mugshots and pictures of the deceased but couldn't recognize any of them as the men she saw.'

Later, when I handed him the notes he informed me that while we were out that morning Carol Trelonic had made a formal complaint that she had been 'harassed' by the police. This, he told me, would have to 'go through the proper channels' but on the grounds that her late husband was a suspect in a major shooting incident, and had still not been completely cleared of involvement, he did not think she would get a sympathetic response.

I just hoped she would not hit a soft target instead.

SIX

I left a message on Patrick's phone with the news that, at the time, Carrick had not omitted to tell him about any complaints and that he would like his practical help after all. I made no mention of any difficulties between us but said that he ought to tell me where he was and what he was doing.

I heard not a word.

Two days later Katie, just back from school, came to find me in the kitchen. 'Mum, you know you said we mustn't go anywhere near the pub?'

'I did,' I agreed, wondering what on earth was coming.

'Had you forgotten that the school bus stops almost right outside now?'

I had, and apologized.

'In the mornings Matthew and I stand a little way off in case that horrible Andrews man sees us and makes more trouble. But when we come home . . .'

'Yes?' I prompted.

'Well, we have to get off nearly right outside, don't we? And just now . . .'

She looked a bit bothered so I sat her down and gave her a drink of juice.

'What's wrong?' I asked, sitting down beside her.

'Matthew stayed behind for cricket so I was on my own. There was a car outside the pub, like ours only black. The windows were made of that dark glass but were open a bit as they were smoking. A man was sitting in the driver's seat and another was talking to Mr Andrews by the pub door. Then I saw another man sitting in the back seat. He looked a bit horrible really, they all did. Then he saw me and gave me a *really* horrible look and shut the window.'

'He deliberately frightened you. That was nasty of him.'

'But it was *Dad*!'

For a moment I was rendered speechless.

'I ran away. I've thought about it now and know he wanted me to run away and not show I'd recognized him.'

'Are you *sure* it was him?'

'Yes. He had his hair all flattened down with that gel stuff and hadn't had a shave but I know it was him.' After a pause, she said, 'He did frighten me actually.'

'That would only be to make sure you stayed right away from any possible danger.'

I could not tell her that when we are working undercover he sometimes frightens me silly too.

'You didn't by any chance get the number of the car?'

She had and not only that gave me quite good descriptions of the other two men. From information I already had from Carrick I knew that the man talking to Andrews had almost certainly been Charlie Gill, who was very fat and given to wearing a suit and loud ties. There was every chance the individual behind the wheel was the 'spavined idiot' so picturesquely described by the DCI.

'I won't say anything to anybody about it,' Katie said in a low voice. 'Not even to Matthew.'

'Especially to Matthew,' I emphasized. 'Only for a while, though, as we don't usually have secrets. I'll find out what's going on.'

Katie had a sudden thought. 'He must be investigating the goings-on at the pub,' she said with shining eyes.

Again, I urged her to keep it to herself but doubted if she could hide what had happened from Matthew for very long. Patrick had obviously forgotten that the school bus no longer stops outside the church as well or he would have kept his window closed. He had taken a huge risk by appearing in Hinton Littlemoor at all but perhaps he had had no choice.

'He was smoking too,' Katie said sadly as she went out of the door.

'He does *sometimes* smoke little cigars,' I said to thin air.

I rang James Carrick.

'I could have done with knowing about this before,' he grumbled.

'You imagine I couldn't?' I retorted.

'Please do your best to get in touch with him.'

*　　*　　*

'Doing my best' would normally involve utilizing one of our ploys, starting with phoning his mobile number, allowing it to ring four times and then hanging up, repeating this several times. I could not do this as Patrick's phone was switched to the messaging service. I had already left him a conventional message before this latest development so decided to wait until at least the next day.

Just before seven the following morning I had a call from Carrick.

'Guess what?' he said, continuing before I could speak with, 'Keith Matlock was found dumped in a wheelie bin just around the corner to the entrance to the nick this morning done up like a parcel.'

'Who's Keith Matlock?'

'Charlie Gill's sometime driver and right-hand moron,' he replied in the tone of voice that suggested I should have known.

'Oh, the spavined idiot!'

'Yes, him.'

'Well, you know who that little present was from, don't you?'

'I do indeed. Has he contacted you?'

'No, but do look through Matlock's pockets.'

'I'm just going in to work. Do you want to be present when I interview him?'

'No, if you don't mind. It's a bit too close to home right now with Patrick in the enemy camp.'

'I'll keep you right in the picture,' he promised. 'Oh, and I've been so up to my neck in work I've had to reschedule interviewing Derek Jessop. I take it you'd like to be there when I do.'

'Yes, please.'

'I'll let you know.'

Three quarters of an hour later he phoned again. 'You were right. There was a note addressed to me containing directions – or at least an OS map reference – of where Gill can be found. I get the impression he might be in the same kind of fix as his henchman. So I'd better send someone out there pronto and call you again later.'

Not ten minutes after this one-sided conversation had taken place I heard someone come in the back door. It was Patrick, still with his stubble, smarmed-down hair and accompanied by a definite aroma of cigar smoke and sweat. He looked as though he might have hiked across fields and through several ditches as there was mud, leaves and twigs affixed to his person as well.

'I'm sorry I went off like that,' was the first thing he said.

'And I'm sorry I forgot to tell you what your mother had told me about Carol Trelonic.'

He walked forward quickly and gave me a kiss. 'Is Katie still here or has she gone to school?'

'She's here and should be down for her breakfast by now. I'll call her.'

We were both in the kitchen when she appeared a minute or so later, Patrick making himself a much-needed mug of coffee. She paused in the doorway when she first saw him and then ran over to give him a hug.

Patrick fished in the pocket of his leather jacket and drew out a small parcel. 'That's to say sorry for scaring you,' he said.

In the box inside the wrapper was a little gold heart on a chain, a single tiny sparkle in its centre.

'It's a real diamond,' he told her.

'It's so pretty,' Katie breathed. And then went on to thank him more times than was really necessary.

'Do I look cool like this?' he asked her, striking a pose.

'Yes, but not the belt,' she said without hesitation. 'It's horrible and silly.'

It is the one he insists brings him luck with the phoney brass buckle in the shape of a grinning skull. Red glass eyes too.

The gift was put into my care and very shortly afterwards she left the house to catch the bus. Matthew had stayed at a friend's house the previous night.

'I nearly blew it,' Patrick said, subsiding into a chair by the kitchen table and tiredly rubbing his hands over his face. 'The last thing I thought he'd do was head here. And stupidly—'

'You had forgotten that the school bus now stops by the pub,' I interrupted.

'Yes. But I couldn't allow frightening her to continue. I had to do something to . . .'

'She wasn't all that scared,' I said when he stopped speaking. 'One of the first things she said to me was that you'd frightened her to make her run away and not show she'd recognized you. What did you do with Gill?'

A reflective and, if I am honest, cruel smile appeared. 'Left him in a barn near Wellow. I take it Carrick got the message.'

'He did. And I should imagine we need to have a debriefing session with him – right now.'

'Hung by his heels,' said James Carrick heavily, having slammed the door of his office.

'Poor guy,' Patrick murmured.

'We had to let him go.'

Becoming exasperated, probably on account of lack of sleep, Patrick said, 'Of course you bloody well had to let him go! The whole idea was that you'd end up as buddies having received a tip-off as to his whereabouts.'

'So what's the story?' the DCI enquired, not at all ruffled. These men are, after all, good friends.

'I did a couple of day's work at HQ on stuff for Greenway and dug out everything I could find about these mobsters. Greenway was still all for the direct approach to Gill but I decided not to go for the maverick cop option on the grounds that I really am one of those. So when I'd run him to earth down here I said I was the man from Uncle.'

'Go on,' Carrick said after I had laughed loudly.

'I told him that my visit was to ensure that he knew precisely where he stood and that he was to do exactly as he was told. Now it's your turn – get in there and offer him police protection as long as he tells you everything he knows.'

'How did you find him?'

'Well, having discovered from mugshots that Matlock looks like a gorilla on an off day and that his last known address was in the London Road I drove down overnight and parked in a back lane, hung around the pubs in that area when they opened at eleven and struck lucky when he rolled into the Carpenters' Arms for something alcoholic to sober himself up from the night before. And as you know, I can act rough.'

I hid my amusement this time.

'And told him to take me to his leader.'

'He swallowed your story then.'

'He was so hung-over as well as naturally stupid he'd have believed me if I'd told him I was the Sugar Plum Fairy. So he rang Gill who demanded to know who I was referring to as Uncle. So I told him – Brad Northwood. That appeared to clinch it and he picked us up outside – I thought you said he was banned? – about twenty minutes later. By which time I decided I would throw a real rage at being kept waiting. That seemed to scare them a bit.'

'Hinton Littlemoor, though?' I prompted, picturing the scene.

'He said he was on his way there to do a little business and did I mind. I said I minded like hell but he'd better get on with it. And then they could buy me lunch. Somewhere else. I don't know how we got there alive as he made Matlock drive and he must have been ten times over the limit.'

I said, 'Matthew and Katie really were on to something then.'

'But we still don't know what it is. I didn't dare get out of the car or show my face to Andrews as he knows me. And if I had asked too many questions they would have suspected my story. But the fact that Gill went to the Ring o' Bells and spoke to Andrews outside does *suggest* that something iffy's involved. One must also bear in mind that he could have simply been booking an evening bash with the boys.'

'He could have done that over the phone,' Carrick observed. 'We must know more before we say anything. In mitigation with Matthew's case, I mean.'

'And we can't mention it to him either,' I said regretfully.

'Thank you for Matlock by the way,' Carrick went on. 'He'll no doubt be banged up for quite a while. But what of Gill? He must know you delivered his henchman into the safe hands of the law.'

'It doesn't matter,' Patrick said. 'Matlock actually carried on drinking at lunchtime despite his boss getting furious with him. Then he passed right out in the car park. Gill by this time was a bit tight too so was in a let's teach the stupid bugger a lesson mood. So Matlock was delivered to the nick with his blessing. I think he thought that if he grovelled a bit to me I'd leave him alone and go home happy with a glowing report for Uncle. Not so.'

'You didn't beat him up, though.'

'No, I don't beat up overweight and unfit men older than me who haven't done me any personal injury,' Patrick replied evenly.

'He refused to say what had happened to him.'

'Good. Did you question him then?'

'No, I thought I'd let him stew for a bit.'

'You might regret that.'

'I don't think so. Where's his car?'

'Oh, I left it on double yellow lines in Wellow village and walked home by the rural route. It was pretty late by the time we'd finished getting Matlock ready for posting so I didn't want to call anyone out to pick me up. Haven't slept under a hedge since army days,' he finished by ruefully saying.

Patrick's service injuries have left him with a right leg of man-made construction below the knee and currently he is taking part in the trial of a prototype that contains springs, a lithium battery and a certain amount of artificial intelligence. Using it has meant the way he now walks is perfectly natural and we plan to pay out a five-figure sum when it comes on to the market. Our automatic Range Rover has been specially adapted with a hand throttle as driving with no sensation in your foot is not easy and something he will only undertake in emergencies or for short distances. Very relevant to this case was that he would not have wanted to bring Gill's vehicle back into Hinton Littlemoor and, worse, be seen driving it.

He smothered a yawn. 'Sorry, I know I didn't do a very good job. I should have worked on Gill a bit longer but I didn't, I cut it short, partly because I didn't want to blow my cover and thought you ought to talk to him. There's also something concerning Katie that Ingrid will tell you about.'

Which I did and Carrick made no comment.

'There are a few more not very important details,' Patrick said afterwards. 'I'll write out a proper report for you.'

'I'll write it, you dictate it to me,' I told him. 'I can email it to James a little later from home.'

Carrick arranged that we were given a lift to where the car had been left and I drove us both home in silence, Patrick half-asleep. The DCI had given no sign that he was disappointed with the outcome of the mission but we both knew that he was.

There was no new or useful intelligence that could be used to move the case forward.

'But at least you got hold of Matlock,' I said when we arrived at the rectory. 'He might sing his heart out.'

'He's next to useless,' Patrick said. 'As well as being on the booze for most of the time the man is genuinely mentally impaired. He forgets just about everything he's told about five minutes afterwards. In my opinion he's on the way to some kind of alcohol-induced early-onset dementia. All I really got out of him was where Gill's living, which he has written down on a piece of paper and keeps in his wallet. He has to remind himself of the address every time he goes there. There was fear there too, not necessarily of me – just fear.'

'Yet he can still drive a car.'

'Sort of.'

'Did it cross your mind that he was pretending to be stupid?'

'Only to begin with. Then he muttered something about being out in Iraq. He's probably an ex-squaddie – with his mind affected by what he's seen and done.'

We met Matthew in the hall.

'This is the job, Matthew,' Patrick said, referring to his state of dishevelment before wearily making his way upstairs for a shower and some sleep. 'Still want it?'

He did not see the boy's reaction but I did.

Oh, brother. Oh, yes. The black jeans and matching leather jacket. That belt, the grinning skull, its red shining eyes. Wow!

Before making a move, and cautious as ever, Carrick had put a watch on Charlie Gill's house, which was in Twerton. Nothing moved. No one went in or out. Then, getting impatient, he sent his temporary sergeant, Frank Keen, and a constable to have a quiet snoop around the exterior. They found an 'open' window and got in. The place was deserted but a TV was switched on and, in the kitchen, food had been removed from the fridge to prepare a meal. In the living room a coffee table had been knocked over and although these combined factors were not particularly sinister in themselves they did suggest that Gill had left in a hurry.

I was still carrying on liaising between SOCA and Bath and

Bristol CID departments. Patrick had contacted Commander Greenway who said he was content, for the present, for the local police to get on with their investigations with us present if needed. Patrick, meanwhile, was finding out all he could about Colin Andrews, the manager of the Ring o' Bells.

As predicted, Carrick got almost nowhere with Matlock in connection with the various charges against him, which were mostly of the oaf-in-attendance at beatings and assaults variety, and he was put on remand with a request for urgent psychiatric reports. Despite Patrick's comments to the contrary the DCI was of the opinion that his suspect was playing dumb. Carrick had already had another setback when the medic at the remand centre had contacted him to tell him that Derek Jessop's condition was no longer considered good enough for him to be interrogated as he had developed a temperature and an infection was feared.

Five days later Charlie Gill's bloated body was fished out of the River Avon. Under the gaze of an audience of tourists who watched avidly from the perfect viewpoint near Pulteney Bridge, the police had removed it, with difficulty, from where it had become jammed on the weir a short distance downstream. After being carried, with even more difficulty, up the narrow steps to road level the corpse was taken away in a plain van.

SEVEN

Gill had been killed with a single shot to the head but not before being subjected to a savage beating.

'We need to know exactly what you did to the man to enable us to know what someone else did to him afterwards,' Carrick said, pausing in a whirlwind progress through the nick when he saw Patrick and me.

'Nothing,' Patrick answered in surprise. 'I told you I didn't.'

'But look, Gill didn't let you tie a rope around his ankles and hang him from a beam without some kind of struggle!'

'Yes, he did. I said I'd been ordered to put him in hospital for a couple of days but was in a tearing hurry. So as I was worried about being watched by Uncle and if Charlie cooperated we could come to a satisfactory arrangement.'

'He's much heavier than you.'

'We arranged a few hay bales underneath; he lay down on the top one and I pulled them away afterwards. You should have questioned him when you found him.'

Carrick threw his arms up in the air and went away.

'Cops don't think like you do,' I explained.

'I gave him that man *on a plate*,' Patrick said furiously. 'And now he's dead, murdered. He should have been questioned and given police protection. As it was he went home, rang Uncle to complain about his treatment and they promptly took him apart and then killed him to teach the interferer a lesson. Uncle – and who the hell else could have done it? – now knows someone's on to him. It wasn't me who screwed up, was it?'

'No,' I agreed calmly. 'But don't forget Joanna's due to give birth at any time and James is dead worried about her. And while I remember it, Matthew has his appointment with the Youth Offending Team a fortnight tomorrow. Will you be there?'

'Of course.'

'What are you going to tell them?'

'The truth.'

'What, about Andrews having a possible connection with criminals?'

'If necessary. That boy's future is far more important than a bloody police investigation.'

Michael Greenway was furious, blaming both Carrick and Patrick for what he called 'their appalling lack of consultation and communication with one other'. As the commander was the latter's immediate superior it was he who received the reprimand, and I am sure, having overheard that bit without difficulty, the fact it was delivered over the phone did not dilute it one iota.

I had tactfully withdrawn from the room – the call had come during that evening only a few minutes after Patrick had come home from work – and when I returned from my little walk around the garden he was pensively pouring himself a tot of whisky.

'I screwed up,' he said. 'Official.'

I refrained from trite statements along the lines of 'you can't win 'em all' and reckoned the oracle was about to be released from her box.

'So what do I do?' he asked.

'You could turn everything around by working with what you've got. As you said yourself Uncle knows someone's on to him but he probably won't think it's the police as cops don't tend to string mobsters up by the heels. I'm sure you've created a certain amount of confusion so Uncle might be on the trail of Mick the Kick right now, assuming he was behind it.'

'And?'

'Stay in character.'

'Go after him, you mean?'

I did not want to say it but did. 'You might have to gain his interest even further in order to get inside his organization.'

'People like him are always on the lookout for specialists.'

'That's right. He might offer you a job in order to get you off his back. He might think that's what you're after.'

'Serious criminals are always on the lookout for experts, in money laundering for example. I've done a bit of work on the ins and outs of international finance but that kind of thing has never been my strong point.' Patrick pulled a wry face. 'He already has an in-house psychopath: Murphy.' He added wistfully, 'I'm good at those.'

'She could always be taken out.'

'Ingrid, you don't normally suggest I top women.'

I tut-tutted and then smiled at his concern. 'I'm not. Surely she's wanted in connection with several crimes – under suspicion for murders committed during the Bath turf war, for one thing. Arrest her.'

'Or I could play the alcoholic, junkie, psychopathic cop with a long tongue that zaps people around the ears like that alien who wears his innards on his head in *Farscape*,' Patrick muttered after a short silence, throwing himself down on to the sofa.

'OK, delete all the above and just go after him.'

'As me.'

'Yes, as you, the man from SOCA.'

'But not in character as a lean, mean, gunning machine?' he asked sadly, very much tongue-in-cheek.

'There's very little difference. Just forget the hair gel and leave off that confounded belt with the skull buckle.'

He went into a reverie and I left him to it to deal with domestic matters, wondering if I had just written myself out of the job.

'I might take your advice,' Patrick said at just before eleven that night, coming into the bedroom. 'But there's something else I want to do first. It's really important to . . .'

The rest of what he was saying was muffled as he pulled his open-necked shirt over his head. Most men undo a few more buttons first.

'Say that last bit again,' I requested.

He delved into a drawer and unearthed a dark blue sweatshirt. 'Find out what's going on at the pub.'

I stared at him. 'Do I take it you're going to break in?'

'Yes.'

'What, *now?*'

'In around an hour's time.'

'You don't need me to list the consequences if it all goes wrong.'

No, and he did not need reminding that he was a cop now

and should have a search warrant; that his MI5 days, when he had not needed one, were over and it would probably be the end of his job with SOCA, etc., etc.

'Are you coming with me, or not?' Patrick asked in the manner of one who had asked the question before and received no response.

Oh, God, the headlines in *The Bath Chronical*: RECTOR'S SON AND DAUGHTER-IN-LAW CAUGHT BREAKING INTO VILLAGE INN. Or: AUTHOR ARRESTED FOR PUB BURGLARY – 'SHE ALWAYS WAS A BIT ODD,' SAYS NEIGHBOUR.

'Are you doing this mostly for Matthew?' I asked.

'Yes, I suppose I am.'

'We may as well hang together,' I said.

At least he and Katie would be immensely proud of us.

There is a gateway in our garden wall that leads directly into the churchyard which has provided a shortcut for the incumbent and his family for several hundred years, initially so they did not have to mingle with potentially verminous villagers in the lane. It was to be very useful to us tonight as it was vital that no one saw anyone acting furtively in the vicinity of the rectory and the Ring o' Bells. Between both properties is a road and the larger-than-average village green and we would not set foot on one inch of it.

It was around midnight as we went through the gate but the church clock would not strike the hour as it had stopped and was awaiting repairs. Patrick led the way and I did not follow right on his heels in order not to cannon into him should he stop suddenly. It was up to me to fend for myself and not trip over any of the gravestones, which was fairly easy to begin with as there is a path that leads around the side of the church to the main door. Before we reached this we struck off across the grass and progressed more slowly and carefully. There was no moon but as often happens in high summer it was not quite dark and the worn stones seemed almost to possess an afterglow from the brilliant sunset.

We came to an older area, the original part of the graveyard that dates back to the Middle Ages, most of the burial sites now just grassy mounds. Then the boundary wall, much higher on this side, reared up before us. There is a gateway here, too, that I knew had once led into glebe land but these days this is the gardens of private houses with a public footpath running between them. Not many people use it now but the ancient iron hinges and latch on the gate are well oiled and silent: one-time MI5 operatives keep their escape routes easily accessible.

The footpath meandered between fencing and hedges for a short distance and then swung hard left and downhill into a lane. I expected Patrick to turn left again but he went the other way and after fifty yards or so went up a bank surmounted by a field hedge. There was a stile in it and we climbed over it, the author swearing under her breath as her dark sweatshirt caught on a thorn. My companion did not wait but loped off into the near darkness. I have never been able to understand how he moves so quietly, catlike.

I followed the hedge for around fifty yards before coming to a gate. What my gaze had slid over as part of the old stone gatepost came alive, making me start, sort of flowed over the gate and was gone. Grimly, I dealt with the gate, not flowing, and set off after him, seemingly in another field, not exactly sure of the direction he had taken. Surely, somewhere, we would have to cross the road that ran through the village.

The hedge curved around to the left. I stopped to listen but all I could hear were the night sounds of the countryside: a distant owl, cows chewing the cud somewhere quite near to me, the light breeze rustling through foliage. Then, close by, a fox yapped. It is a strange sound, not much like that made by a dog. I went in the direction I had heard it, leaving the hedge to strike across what appeared to be a narrow tapering corner of the field as I soon came to another boundary hedge. A piece of shadow, the fox, moved and went over another stile; at least that was what it turned out to be when I groped for it in the dark. The foot rest on the other side of it was slippery, my foot skated off it and I went down heavily, hitting my head on a branch. No stars, just pain.

In the earthy blackness a tiny beam of light found my face, went on a short exploration and snapped off again: Patrick's 'burglars' torch. Nothing was said. I got to my feet and stood quite still in the blackness of what was probably a little wood. I knew he was nearby, waiting – waiting patiently, I suddenly realized, for me to recover and the training in night surveillance he had given me some years previously when we were still with MI5 to kick in.

Something that is part of his make-up after special services training and happens without him thinking about it had taken time for me to acquire. You have to learn to switch on those senses other than sight and, told to follow him in a Dartmoor forest on several cold winter's nights, I did, after walking into umpteen trees, get quite good at it.

And no, don't speak.

He was still standing very close to me, I knew that; I could actually feel the warmth of his body. Then there was the soft rustle of his clothing as he turned and went away from me. My eyes were more accustomed to the darkness by now and I could make out the outlines of the trunks of trees, the low branches that might hit me in the face, the trailing leaves. I could just pick up his soft footfalls.

It quickly became lighter ahead, the tree cover opening out and then we were walking down a stony track. Patrick almost immediately – I could see him clearly now – turned aside, crouched and then disappeared downwards. He had slithered down an embankment and I did likewise, arriving on what I now knew to be the track bed of the old Somerset and Dorset railway line. We turned to the left, going beneath a road bridge and I heard a vehicle whoosh across it above our heads.

A minute or so later we climbed the embankment on the other side, emerging on a rough path that led gently downhill and into a lane with high hedges. Before us was the clear outline of a huge weeping willow against the night sky. I knew where I was now as I had explored some of these little back ways since moving to the village. We were around a minute's walk from the rear of the Ring o' Bells.

Even without the 'no talking' rule I would not have asked about hazards like alarm systems, dogs, people living on the premises and so forth as I knew they had already been taken into consideration. This did not mean that I was not sweating from nerves: our sortie was far too close to home and had all the potential to be a disaster.

The dark, long shape and the irregular roof of the building loomed before us. There was a gated yard at the rear where deliveries by brewery vehicles were made and which also provided access to the public bar and kitchen. As we got closer I was able to make out that the heavy wooden gates to the yard were open. Patrick did not hesitate and we ghosted through them and made our way over to one side where, if anything, it was darker.

I expected security lights to blaze down on us but we remained in darkness. Two cars were parked there: one the large Japanese four-by-four that I knew belonged to Andrews, the other a small hatchback of some kind. I quickly made a note of its registration number. A single light was switched on in an upstairs room of the building, the window of which was open, the curtains wafted outwards by an inner draught. Sounds were emerging through the open window as well, quite unmistakably those made by people engaged in very vigorous sexual intercourse.

Patrick nudged me and we made our way over towards one of the rear doors, which eventually led into the public bar. It was unlocked. All within was in utter darkness but for tiny red and green indicator lights probably on fridges and freezers in what I seemed to remember was a utility room off to our left. Closing the door behind us Patrick then risked switching on his tiny torch, its pencil-like beam at least preventing us from walking headlong into solid objects.

I drew him around to a passageway off to the right in case he did not know where the office was situated. Events upstairs were getting even more exciting, the cries of pleasure the woman was uttering reaching us down the narrow winding staircase that led up from the junction of corridors. I reckoned there was not much time before they hit a resounding jackpot and then possibly, after getting their breath back, someone would come downstairs for refreshments.

The office door was locked but the lock was old-fashioned and soon yielded to Patrick's skeleton keys. He went in; I stayed just outside on watch.

Ye gods, you could even hear the floorboards creaking as the bed bounced up and down.

By the illumination provided by the tiny torch Patrick was going through what appeared to be files and folders so perhaps there was no computer for records. If so this was odd for someone running a business – unless there was one and it was kept upstairs for added security.

Upstairs, The Moment arrived, the female shrieking like a banshee: bed, floorboards and presumably the rest of the furniture, curtains and wallpaper uniting in one long reverberating clamour that moaned down slowly into silence but for exhausted panting.

I went into the room and hissed, 'I think we ought to go now.'

Patrick appeared to be half inside the deep bottom drawer of a wooden desk, on which there was his pen and note pad, and did not react.

'They might hear us now,' I fretted.

'Five minutes,' he murmured. 'Close the door.'

At the end of what seemed like a good quarter of an hour I heard creaks as someone came down the wooden staircase. A downstairs light was switched on, the door of the office suddenly framed by a thin band of brightness. We stood by the wall close to it so that we would be out of sight if it was opened.

Nothing happened and then came the sound of a kettle being filled. After another pause crockery rattled.

'Right,' Patrick whispered in my ear. 'It's coming up the boil so she won't hear us.'

I was nearest so opened the door a cranny and peeped through it into the empty passageway. All we had to do was go the few yards to where it joined the main corridor and then make for the exit.

'D'you want something to eat?' a woman's voice yelled close by. I couldn't decide whether it sounded vaguely familiar or not.

No reply.

'He's asleep, you silly cow,' Patrick whispered.

'Colin, d'you want something to eat?' she bawled, even closer.

There was a loud snoring kind of grunt from upstairs. Then, 'Yeah, I'll have a burger.'

'Well, you can do it then. I'm not in the mood for cooking anything complicated.'

The woman then returned to the kitchen. Crockery clattered as though she was slamming around mugs in a temper.

We left as silently and as quickly as possible and did not pause until we reached the gate into the churchyard.

'Wow!' Patrick exclaimed, short of breath, locking up again. 'That was interesting.'

I had one thing on my mind. 'How did you know it was a woman who had come downstairs?'

'Women always make the tea afterwards.'

'We never have tea afterwards.'

'No, but I nearly always go to sleep, don't I? The practicalities of sex, my dear Watson. Did you get the registration of the second car?'

'I did. What did you find out?'

'Names of various suppliers. Also customers.'

'What kind of customers?'

'It would appear the pub has clients in the service industries – does the catering for corporate bashes, weddings and so forth.'

'I find that a little hard to believe.'

'So do I.'

We returned the way we had come.

Matthew was in the kitchen, huddled around a glass of milk on the table before him and looked very surprised to see us.

'I couldn't sleep,' he said, obviously feeling that his explanation might be the more pressing of the two.

'Are you worried about your interview with the Youth Offending Team?' Patrick asked him.

'It's only a short time away.'

Patrick sat at the table with him.

I said, 'Would you like that turned into hot chocolate?'

Matthew's face lit up. 'Oh, yes, please.'

'As I've already said, we'll both be there with you,' Patrick assured him. 'All you have to do is tell the truth.'

'Katie said she'd seen you pretending to be a crook of some kind. In the village.'

'She did. It was unfortunate.'

'And you've been somewhere tonight.'

'Yes, and I'm not going to lie to you by saying we couldn't sleep either and went for a walk. Sometimes you have to let people get on with things and not ask questions.'

There had been a hint of steel in this last remark and Matthew dropped his gaze. He found a smile for me when I gave him his hot drink and went off back to his bedroom.

'He needs something to be happy about to take his mind off it,' I said.

'OK, we'll start the self-defence lessons tomorrow.'

I was aware that Carrick had been restrained by the stringent rules of police interrogation when he had broken off from questioning Derek Jessop, who had looked as though he was genuinely feeling faint. It was to be hoped that a short time on remand and being put on a course of antibiotics had not strengthened him sufficiently to make him clam up altogether when required to search his memory on certain matters. My fears appeared to be realized when I first entered the interview room at ten a.m. a couple of days later with James Carrick and the man's face displayed a defiant smirk.

'You're permitted to have a solicitor present,' the DCI pointed out.

Jessop mouthed something obscene at him which is not worth repeating.

'As you wish.' Carrick then went on to open the interview formally and started the recording machine.

'So, from what you said last time we spoke to you we know you were in Bath the night of the mass shootings and were part of a gang run by a London mobster who got his female sidekick to recruit men local to here to swell his numbers,' Carrick began. 'You and your brother Billy were both shot and injured whereupon—'

There was an urgent-sounding rap on the door and DS Frank Keen put his head around it. 'Phone call for you, sir.'

'Can't you take it?' Carrick asked, frowning.

'It's a private call.'

Carrick stopped the interview, asked Keen to stay with me and left the room. Jessop gave me a dirty leer.

'Shoulder better?' I enquired breezily. Actually I was experiencing a pang of guilt: the man was still using a stick following the flesh wound I had caused him.

Moments later Carrick called to me from the doorway. When we were outside, he said, 'It was Joanna. Her waters have broken and she's called an ambulance in case I can't get home in time to take her to the hospital. I *must* go.'

'Go,' I urged. 'She needs you. Give her our love.'

'I'll have to postpone this again.'

'It's not really fair on Jessop. Patrick's working on something in the main office. Can't he do it?'

For once Carrick did not pause to ponder. 'Yes, you're quite right. I'll get him to come in.'

EIGHT

Jessop had cheered up visibly when told that there was to be a different interviewer and the smirk had returned. I saw no reason to spoil things for him. In fact, when the substitute entered the room he was met with a sneer. This might have been because earlier my husband had been out in the city centre walking the route of the gang war, endeavouring to re-enact what had happened in his mind and, judging by the state of the old T-shirt and jeans worn specially for the job, had crawled into various nooks and crannies in case scenes of crime personnel had missed anything.

Patrick, carrying the case file, dropped it on the table, introduced himself to our suspect, thanked the departing DS Keen and switched on the tape machine to listen to what had taken place in the past few minutes.

'Any problems with that?' he asked the man before him.

'Yes, I didn't say any of it.'

'You did,' I told him. 'I was there and wrote it down.'

'Well, yer must have made it up then.'

'Look, DCI Carrick will swear in court that's what you said.'

'Then it just goes to show how corrupt you lot are, doesn't it?'

'So you and Billy were ambushed by Afghan insurgents as you returned from Tesco's?' Patrick asked, opening the file and flipping through it. This was play-acting, he could probably quote large chunks of it from memory.

'You're a real stupid arse, aren't you?' Jessop shouted.

'Yes, I suppose I am. You're having to put up with a new boy, I'm afraid.'

'We were on our way home after a few beers and got caught in crossfire.'

'And all this stuff in the file about having your wallets stolen by the woman who hired you together with Billy's gun is also cobblers, is it?'

'Yes,' Jessop answered grimly.

'But you did have a gun. You tried to kill DCI Carrick with it when he came to talk to you.'

'I panicked. I found it on the pavement when we was shot and used it to defend the pair of us.'

'Completely innocent people don't normally hightail it away when they're hurt. They keep their heads down and pray for an ambulance.'

'I thought they was going to kill us. I half-carried Billy and we got a taxi.'

No taxi drivers had come forward to report that they had transported anyone injured that night.

Patrick said, 'And yet there's a witness who's identified both of you from mugshots as taking an active part in the war. Would you care to explain that?'

'Who, the bloke in the shop doorway? He was only a down-and-out. A meths drinker. Stoned out of his skull most likely.'

'He did mention running away and climbing over a wall into the car park of a university facility to get away from the murderous bunch going on the rampage. Not all that drunk then.' Patrick closed the file gently. 'You know perfectly well the account accurately records what you said.'

'OK, I made it up.'

'Why concoct such a wild story if it wasn't true?'

'Because they was leaning on me.' Jessop jerked his head in my direction. 'Her and Carrick. Making threats if I didn't talk. I was feeling terrible so I said anything to get rid of 'em.'

Patrick leaned back in his seat and regarded Jessop narrowly. 'Well, no, actually,' he said quietly. 'Also in the room with you were three elderly patients who were watching television. Since you went to the remand centre Detective Sergeant Keen, who you saw just now, has been to the hospital to talk to male patients with whom you might have come into contact to see if you'd said anything that might be of interest to us. Two of those in question were still in hospital and they both said how you'd shouted and raved at the police who had come to inter-view you in the patients' lounge. They heard almost every word of what was said, mostly on account of turning the sound down on the TV as what was going on right there in the room was much more interesting. No threats were made; in fact, DCI Carrick stopped the interview when it was obvious you were feeling unwell.'

There was a longish silence.

'Shall we begin again?' Patrick asked. Then, when nothing appeared to be forthcoming, he added, 'I don't like it when people waste my time.'

Jessop, who had had his gaze stonily focused on the table top, glanced up and discovered that when his interrogator did not like something events could get rather . . . unpleasant.

I was sitting next to Patrick but did not have to look at him to know what was going on and as intimated before I have never been able to discover how this sense of menace is achieved. It is just that, all at once, without his facial expression changing, it is there. I am Patrick's wife, have known him for almost always and love him to bits but when he is like this he is too big, too close, too damned dangerous.

'You said you were a new boy,' Jessop muttered.

'In a manner of speaking,' he was told. 'I'm fairly new to the Serious Organized Crime Agency. Before that I worked for MI5.' He smiled humourlessly. 'No restrictions there.'

Although nothing was actually said it was at this point that Jessop decided to cooperate. For the moment.

'Charlie Gill's dead, by the way,' Patrick said in offhand fashion.

'He was nothing to me,' Jessop said in an undertone. 'Just a local villain who tried to look like some kind of Mr Big.'

'Of course he was and I know you weren't working for him directly. I just mentioned it because I'm sure it was Uncle who had him savagely beaten and then killed with a single shot to the head. It gives you a better idea of what will happen if this crook and his murderous minder get a hold in Bath.'

'Uncle?'

'Yes, the London mobster. That's what people call him after he murdered his nephew. The woman who hired you and then stole your wallets was almost certainly Joy Murphy. She's probably a psychopath.'

'Billy nearly died,' Jessop brooded. 'They took me to see him and he didn't even know me.'

'So they need banging up for just about for ever. What of Gilly Darke and her boyfriend, the one with ginger hair?'

'They were Gill's people.'

'Chums of yours?'

'No, of course not! She's just a sozzled tart!'

'What's his name?'

'God knows. He was just known as Red. Always seemed to be whispering in corners with the bosses and treated the rest of us like dirt. I didn't see him at all after the second meeting.'

'What did he look like?'

'Short, thin, eyes like a ferret I once used to have. Shifty-like.'

'What were his and Darke's roles then?'

'Kind of organizing things. It was him what did it all, though. He insisted he brought her along so perhaps he had a quick screw with her when he felt like it. When there was a meeting . . .'

'Just keep talking,' he was urged when he stopped speaking. 'I take it the meetings were between Gill's lot and the London gang to arrange the war.'

Jessop nodded.

'Where were they held?'

'In the back rooms of pubs.'

'And Mick the Kick?'

'He was tricked into coming into Bath that night. I don't know how.'

'Does the name Adam Trelonic mean anything to you?'

'I've been asked that before. No.'

To me, Patrick said, 'Do we know the name Trelonic used for his social security scam?'

'No, but it'll be in the records,' I replied.

'I'll look later.' And then to Jessop, 'Did you ever actually see this Uncle character?'

'Yes, he was there once, with *her.* When she's not all smiles she's like something crazy in a Batman film.'

'What does he look like?'

'He's a square sort of bloke, short and broad. But he's not

fat, it's all muscle. Blond – out of a bottle, mind. Little blue eyes – pig's eyes, now I come to think of it. Gave us all this crap about how soon we'd be rich men like him as long as we did as we was told.'

'Has it crossed your mind since that he was hoping all the local opposition would shoot each other, leaving him with a nicely cleared-out manor?'

'No, but . . .' Jessop brooded some more and I could almost read his mind. That theory seemed all too likely now.

Patrick said, 'Shall we start the story right from the beginning when Murphy was in a pub somewhere quietly asking drinkers if they fancied a job with lots of money, travel and excitement?'

The man stirred restlessly in his seat. 'It was Billy what got spoke to and took the job. I just went along that night to keep an eye on him.'

'Oh?'

'That's the truth.'

'According to Carlton Huggins's wife it was Derek someone her husband told her was in the pub.'

'Huggins! That load of thievin' tinkers!'

'She's lying then?'

'None of them have spoken a true word in their lives!'

'Why would she lie?'

'How the hell should I know?'

'The woman has no reason to lie; she doesn't even know who you are.'

Jessop's right fist came flying but the hand was caught and smashed down on to the table.

'I know what this is all about,' Patrick said in a deadly whisper, his face inches from the other man's, the hand still in a tight grip. 'You and that overgrown brat brother of yours played a much bigger part in the shootings than we have so far thought.' He added, for the benefit of the tape, that the suspect had just attempted to strike him.

There was a short silence during which Jessop obviously wished fervently he was somewhere else. Finally, he was released.

'Let's think what that might be,' Patrick went on. 'We have

these two men who we think are of mid-European extraction who were cornered in Abbey Churchyard, easily shot because they had run out of ammunition and who were then, possibly while still alive, knifed to the extent of being disembowelled. No one's a lousy shot at point-blank range, Jessop, and that's what we're talking about here. I reckon that was you and Billy boy and then Murphy did the fancy knife-work. It was after this, when you were running through the Stall Street area blasting at everyone who moved that the pair of you were wounded. Did you pick off the waitress going home from work and the stage hand whose body was found in a skip? And then when you'd been taken out Murphy relieved you of one of the weapons they'd given you and your money just to tidy things up a little.'

'I didn't do nothing to people just goin' home!' Jessop shouted, visibly trembling.

'But you killed the other two, didn't you? Quite safe targets too, no risk to you at all. Perfect for beginners to try their hand on, eh?'

'I want a solicitor,' Jessop said, barely audibly.

'Is that a confession?'

'They . . . they was armed though, wasn't they? We didn't know they'd run out of ammo. All I saw was two nasty little gypsy types. It was them or us. Besides, she made us do it.'

'You're going to need your solicitor.'

'It's all falling into place,' I said over coffee in the canteen.

'Too slowly,' Patrick said, pulling a face after draining the polystyrene cup.

'Have you had time to look into the info you wrote down in the pub last night?'

'No. But I did look up the registration of the car. It was Carol Trelonic's. In her name, not her husband's.'

'So she and Andrews . . .' Words failed me for a moment.

'Unless she lent the vehicle to someone.'

Adam Trelonic had used the name Brian Law, a false identity acquired from 'a bloke in a pub' from whom he had bought stolen credit cards, a passport and a cheque book. For this Trelonic had served a six-month jail sentence.

But when asked about this, Jessop, awaiting the arrival of someone to represent him who we gathered was on her way, refused to answer. When interviewed later he still refused to give the names of anyone with whom he and Billy had been involved. Patrick had to resign himself to this for now as he could not utilize the methods he once did when working for MI5 in order to get to the truth.

'Trelonic's dead but I still want to drop him right in it,' he admitted.

'Please don't let it become personal,' I said.

'I'm sure that wife of his knows all about what he got up to and is even involved herself.'

'There must have been a PM. Usually there are chemical residues if someone's fired a gun.'

'Yes, lead, barium, antimony and soot. I've already looked up the PM findings and there were no residues found on the body or clothing. But that doesn't mean he didn't fire a weapon as there only has to be a breeze or crosswind that blows any traces away for the test to show a negative result. He'd been killed by two shots in the back from fairly close range.'

'Therefore, in law, there's still uncertainty with regards to his participation.'

'Exactly.'

'Were there any weddings last weekend?' Patrick asked his father that evening.

'Not at this church,' was the reply. 'And not to my certain knowledge at Wellow.'

We had invited Elspeth and John in for pre-dinner drinks.

'You don't happen to know if there was a reception over at the pub following, say, a civil ceremony?'

'It could only have been a very small one if there was,' Elspeth replied. 'The place simply isn't large enough so they normally have to hire a marquee and have it erected at the front on the green. After applying for permission, of course. I can't remember that happening since the early spring. It poured down with rain all day and I felt so sorry for everyone. Why are you asking?'

'Oh, local research. So you don't think there's been any kind of big bash over there for four or five months?'

'Nothing of the size you seem to be talking about,' said John. 'We can't help but notice really due to the loud pop music that people can't seem to live without these days.'

'Do they have many coach parties?'

The couple exchanged looks and John shook his head.

'They must sometimes but we really can't say,' Elspeth said. 'I'd probably notice if I was here as they'd have to leave it in full view – there's only a small car park with that big oak tree overhanging the entrance.'

'And you haven't seen anything like that lately?'

'No.'

Patrick changed the subject.

'I can't imagine they do much in the way of outside catering either,' he reflected later, his mind still obviously on the pub.

'Were there records of lots of bookings?' I asked.

'Yes, dates in connection with discos, wedding receptions, office outings – but I realize the latter could probably be accommodated inside – birthday parties; one, like the weddings, with a marquee booked plus oceans of champagne, and Christmas bashes, only those are quite likely genuine. It adds up to a lot more events than it would appear have actually taken place. And according to Andrews' records there's a big customer in a service industry, an insurance company based in Bristol to which he provides catering for meetings and training sessions, etc. That's the only thing I've had a chance to check up on. The company doesn't exist.'

'What's it all about then?'

'Money laundering. To explain high profits. But the money's mostly coming in through the door in cardboard boxes disguised as something along the lines of food ordered for the kitchen. It's likely there are other scams involving stolen goods. It's the kind of thing Greenway was talking about.'

I went cold. 'Matthew could have been killed.'

We gazed soberly at one another.

'D'you think he's safe here?' I wondered. 'Andrews must know you work for SOCA.'

'I shall have to involve Greenway and Carrick.'

'He could have been made just to disappear without trace if

they thought he'd been nosing around in the office. He still could be.'

'I'm staggered Andrews hasn't dropped the charges in an effort to draw attention away from the place. That's poor judgement.'

'I don't think he's very intelligent – as well as being spiteful.'

'You're probably right.'

'Patrick, what are we going to *do* about this?'

'The biggest problem is lack of formal evidence. I'm already going to get it in the neck over what we've discovered already.'

'Look, I'm talking about *Matthew*. We ought to send him away somewhere safe.'

My mobile rang.

'It's a girl!' James Carrick said jubilantly.

'A daughter and both doing fine,' I reported to Patrick after conveying all due congratulations.

'Yes, I'm talking about Matthew too,' he said, as though the call had not occurred. Then, 'Do we have a bottle of fizz in the house?'

'We usually do.'

'I'll take it over when Carrick's home and talk to him about it.'

'His brain'll be blown from lack of sleep and becoming a father.'

'Surely not,' Patrick said absently. He went from the room to rummage in the kitchen.

Whatever the reason, Patrick could raise no one at the Carrick's old farmhouse when he drove over later, even though the DCI's car was parked outside.

Anxiety gnawed, like rats, at me. All the last of the tests and exams were over at school and the children were due to break up for the summer holiday in around a week's time. I felt I could not raise my concerns with the Youth Offending Team as to explain my worries would involve giving details of an ongoing police investigation. So there was the choice of either taking Matthew out of school and spiriting him away somewhere, possibly to my sister in Surrey, or not allowing him out of our sight. No, we had to talk to Carrick.

'He's having a few days paternity leave,' Patrick reported

early the following morning. 'He's concerned about Matthew, of course, but not really interested in the reasons for our worries, even though I'd stepped out of line to get what is potentially new evidence. As you said, brain a bit blown. But he *will* contact the relevant Youth Offending bod and tell her we're taking the boy away for a while for his own safety. He doesn't have to go into details apparently as he's the officer in charge of the case.'

Relief washed over me.

'Where does Matthew go then?' Patrick went on to ask. 'It's a bit difficult with your sister in the States.'

I had forgotten all about their holiday in Florida. Sending him to his other grandmother was absolutely out of the question as she would doubtless forget to feed him and send him out to buy her cigarettes and booze. I do not get on with my mother – she has never forgiven me for marrying Patrick – and has always made herself so obnoxious to everyone, even those trying to help her, that I am afraid, one day, she is going to end up one of those elderly people who are discovered in their homes very, very dead.

'DS Keen is running Carrick's cases, keeping in contact with him by phone,' Patrick went on. 'I shall have to go in and assist.' He groaned. 'Confession time again – to Mike.'

I did not learn of any consequences, if any, of that conversation until later when the pre-school chaos was over, leaving Matthew, puzzled as to why he had been told to stay at home, having a more leisurely than normal breakfast in the kitchen.

'I'm missing the trip to Cheddar Gorge,' he said quietly.

'We'll take you another time,' I promised.

'Will someone phone in and say why I'm not there?'

'Of course.'

'*Why* aren't I going?'

Patrick had come in and heard the last question.

'Because you're going to stay with someone in Berkshire who has a very large garden and wants you to help him with it as he hurt his shoulder a while back,' he said. 'How are the muscles?'

Matthew looked down at his wiry arms. 'I don't think I've got any. Do I have to go?'

'I was only joking about the gardening. So cheer up – Mike has a lad about your age. But to answer the question properly – yes, you do.'

'When are we going then?'

'This afternoon. Now then . . .' Patrick drew a chair up to the table. 'I'd like you to tell me *everything* you saw when you had your second little snoop around the Ring o' Bells.'

Matthew's face fell. 'Am I in more trouble?'

'There's no need to look like a policeman,' I said quietly to Patrick.

'No, my apologies and to be sure we're all in this together now,' Patrick responded in a strong Irish accent. Then in his own voice, 'But this *is* work. Cast your mind back to that night. You climbed out of your bedroom window. What then?'

Matthew frowned. 'I walked through the garden into the churchyard. It was quite light still so I could see where I was going. I went through the gate and crossed the road a bit farther down so I wouldn't have to walk across the middle of the village green where people might see me.'

'Good thinking. Then what?'

'I didn't see anyone except old Mrs Taylor taking her little dog for a walk and when I got there a man was sitting smoking outside the pub.'

'What did he look like?'

'I couldn't really see his face as I wasn't that close but he had red hair.'

'Had you ever seen him before?'

'I don't *think* so.'

'OK, go on.'

'I didn't dare go near the front of the place at all and tried to look as though I was going to see someone in one of the houses up the lane at the back. But I went in through the gates behind the pub. There wasn't anyone around.'

'No, it was almost closing time. Any cars parked there?'

'Only the big four-by-four that belongs to Mr Andrews. I couldn't see the car park from where I was but there were several cars out the front.'

'One of which could have belonged to the man with red hair.'

'He was sitting quite close to a nice green sports car.'

'D'you know what it was?'

'No, but it was old. An MG or something like that.'

'Then you went in the rear door?'

'After I'd stood quietly for a little while in case someone came. I went straight back to the office where the computer was and—'

'There was a computer?'

'Yes, a Dell.'

Patrick turned to me. 'Did you notice it when you were called there?'

I shook my head. 'No, I was too worried about the kids to notice much at all.'

'I'd started playing around with it when Katie and I were there earlier,' Matthew continued. 'People use the stupidest obvious passwords. I'd already got into it just by keying in ROB and had just managed to shut it down when we'd heard Andrews coming and ran back into the storeroom. That's why I went back, to try to find out more.'

'Please try to remember anything that might be useful.'

'I couldn't possibly remember all of it. It was mostly loads of names and figures.'

'No, of course not,' Patrick said with a sympathetic smile.

'So I sent that file and a couple of others to my computer here. Then the dog found me.' Ruefully Matthew added, 'I kept quiet about what I'd done in case I got into even more trouble.'

Sometimes, moments of pure pleasure have to be prolonged and there was an appropriate silence.

'Do you still have all this stuff?' Patrick asked.

'Yes.'

'May SOCA have it?'

'Of course,' Matthew answered with a grin.

Patrick took a deep breath and let it go on a delighted sigh. 'You know, Ingrid, sometimes adults can be really *thick.* If someone had enquired of this young man a little further before now . . .' And then to Matthew, 'What everyone's been telling you about trespassing still applies. *Don't* do it. You'll still prob-ably get some kind of official telling off but my reprimand will be in the form of a hundred quid spending money for your holiday provided you don't ask any more questions about this, *whatever happens,* and keep it all very much to yourself. Promise?'

'I promise,' Matthew said.

NINE

Moments later DS Keen rang in a state of some excitement with the news that Gilly Darke had been arrested the night before for being drunk and disorderly. Despite diligent searching she had not been located since the night when Lynn Outhwaite had spotted her in the restaurant and was now, having been put in a cell overnight to sober up, spitting mad at being further detained.

The answer to his question to Patrick as to whether he would like to question her was predictable.

I had thought Lynn's summing up of the woman's outward appearance to be the product of boredom, resentment and a leg in plaster but on following Patrick into interview room one I had to give the girl her due. In fact, to describe Darke, who was probably in her late forties, as resembling anything to do with that most clean of animals was an unkindness to pigs. In short, she was filthy. Spending the night in a police cell notwithstanding it was not so much the musty-smelling clothing, muzzed-up dyed black hair and smeared make-up as the obvious fact that the latter had been applied over grime. Her fingernails beneath chipped bright red polish were full of dirt, the black high-heeled shoes scuffed – this last fact perfectly obvious because as we entered she snatched off one of them and wildly threw it at Patrick. He caught it.

'I'll have the other one too, if you don't mind,' he said quietly.

'Fuck off,' the woman mouthed at him.

'Otherwise we'll upend you on the floor and remove it ourselves.'

'I know my rights,' she whispered with a triumphant smirk.

Patrick looked at me. 'OK?'

We moved in on her.

'OK, OK, keep your soddin' hair on!' Darke whinnied, pulling the remaining shoe off and throwing that too, at me this time, but Patrick still fielded it. No doubt relieved at not having to touch her, he took them outside.

The formalities over, Patrick said, 'You'll shortly be charged with being drunk and disorderly last night but as far as this little chat's concerned you're not actually under arrest in connection with the recent shootings in the city; I just want to ask you a few questions.'

'Shootings!' the woman blared. 'I didn't have nothin' to do with that!'

'It'll save a lot of bother and wasted time if you cooperate,' Patrick went on as inexorably as a combine harvester. 'You were seen in a Bath restaurant just after it happened by a police officer, in the company of any number of hoodlums, local and otherwise. It's a waste of breath to deny it.'

Darke tossed her head but could not hide her dismay.

'Charlie Gill's been murdered. Did you know that?'

'Who's Charlie Gill?'

'You were with him, in the restaurant.'

'Oh, the fat greasy sod, you mean. He's no friend of mine.'

'You agree that you were there then?'

'Er – yes, I've just remembered, haven't I? It was some geezer's birthday and my boyfriend had an invite and took me along.'

'The man with red hair?'

'Yes.'

'What's his name?'

'I only know him as Red.'

'Known him long?' I asked.

'I'd just met him that evening.'

'That's not true though, is it? You'd been going around with him for a while. To meetings. With at least two other people who were there that night.'

'Yes, do stop lying,' Patrick said, playing with a pen on the table before him. 'One of whom is a London mobster and the other is his sidekick, a woman with a very handy line in all kinds of death. You're actually a very stupid woman, Gilly, and I want to know *exactly* what your role was in all this.'

'I ain't stupid and I didn't have no role. Red just liked to have me along, that's all.'

'He fancied you,' I said.

''Course. Why shouldn't he?'

OK, perhaps she'd had a bath that particular week.

'How did Red get involved with these people?' Patrick wanted to know.

'God knows.'

'And his responsibility was what?'

'Not a clue. The blokes always got in a huddle together and whispered.'

'Look,' Patrick said with amazing patience. 'This mob were planning gang warfare on a large scale. Your only claim to fame so far in the criminal stakes is to get drunk far too often and stand on street corners, soliciting. That isn't quite what professional criminals are looking for by way of talent. *Why* were you at the meetings?'

'I've already told yer, Red liked me there.'

'Where is he now?'

'I don't know.'

'Chucked you over?' I queried.

'No!'

'But he's gone off somewhere.'

'He isn't from round here – works in London for most of the time.'

'Doing what?'

'God knows.'

'Didn't you ask him?'

'No, he wasn't the sort of bloke you pestered with questions.'

Patrick asked, 'Was he a close friend of Uncle?'

'Look, I ain't got nothing to do with shootings.' The woman muzzed up her hair a bit more, her fingers raking through it. 'I want to go home.'

'Please answer the question.'

'I don't know any uncles.'

'The geezer whose birthday it was.'

'Oh, him! That was Brad. He was horrible – and that bag with him.'

'Was he chummy with Red?'

'Yes, but Red was very polite to him.'

'Did Red carry a gun?'

'I – I don't know.'

'Yes, you do. *Did* he?'

'At the meetings he did.'

'Where were these meetings held?'

'At pubs in the sticks. I can't remember the names.'

'Was one of them the Ring o' Bells at Hinton Littlemore?'

'I think so.'

'I still can't understand why they recruited you.'

'I told you, it was Red. He – he's a bit strange, mind.'

'In what way?'

'Nothin' you could put your finger on. But he did like a lot of sex. All the time – in the toilets, anywhere.'

'Which you were paid for.'

'Well, of course! Would you work for nuffin?'

'Was he around the night of the turf war? Did he take part?'

'I don't know. No, really, I've no idea.'

'Were you?'

Silence.

'Yes,' Darke finally whispered.

'Tell us what you were asked to do,' Patrick requested.

'Will it help me if I tell you?'

'It might. I can't guarantee anything. I'm not in charge of the case.'

After a short pause while she undertook some mental wrangling, Darke said, 'I was just a sort of lookout. I had to stand on a corner in George Street where I sometimes do and ring a number on a mobile they gave me – just let it ring a few times and then hang up – when I saw certain people coming along.'

'How were you supposed to know what these people would look like?'

'They just said watch out for a load of blokes either getting out of cars or already on foot. I was to call out to them and keep them talking for a bit, chat them up.'

'To give other people time to get into position?'

'S'pose. I didn't stay around to find out what happened. I went home.'

'But you knew they'd be ambushed in some way.'

'I wasn't told.'

'You're lying.'

'But it all went wrong, didn't it?' the woman cried out. 'They came in cars and didn't stop for me to chat them up. Just drove right past and stopped on the corner of Milsom Street.'

'It didn't make any difference to the outcome though, did it?' Patrick said. 'Most of them were either killed or injured and a couple ended up being mutilated, probably by the woman you've just described as horrible. She is, literally, bloody horrible. Then, a few days later, you all met up to celebrate.'

'It was Brad's birthday,' Darke muttered. 'Or so he said.'

'What did you talk about? How well the war had gone? How Brad soon planned to go into partnership with Charlie Gill and have Bath all sewn up between them?'

'They did have a toast to . . . future business. I didn't understand it really.'

'What on earth did you think the shoot-out was all about then?'

'I don't know. I didn't care a lot. I just wanted to have an evening out. I don't normally get taken to eateries like that.'

'Have you seen Red since that night?' Patrick wanted to know, unable to prevent the expression of disgust on his face.

'No.'

'Nor any of the others?'

'No, he paid me off and told me to get lost.'

'He being Brad.'

'Yes.'

'You'll be charged with being an accessory to murder.'

'But I didn't do nuffin!'

'You were there. You took part in the planning. You took money, knowing full well what was going to happen.'

'They was just a bunch of scum! It was Mick the Kick's lot. They all deserved to die like dogs.'

'How are they different from the mobsters you were working for?'

'Brad's clever. I was really frightened of him but he's got brains. He said – '

'What?' Patrick snapped when she stopped speaking.

'He said he'd soon have all the police eating out of his hand

and looked at Red. Red laughed. He will, you watch.' With a
self-satisfied smile she added, 'Everyone's got their price, even
you sitting there so cold and posh. You're no different to me
when all's said and done.'

Speaking very softly, Patrick said, 'Did he say he'd soon
have *all* the police eating out of his hand?'

'That's what I've just said, haven't I?'

'Did he emphasize "all"?'

'Yes, but what difference does it make?' Darke asked,
bewildered.

'I'll make sure you're remanded in custody – for your own
safety.'

His face tight, Patrick got to his feet without another word
and we left the room.

'What do we have?' he said, coming to a halt in the corridor
that led towards Carrick's office. 'Working undercover, but bent?
Undercover, threatened? Undercover, bought just for this one
job? Who is he? Who does he work for? The Met in the shape
of F9? Special Branch? No, that's unlikely. Or even SOCA, for
God's sake. I need to talk to Mike – now.'

'Red laughed,' I reminded him. 'So it's unlikely he was
threatened.'

'Yes, you're right. And now he's safely at home and any
number of Bath cops could have been gunned down that night,
never mind the innocent passers-by who actually were.'

Furious, Patrick slammed into the DCI's room, severely startling DS Keen in the process.

'My apologies, I didn't know you were in here,' Patrick said.
'But I think we have a maggot in the apple.'

The commander was in a meeting so we deferred telling him
the latest developments until later that afternoon when we could
talk to him face to face.

True to his promise Matthew asked no questions, helping to
load his case and a few other possessions he felt he could not
do without into the Range Rover. I knew he would ache for his
computer but realized that it was not practical to take that too.
The files he had sent to it from the pub were now safely stored
on CD-ROMs and were in Patrick's briefcase. I knew that the

next Christmas present request would be for a state-of-the-art laptop. He would probably get it.

'I wish Katie was coming really,' he said wistfully.

'I'm sure you know how excited she is about going off to a friend's for a week or so,' I said.

We left an almost speechless with shyness Matthew in the care of Michael Greenway's wife, Erin, at a large house in north Ascot and pressed on for SOCA's HQ in Kensington. The commander was in yet another meeting and while we waited for him Patrick slipped one of the CDs into the computer he uses when working in the building.

'These'll take hours to go through,' he murmured. 'We need to give it to a boffin in the general office for a detailed analysis. This one seems to consist mostly of accounts with some words in some kind of home-made code.'

'Nothing leaps out at you, though.'

'No.'

'I'm still not sure why this Red character, who we mustn't forget Matthew might have seen outside the pub that night, took Darke along.'

'To give himself some kind of low-life cred, I expect. And for on-tap bonking.'

'He isn't fussy then.'

I found myself on the receiving end of a lustful smile. 'No, it's only the cold, posh types who are fussy.'

Any further conversation along these lines was then out of the question as Mike Greenway entered. We immediately thanked him for coming to the rescue.

'No, it suits us well,' Greenway said with one of his big smiles. He is a big man. 'I have an idea that lad of yours is keen on the outdoors and fresh air. It'll be a good thing to get Benedict away from his computer for a while.'

I desisted from catching Patrick's eye.

'So this is the stuff Matthew gleaned from your village pub,' said Greenway, in receipt of the CD-ROMs. 'Worth looking at?'

'The local mobsters held some of their planning meetings there,' Patrick told him. 'I'm assuming that was in the long back room that used to be a skittle alley.' He placed another

small packet on the commander's desk. 'That's an unofficial
official tape of an interview we conducted this morning with
the Darke woman. She's confessed to acting as lookout and
will be charged accordingly. I think we have the beginning of
a case against Uncle – or Brad Northwood as he's calling himself
now. Darke knew the man in the restaurant as Brad and he and
Gill drank a toast to future business. Also, I think the man with
red hair, ostensibly Darke's boyfriend, is a cop.'

Greenway swore under his breath, whispered an apology to
me and then said, 'I've got some news for you about him, or at
least a man with red hair. He's been seen at Brad Northwood's
place in Hammersmith, just coming and going. He drives an old
British racing green MG sports car which is registered in the
name of Anthony Beardshaw with an address in Woodford Green,
Essex. Mr Beardshaw reported this motor stolen four months
ago so God knows where it's been hidden away until now. He's
been interviewed, is perfectly on the line and as bald as a coot.
The Met has asked him to cooperate with them by keeping quiet
and patient as we don't want to grab red head *yet.*'

'Do you have a photo of him?' Patrick enquired.

Greenway stabbed at his computer keyboard a few times and
then swivelled the whole thing around for us to see what was
on the screen.

'Derek Jessop described him as short, thin and with ferrety
eyes,' I recollected, gazing at the fairly clear image on the screen
before me. 'That's about right, even though you can't see his
eyes.'

The picture had been taken on the doorstep of a house that
appeared to be part of a terrace, the man in the act of looking
round, a hand raised to ring the doorbell.

'Not much change out of a small fortune for that place,'
Patrick commented. 'The surveillance is obviously taking place
in a house just about opposite. Do you want me to find out
more?'

An admonishing finger was wagged at him. 'No, not in the
way I think you mean, going down the chimney or whatever.
But we have a reliable source of info that says he's hiring.
Interested?'

'Ingrid and I have talked about this and I've given it some

thought since. If you remember I reinvented myself as a mobster in order to get inside the empire of a Romford-based minor ditto not all that long ago. So, no, it's too risky, there might be an overlap of honchos.'

'You got quite seriously done over too,' the commander mused.

'Yes, and although I regard that as all part of the job there doesn't seem to be much point in risking actually cracking under questioning this time when it's not necessary to go under-cover in the first place, not to mention getting shot on sight because someone recognizes me.'

'So what do you suggest?'

Patrick smiled winningly. 'I take it you won't let me loose with a sniper's rifle.'

'No,' Greenway replied heavily.

'Only joking.'

Yes, but if he was ordered to he would.

'Is this red-haired man sacrosanct?' Patrick went on to ask.

'Only from the point of view that if the law grabs him the rest might scatter and we'll lose the lot.'

'Suppose he's taken ill, say, in a restaurant.'

'I'm listening.'

'Or trips over something in the street and breaks his ankle – taken out of circulation to be questioned that way.'

'I agree. It probably wouldn't arouse suspicion.'

'Then my question stands and you really mustn't let your imagination run riot. Would you like me to find out more?'

'You'll have to sell it to me a bit more,' Greenway murmured.

'Has he been followed to where he lives?'

'No, not yet. It's only within the past couple of days that he's been spotted at the address in London.'

'Could you arrange it? I'm not volunteering as it's possible he's been hanging around in Hinton Littlemore.'

'OK, I'll do that.'

'Then we'll be able to work out his routines. If he's got any – he might just have been visiting when Matthew saw him.'

'I'd rather you didn't kick your heels while the job's being done,' the commander said as we all rose to leave. 'No, sorry, that sounded as though I think you're in the habit of—'

'Kicking my heels?' Patrick interrupted with a smile. 'Ingrid and I will use some of the time for firearms training. This affair isn't going to end with everyone handing around bunches of flowers. Did you have another job in mind?'

'We've discovered that Joy Murphy doesn't live at the Hammersmith address but has a top floor flat in a high-rise block in Notting Hill. Have a quiet look round. But don't under any circumstances make contact with her.'

The kind of weapons training that Patrick and I undergo is not merely firing at targets on an indoor range, although that is part of it. Far more interesting, useful and terrifying is the next stage where one is tossed, sometimes literally, into a mock-up in the bowels of a Ministry of Defence building where any kind of scenario can be created. Maze-like constructions, with interconnecting tunnels and cellars, are constructed out of blockboard, polystyrene and other materials supported by scaffolding and fronted by camouflage netting and painted cloths similar to those used on film and stage sets. There are always teetering stacks of fairly lightweight 'stone pillars' – once upon a time it had been piles of tea chests – that can be nudged over by hidden gizmos to complicate matters together with the added interest of bare live but low voltage wires with a few potential water leaks to make them really bite. As its situation would suggest this second training ground is nothing to do with the police but belongs to the military. It is probably the fact that he helped set it up and wrote most of the original 'scripts' that has ensured that Patrick appears to be a life member.

There were new authors now, of course, but the challenge remains: you start at one end and have to make your way to reach the other, usually a high point, perhaps a tower of some kind. There is a time limit. We use live ammunition on the mobile cardboard targets – the usual figure of an armed man carrying a sub-machine gun – that pop up like magic when things get difficult and if you do not hit them meaningfully within five seconds you lose a 'life', of which you are given three. This goes on while operatives with a handy line in unarmed combat stalk the tunnels and others, from up on a gantry by the control room, take careful aim at you with handguns, loaded with, yes, live rounds. It is a point of honour with Patrick that he gets round inside the time limit without losing a life and there is a tradition that they try to overpower him before he goes in for some serious demolition just for the hell of it.

People often end up needing hospital treatment – health and safety there is absolutely none and I know for a fact that Commander Greenway is completely unaware of our participation. Otherwise he would want to have a go as well and the answer would be no. The reason for this is that, although the set-up is sometimes used by the police, for those without the right preliminary training, which Patrick and I received when working for MI5, it is very dangerous.

'We're bloody rusty,' was Patrick's magnificently encouraging conclusion on having completed the first stage at another venue, driven a short distance across London and, having arrived, travelled downwards for what had seemed half a mile in a lift.

We donned dark blue tracksuits and non-slip boots, the latter I reckoned being the only generous nod to us staying in one piece. There were no ear defenders as with them we would not be able to hear people creeping up behind us.

'As you're with me they won't play too dirty,' he added.

'It hasn't felt like that on previous occasions,' I commented dourly, thinking my accuracy so far had not been too bad. 'If a bloke grabs me can I kick him in the goolies?'

'No!'

'I distinctly remember a marine shoving a freezing-cold soaking-wet sponge into my knickers.'

Patrick tut-tutted and went off.

Was it irresponsible doing what we did with five young people to look after? I was sure it was. Nothing could change that. But from the moment Patrick, at the age of almost eighteen, had walked into my parents' kitchen – our fathers had arranged that he helped me with my physics homework – seated himself and glowered at me, my life had been set on this path. Drawing a neat line under the words specific gravity I had known, instantly – and there are those who would sneer at such sentiments – that here was the man I wanted for ever and ever.

There would be no halfway measures: you were either with him or you were not.

My one and only claim to fame at school was that I had nabbed the head boy. Eventually we had married but by that time everything had changed. Patrick had joined the police on leaving school but left, finding it not exciting enough, and opted for the Devon and Dorset Regiment instead. Suddenly he had a life where there were places to visit, adventures to be had; the whole world at his feet. Despite this, he wanted children. I did not. We saw less and less of one another, and on his leaves there seemed only to be a newly arrogant and aggressive man with whom I had bitter rows. This culminated one night when I threw his classical guitar down the stairs, smashing it and then threw him out too: it was my cottage, bought with the royalties from my books and some money left to me by my father. Eventually, we divorced.

Then, on secret operations in the Falklands, the second youngest major in the British army, there was an accident with a hand grenade, not of his doing, and he was horribly injured. Strangely, no one was more horrified about it than the perpetrator, an Argentine undercover soldier they had captured who Patrick interrogated and who had come to quite like and admire him. Initially terrified – an old pony had come in out of the rain into the shepherd's hut they were hiding in, laid down and fallen so soundly asleep that Patrick was leaning back on it, using it as a sofa – and the man thought they had killed it to sit on. But the following morning, by which time the pony had gone, he had tried to warn his own side by grabbing a grenade and throwing it, only for it to bounce off a rock and explode inside the hut.

What Patrick has revealed about it – not everything, I feel – still haunts me. He could not understand how his sergeant, who had been blown against a wall and was only suffering from a broken arm, could scream with his mouth closed. Then he realized that it was him. Carlos Savadra, the Argentinian, he remembers, knelt by his side weeping, praying and begging his forgiveness all at once while the others gave him first aid. The enemy did not notice that small bang in the hills above Port Stanley.

Several operations and lengthy stays in hospital later he was offered a job with MI5, the only stipulation, as socializing was involved, being to find a female partner. It was reckoned that lone men, especially one with a bad limp and a somewhat saturnine demeanour, were conspicuous. The injuries having left him with a severe lack of self-confidence as far as the opposite sex was concerned, he asked the only woman on the planet he knew would not want to go to bed with him: me. How could I refuse to help the man I had once been deeply in love with, who was convinced he was crippled for life? He wasn't. He was wrong and we sorted out the sex bit. A little later we had remarried. And now? Three children of our own and two adopted? Sometimes when the house is in uproar with them we just look at one another and laugh.

I caught up with him in the armory where he was in receipt of his own Glock 17, handed in to be thoroughly checked over while we had got changed. The short-barrelled Smith and Wesson was still in the secret cubbybox in the Range Rover – it is always kept there – as I am not the slightest bit superstitious when it comes to using anything but my own, unlike Patrick – any one will do. They are not really standard issue any more but I am permitted to keep it as I am not called upon to use firearms very often. Not only that, but specialist training with a new weapon would also cost money and the Ministry of Defence budget was being sliced to the marrow.

We would not know what kind of scenario we would be faced with until we actually arrived.

'OK, as you're together you have three lives between you,' said a gimlet-eyed combats-clad man in an if-rhinos-could-speak voice. He gave me a thunderous frown that told me that a woman's presence was about to seriously pollute his fantastic piece of theatre.

In receipt of my weapon I beamed sunnily by way of a reply. It was all part of the process, together with giving us only three lives: moves designed to undermine self-confidence and give a little frisson of fear.

Damn their professionalism.

TEN

I t started before we had even reached the door at the end of the short, gloomy tunnel that led into the complex, a couple of dark figures springing from nowhere to grab Patrick and wrestle him to the floor. At least, that was the idea but he had anticipated something might happen and, like me, had both hands free, our weapons in shoulder harnesses. One went bowling head over heels back the way he had come; the other had his arm twisted up his back until he grunted his surrender. He was released and we proceeded and I was not worried about them at all for they were fit young servicemen who would laugh about it afterwards with a man twice their age.

Any warm feelings I might be harbouring now were ruthlessly negated when suddenly I was seized, hauled backwards, feet trailing, and then slid head first down a chute of some kind. After an impossibly long descent with a few bends in it there was a heart-stopping drop on to what felt like damp cardboard boxes. They turned out to be exactly that, with a nice built-in smell of bad drains just for me. They do usually try to split up the pair of us at some stage in the proceedings but this simply was not cricket. I rolled off the stinking pile and crouched down, drew the Smith and Wesson and listened.

My surroundings resembled a large sewer and as I was standing in around four inches of stinking liquid perhaps they had dug down and borrowed one from Thames Water. The only light, albeit dim, was coming from somewhere ahead in a tunnel and through a small round hole in the planking above my head. Some kind of continental-style urinal? Over to my left was a dark opening of some kind. The only sounds were the slow drip of water and a strange humming noise which I put down to the set-up's running gear. I then thought of the time limit: no one had said what it was.

I moved off and as soon as I did a target popped up in the tunnel ahead of me. Getting it comprehensively right in the heart, the shot oddly muffled by my surroundings, and knowing from past experience that it was in a dead end I headed for the dark opening, pausing at the entrance. It was absolutely pitch dark down there. I set off, dreading holes it was planned I should fall into.

'Boo!' someone whispered right behind me.

'How did you get here?' I hissed, having jumped out of my skin.

'Down some stairs and through a door,' Patrick answered, pushing past me. 'Did you hit the target?'

'Of course. How much time do we have?'

'God knows. Don't follow me too closely.'

Fat chance, he had gone.

There was no indication that anything nasty had happened to him so I set off in his wake, groping, aware he would be really, really mad with me if I walked into him at a crucial moment. But nothing happened and we emerged a few yards after rounding a right-angled bend into a dimly lit and slightly wider area with a tall set of steps in it that appeared to give access to an aperture in the ceiling above. I had learned never to take anything for granted in connection with this war games complex.

'You go first,' Patrick whispered. 'Then if these damned things are designed to collapse I can catch you.'

The steps were wobbly but I went up them and poked my head out through the opening and gazed around. There was not much to see, just a very small room with three corridors off. At least the lights were on.

There was a slight click behind me, like an old-fashioned gun being cocked, but I knew what it was. I straightened my knees, spun round off-balance, and somehow got the target in the guts. Then got goosed from below by Patrick in a real hurry and jumped off the top of the steps still off-balance, tripped over my own feet and crashed on to the boarded floor. He dealt with another target, firing across me like a cowboy taking cover behind his dead horse.

'I suppose that could have looked as though we meant it,' he muttered.

'It was your fault for tweaking me like that,' I countered.

'The bastards sent a few volts through the steps.'

And we were, of course, being watched and overheard over most of the course courtesy of CCTV cameras and microphones.

Two targets down, one corridor remaining. We went down it at a thoughtful speed – it pays to be cautious – arriving at a door. The handle was nice shiny metal and there was a distinct fizzing noise coming from the vicinity of it.

'They're not really trying to kill us,' Patrick said, grasping it and opening the door. His hair did not stand on end so I reckoned we were safe.

A large open space lay before us, a pitiless indoor landscape of sand, shingle, phoney boulders and rocks, some of which were huge, and a lot of dead branches with camouflage netting draped over them which could conceal anything. What looked like the entrance to a 'cave' was on the far side. The 'roof' was just a blackness with a few tiny lights like stars and some kind of hidden illumination that gave the impression of moonlight. I risked a glance high up into one corner and spotted one end of the control centre, a structure with a wide curving bulletproof glass window. I have been inside it and, to me, the instrument panel looks as complicated as the cockpit of a jumbo jet.

'Is Ken still in charge here?' I whispered when we paused momentarily in the comparative cover of an overhanging 'rock' after dashing across the first open space. Ken was difficult to forget: a fine marksman, the mind of a slightly sadistic genius, hair like a full-blown marigold. His and Patrick's rivalry went back years.

'No idea. Possibly,' Patrick snapped, concentrating.

A shot pinged off the metal underpinnings of our rock, scattering us with bits of what were probably fibreglass. Then the world went mad. A thunderflash went off seemingly right behind us and, regrettably, my instinctive and first reaction to this was to bolt. This was severely curtailed by my husband grabbing a handful of spare tracksuit material between my shoulder blades, hauling me to a standstill and then back.

'Think!' he bellowed right in my face through the smoke.

'That was a grenade,' a disembodied voice said silkily. 'You're both dead. Two lives left.'

In the next moment there was another bright flash and deaf-
ening bang but we were already moving and travelling at speed
to the left towards another rock. A shot kicked up the sand at
out feet.

Patrick carried on shouting. 'He's supposed to be firing high!'

Another dead target later and we were making our way, bent
low around the base of the rock which turned out to be the first
in a group of three. The farthest was very large and had a
tumbledown shack of sorts leaning up against it, constructed
out of planks and what looked in the dim light like a piece of
tarpaulin. It appeared to be a very safe way of reaching the
cave entrance somewhere on the far side of it.

Patrick picked up a small rock, real, and hefted it. It landed
somewhere on top of the structure with a crash and the whole
thing went down like a pack of cards in a cloud of dust and
bits of rotten wood.

'I demand lost lives back!' Patrick yelled. 'For breaking rule
ten by making something likely to cause real injury.'

No response.

'Right,' he muttered, getting another target in the head. 'War.'

Secretly, I thought he was getting a bit too exercised by
everything but, after all, he had written the original set of rules.

And with that we got the equivalent of a bathful of cold
water tipped over us.

The shock was enough to make me forget, for a moment,
where I was and what I was supposed to be doing. My hand
was grabbed and we went like hell, jumping and scrambling
over and through the remains of the shack and then out across
an open sandy and stone-strewn space towards the entrance to
the cave. A target popped up in the entrance – how could a
mere slab of cardboard, a SAPU, a Small Arms Pop-Up,
engender such alarm? – which Patrick slew on the run and we
carried on, crashing past the holed target into the dark space
beyond.

'It must be a dead end,' I gasped. 'It always is.'

'Then goody we've gone the wrong way,' Patrick responded.

Someone jumped on him, a tall, broad someone who got him
around the throat with a crooked arm. I did think this time,
jumped out of the way so Patrick could work some rather dirty

magic and when the man flew through the air and thumped down on to his back I sat on him hard enough to hear the rest of the breath leave his lungs.

Lights suddenly blazed, dazzlingly, and there in the cave entrance was another target. From my seated position I got it at the second attempt and then scrambled up and ran to where I could see Patrick going down a passageway off to my right. As soon as I entered it the ceiling fell in on me. It was only made of large polystyrene blocks but that did not stop me from tripping over some of them and being buried by the rest. I fought my way out and, slipping and sliding over the squeaky and unstable pile, tried to carry on in the direction I wanted to go. It was hopeless. There was a much larger amount than one ceiling's-worth: a small mountain of it.

So be it. I had one shot left and I had not been given any more ammunition. Patrick had started off with seventeen.

Squeezing past the 'dead' targets in the entrance I gazed around outside. No one was in sight. Soaked through and shivering, my hair plastered to my head, I trotted off to the right, moving along a mock rock-face in what I hoped was a roughly parallel course to the one Patrick had taken. The 'moonlight' was even dimmer now and, yes, I really was thinking. When I had fired my last shot and in order not to lose any more lives by not being able to shoot at targets I would have to catch up with him. I had wasted one shot already.

Incongruously, I came to a door. No fizz, no electric shock either. Just locked. I shoulder-charged it and someone opened it just as I got there leaving me staggering in another dark space, finally crashing into the door opener who wasn't Patrick as he was not wet and anyway smelt of very cheap, handy for drains, aftershave. I got a bit cross with him, took a wild swing in the dark and smacked him hard around the face, which startled him sufficiently enough to call me a bitch.

'I can get a lot bitchier than that!' I yelled at him. 'This is supposed to be target practice, not dungeons and effin' dragons!'

Gut feelings told me that the effin' dragon was about to try something else so I ran back to the opening and when he followed me outside tripped him so he bellyflopped with a loud 'Ooof!', hopefully getting a mouthful of sand. Only a little twerp after all. I dashed back through the door, slammed it behind me and then made for a corner from which faint light was emanating. This proved to be yet another tunnel and when I was around ten yards inside it a target slid into place at the end of it. I got it in the head, turned right into a side passage I had not previously noticed but quickly came to a dead end. I was now out of ammo.

There were then three shots in quick succession, not all from the same weapon, impossible to tell exactly from which direction but not alarmingly close by. I decided that the first had been fired by a Glock and ran back and out through the door into the Lawrence of Arabia scenario, which I was beginning to loathe. No, hang on, I'd loathed it right from the start.

There was another shot, seemingly from above and a ricochet whanged off something. Half-crouching I scurried along the mock rock-face which curved away and then sloped steeply upwards. Damning all men I raced, slithering, up the sand and gravel with which it was surfaced and emerged at last and on all fours on a flat wooden platform just above a roof of sorts over the maze, tunnels and cave complex. Again, it was very dim and the platform rocked and swayed, appearing to be suspended on ropes. Crawling, I started to make my way along it.

'I'm here,' said a voice somewhere to the rear of me.

As soon as he had spoken a target jumped up in the darkness ahead. I flattened myself, pronto, and there was a shot which made such a good job of it that the SAPU actually fell over, something in the mechanism smashed. I wriggled backwards for quite a distance from the point where I had reached the platform.

'It is Ken,' Patrick said, stretching out a hand to touch me in order to further inform me that I had arrived. I turned around to see that he was sitting down, very still.

'What's wrong?' I asked, seeing the expression on his face.

He handed me the Glock. 'You must be out of ammo.'

'Patrick, what's *wrong*?'

'He seems to be taking it a bit too seriously.'

'Are you hit?'

'He's wrecked my right ankle joint. Firing low, utterly forbidden.'

'Then let's stop this!'

'I think Ken's finally lost it.'

Memories returned. The computer geek with the wild ginger hair, the obsessive whose brainchild this set-up had partly been and whose mental state some years ago Patrick had been very, very worried about.

A voice boomed out. 'You're getting seriously close to the time limit. One minute left.'

'That's not Ken's voice,' I said.

'No, I spotted him out on the upper gantry by the control room – he's only supposed to be firing safe but disconcerting shots at us.'

'It might have been an accident.'

'It wasn't. He's just about the finest shot in the country and we're talking about a deliberate attempt to cripple.'

'Are you *sure* it was him?'

'You can't miss that ginger hair.'

'But there's possibly a bent cop with red hair mixed up in the turf war.'

His mind was on other things. 'I'm sorry, I'm completely useless.'

'Then stay here where you're reasonably safe.'

'I simply can't dodge around quickly enough,' Patrick raged.

I blew him a kiss.

'For God's sake, be careful. I simply can't believe you're in the equation but shoot him if you really think he's gone raving mad.'

It was too dark for cameras up here and I was not sure if there would be any mikes to hear me raising the alarm. I crawled back to the top of the incline and slid down it on my behind back into the desert area. A shot was immediately fired at me that probably did not miss by much.

'Oi!' I yelled. 'Stop this now! My husband's been shot in the leg!'

Someone laughed. 'They can't hear you, ducky – I've turned all the mikes off. Shouting will get you nowhere.'

He fired again and I got the distinct impression that the bullet whistled just above my head.

This was not Ken, the voice was quite different.

How to raise the alarm? How to get up on to the gantry without being spotted by this bastard? I raided all recollections I had of the place and remembered an iron staircase, like a fire escape that was at one end, the end farthest from the control room. But surely I could draw someone's attention to what was going on. What about all the *other* people here, for God's sake? No doubt job done they had probably gone off for their tea break.

No, whatever he was after I was not going to play this man's game.

Jinking, I dashed squelchingly across the sandy area, using the rocks as cover, hearing shots fired at me but, hey, this wasn't Ken and he wasn't so good. The door on the far side was still open and I hurtled through that and then along the corridors, somehow finding my way back to where we had come up through the hole in the floor. The steps had gone so I sat down with my legs dangling through the aperture and then dropped. All my body protested at the impact: you're too old for this, woman. I could not remember two passageways but there were now and I initially chose the wrong one, ending up in a dead end. Reduced to swearing now I went back, ran around the right-angled bend and then the dark tunnel loomed before me.

A kind of stand-by-your-man madness came over me and I tore through it, almost slithering over and into the water on the slippery floor where I had first landed on the pile of cardboard. Patrick had said he had come down steps and through a door. I found it, or at least what seemed to be a doorknob in the wall, but although it turned the door would not open. I fought with it but it would not shift.

With the steps gone I was trapped down here as there was no possibility of climbing up the chute down which I had arrived. Forcing myself to be calm I examined the walls of this dank little room for other exits but found nothing. Then I heard footsteps approaching, descending stone steps on the other side of the door. They came to a halt and a key turned in the lock. I retreated to stand in the mouth of the tunnel.

He opened the door, entered and, detecting my presence, chuckled. He then walked forward and there in the thin beam of light shining through the hole in the ceiling, as though under a spotlamp, stood the man referred to as Red: short, thin and with ferrety eyes, who had been photographed entering Brad Northwood's house here in London. He was still holding the sniper's rifle but not aiming it directly at me.

'Ever fired one of those before?' he enquired, nodding in the direction of the Glock, which was pointing at him.

'No.'

'Just familiar with the Smith and Wesson?'

'That's right.'

'Your husband, who I shall go and find after I've done with you, will have put on the safety catch before handing it over. Know where it is, eh?'

'No.'

'And you wouldn't be able to find it in the dark.'

'Probably not.'

'That's a real pity.'

'If you say so.'

'For you. It means I've plenty of time to kill you before you suss out where it is, haven't I?'

He began to swing the barrel of the rifle towards me, taking his time, enjoying himself.

'No,' I said.

'No?' he whispered with a big smile, very relaxed about it all, the rifle coming to a halt. 'Are you begging for your life?'

I said, 'The Glock's three safety mechanisms are automatically disengaged when you squeeze the trigger.' Which I did.

Patrick always tells me never to shoot to wound an armed man: 'It'll be the death of you one day.'

I had never shot to kill.

Until now.

'So was he naive, or what?' Michael Greenway demanded to know. 'Didn't he know about Glocks, even though he appears to have been familiar with arms?'

'I think he was trying to get me all flustered just in case I did pull the trigger,' I said. 'But was complacent to the point of stupidity.'

The man now in a body bag had been wrong in that he had only succeeded in switching off the microphones in the desert mock-up area. This meant that the conversation between the two of us had had been recorded, every word of it. Needless to say, an inquiry into the breach of security and other lax operational practices had been set up as well as frantic enquiries into the dead man's identity.

The commander had decided to survey the scene himself after I had phoned him to report what had happened and I gather had arrived at the same time with what appeared to be half the Met. So far he had not had the opportunity to comment on our presence in the training complex as I had only just come back to the reception area from answering questions, making a statement and getting into dry clothes. Patrick's Glock had been taken away for examination, routine I knew, and I hoped they would not keep it for very long.

The smashed ankle joint would probably take a while to put right and Patrick, after satisfying himself that I was safe and sound, had brushed aside all police endeavours to question him and taken a taxi to the specialist clinic where something could be done about it.

'I listened to the recording,' Greenway said all at once, startling me slightly from my musings. 'He underestimated you, didn't he?'

'Blind drunk on how clever he was,' I said.

'He got in here by showing a warrant card. I've seen it and it gives every appearance of being genuine issue although the name on it is that of someone who is now dead, a special branch sergeant who was killed in a powerboat accident while on holiday three years ago.' He gazed at me gravely. 'Are you all right, Ingrid?'

'Sorry, no,' I muttered. I had been trying to conceal the fact that I was shaking like a piece of tissue paper in a gale.

He crooked an arm, which I took, and after a short journey in the fresh air I was seated on a very comfortable padded bench seat in the bar of an Italian restaurant. A Bombay Sapphire gin and tonic with plenty of ice was placed before me.

'It was either you or him, you know,' Greenway said, seating himself. He was drinking orange juice.

'I'm usually the one who takes out tyres and windscreens,' I said with a failed attempt at a laugh.

'Which don't bleed all over the floor.'

'No.' The murky water around my feet had run red.

There was a little silence and then Greenway said, 'So who knew you were coming here?'

'No one. Even I didn't.'

'*He* did. And worse, probably so did Uncle.'

'Patrick doesn't write things like that down in a business diary. It's in his head.'

'Then we must assume that that particular security leak was right here. I'm even more perturbed that serious criminals know about the pair of you at all.'

'I think I've already mentioned that in Hinton Littlemore it's no secret that Patrick works for SOCA. That could be the connection we've been looking for, the pub. Carol Trelonic, the widow of a man killed during the Bath turf war who James Carrick would like very much to connect with the gangs involved, is having an affair with the landlord, Colin Andrews. That was something else we discovered when we went to the Ring o' Bells that night but I'm afraid we forgot to mention it.'

'And if the Trelonic woman's part of Uncle's set-up . . .'

'Easy to pass on the info. But that doesn't explain how they knew we were coming here.'

'We have to get evidence that Brad Northwood was right there in the Bath shootings. I want him behind bars. When your husband gets off the ramps carry on with what you were going to do – have a quiet look at the address where this harridan Murphy's been known to live. Don't rattle the bars of her cage. Meanwhile, we have find out who this Red character really was and how he knew you were coming here today.'

ELEVEN

'The entire place was crawling with scenes of crime bods when I left,' I told Patrick around three hours later at our hotel.

'I'm glad it wasn't Ken,' he said. 'I made enquiries when I got back and had given my statement. Having got married he's now living in Australia doing a similar job with their special forces.' He gave me the same kind of searching gaze as had Greenway. 'I'm sorry it had to be like this.'

'So am I. Perhaps I should have wounded him and then he could have been questioned.'

'No. He might still have fired and hit you. I want to apologize too for being so bloody useless when you needed me.'

'Look at it this way: if you had your own foot you'd be seriously injured in hospital right now and probably out of action for months.'

An emergency repair had been carried out, nothing that would fail but using parts straight off the shelf without any time for delicate calibration to take place with regard to the user's deportment. The end result did not look any different to me.

'Joy Murphy then,' I said. 'Tomorrow.'

'Tomorrow. Mike told me to take you out to dinner tonight.'

'He's very kind.'

'Heard from Matthew?'

'Yes, he sent me a text. Benedict has a fantastic computer, much better than his.'

We both groaned.

Overnight there was a breakthrough: the man Red identified as a one-time detective sergeant with the Wessex Constabulary by the name of Warren Rouse. Some five years previously Rouse had been convicted of falsifying evidence, receiving bribes, perverting the course of justice and had served two years in prison and been dismissed from the force. Further digging revealed that the cases involved, three in number, had all been in connection with existing, or would-be, crime bosses who then, let off the hook, had gone on to much greater things in London and Birmingham. One of the names was Joy Murphy.

'She kept a job nice and warm for him,' I said, in receipt of this information from Greenway over breakfast.

Patrick put his mobile back in his pocket. 'It's another connection.'

'You'll have to be very careful. This lot know about you and might have even dug out a photo of you from somewhere. You've been pictured in the national press at least a couple of times.'

'It was a real shame the Met didn't tail Rouse when he first turned up at Northwood's place. Then we'd have an address to search.'

'And where's the sports car? I'm assuming he didn't have the nerve to use it to get to the weapons training centre.'

'Greenway didn't mention it. I'll check.'

He went into the lobby to phone: we both have a real thing about people who persist in hollering into mobiles in bars and restaurants.

The stolen car had indeed been found parked there and subsequently taken away for examination. It had a cloned tax disc. After more investigation during the following days fingerprints in the vehicle would be found to match those of the dead man together with a couple of good thumbprints made by the real owner. Rouse had initially been identified from mugshots and it appeared that there were not all that many criminals with red hair. I wondered why he had not dyed it. The same arrogant mindset, perhaps.

'It's vital that we find out how Rouse knew we were down for weapons training,' I said. 'Who did you tell?'

'No one. I never do.'

'Please think.'

'I never even mention that kind of thing at home but—'

'What?'

'Last weekend Elspeth said she was going on a trip with the WI to London to the Imperial War Museum and other places. I remember saying that I'd be just around the corner from there on the same day for a training session.'

'Someone might have overheard then. Who else was in the house?'

'Well, you, Carrie and the little ones were in the main rectory but I was talking to Mum in hcr own kitchen. The front door to the annex was open as I was just dropping off some shopping I'd got for them. I think the new cleaning woman was around somewhere nearby.'

'I don't like her very much.' Betty Smithers, who had helped Elspeth for years, had retired.

'It really is a terrific long shot that she's some kind of mole. But I'll investigate.'

'We're still tiptoeing around this case,' Patrick said later when we were on our way to Notting Hill. 'No, poking ineffectually around the edges,' he continued and I could detect the frustration and simmering anger. 'We know where this Northwood bastard lives, we know he's trying to take over Bath, we know he's murdered several people with the help of some bloodthirsty bitch, and that's only recently. God knows what's gone on before. We *know* all these things but can't prove them. So how *do* we prove them? Pity we can't just grab him and take him apart until he talks. I'd volunteer, any day of the week.'

'Feel a bit better now?' I queried gently when he stopped talking.

'Not really. What does the oracle say?'

'The oracle originally recommended arresting him rather than going in for an undercover operation if you remember but, as you say, we need evidence. We all know that if you get hold of minions and they talk they often change their minds just before or during the trial as they've been threatened or end up being fished out of the nearest river. I don't want to say this but you'll need to go to the top.'

'Northwood himself?'

'Not necessarily. Has Mick the Kick been located?'

'Not to my knowledge. I can contact Bath CID to find out.'

'Derek Jessop said Mick and his gang were tricked into coming into Bath that night so he must be burning with resentment after what happened on at least two counts. Get hold of him, but in a fairly friendly fashion, and see what you can do between you. He might even really cooperate and you could set up some kind of reverse sting operation.'

Patrick thought about it for a few moments and then gently punched my shoulder.

Saying that he was hanged if he was going to adopt some kind of Marx Brothers-style disguise Patrick nevertheless did part with a twenty-pound note in exchange for a stack of religious tracts being hawked about by a strange dreadlocked man in Notting Hill. Thus armed with the means of avoiding eternal hell and damnation we made for the block of flats where Joy Murphy had been known to live and started knocking on all the doors, stuffing leaflets through the letterboxes of those where there was no reply.

'Look, we won't be taken seriously if you keep giggling,' he protested after our third call as we worked our way up the building.

Thus reprimanded I hid my face in my hands and howled with laughter.

'I can't think I'm that funny,' he said stiffly.

'It's the mid-west accent,' I cackled. 'Repent now and worship the Loorrrrd.'

It must be said that, so far, we had been given very short shrift.

'I'm going over the top deliberately so people don't connect us with the cops and start to gossip about this place being checked up on.'

To annoy me even further he then went up an octave and adopted a truly manic twitch which was inflicted on all but the very young and elderly and we arrived, finally – both lifts were out of order – at the flat next to Murphy's. A dejected-looking middle-aged man answered the door and was treated to the usual opener of being in the presence of a representative of the Church of the Brethren of Hickory Smokers.

'Is your neighbour at home, do you know?' Patrick asked, oozing charm, when the door was about to be closed in our faces.

There was a rapid change of interest. 'Nah, she's not been here in ages. I always know, like, 'cos of the racket she makes.'

'Racket?' Patrick echoed.

'Yeh, headbanging music stuff and some kind of DIY that involves knockin' down walls. Drives me daft. I knocked once to complain and she came to the door and sort of snarled at me like a mad dog. Scared me silly, I can tell ya.'

'I have a good friend who works for the local council's noise abatement department,' he was earnestly informed. 'Would you like me to get him to call round? People can be taken to court, you know.'

'Better not. She might come gunnin' for me.'

'Not weapons!' Patrick cried in horror. 'The brethren are absolutely against the right to carry arms.'

'Yeh, guns. I reckon it's not just the music and DIY when you hear bangs. She's lettin' off shooters in there. Mad as mustard if you ask me.' A crafty look came over his face. 'She might need lockin' up, like.'

'If I could only give my friend some real evidence . . .' Patrick said sadly. 'We might just be able to—'

'I promise I'll look the other way if ya want to git in there,' interrupted the man, eagerly. 'I mean, people like her usually end up killin' someone, don't they?'

'Truly, they do, they do,' my husband warbled. He went away along the outside walkway for a few yards and eyed up the door. 'But one can hardly—'

'The kitchen window round the back ain't too good,' he was encouraged. 'I went round there once when we could smell somefink 'orrible but it wasn't comin' from 'er place. Poor old Mrs P in the flat below had gorn and died. Bin in there for nigh on four months lyin' on the floor.'

'God rest her soul,' Patrick murmured in his own voice. He rushed back and warmly wrung the man's hand. 'Friend, you are one of the Lord's very own.'

'I ain't a church person really,' said the man with a hint of sadness in his voice as we were walking away.

'It can be very helpful if you're lonely,' Patrick told him.

We followed the balcony in the direction that the man had indicated. It narrowed slightly at the side of the building and then continued past rubbish chutes – down one of which Patrick lobbed the remaining leaflets – and a fire escape together with more utilities: fire hydrants and so forth. Turning again and continuing along the rear we started counting windows: there were no back doors. Any doubts we might have had were allayed when we came to one where the catch had broken, the window being kept closed by having a folded strip of newspaper jammed in it, one end of which flapped in the minor gale that blew up here.

'I do urge caution,' I said. 'This woman is mad and bad and might have set traps for unwanted visitors.'

'And if she's not reckoned to be at Hammersmith with Northwood and the bloke doesn't think she's here where the hell is she?'

'In Bath?' I ventured.

'When we're through here I'll phone Carrick about Mick the Kick. I'm warming to your idea. I'm convinced that Bath is where all this will end.'

He got the tips of his fingers under the edge of the window and pulled. It opened with a jerk, the opening adjuster at the bottom inside knocking something off the ledge into the kitchen sink. We froze, listening, and I glanced fearfully over my shoulder. But all there was to be seen was the back of a derelict factory with equally disused rusting railway lines running along at the rear of it.

'I think you ought to remain out here,' Patrick said, preparing to climb in.

'And I think two pairs of eyes are better than one.'

We stared at one another for couple of seconds then he gave me a leg-up and I wriggled in, removing a couple of other items from the window ledge as I did so and placing them out of the way on an adjacent worktop. Not many moments later we were both standing, a little surprised, in an immaculate minimalist and mostly stainless steel kitchen. The first thing I noticed were the two sets of top-of-the-range knives sort of staring at me from the other side of the room.

Patrick noticed them too but made no comment, motioning to me to stay where I was and moving over towards the door. I gazed carefully around every inch of the room. Everything was sparkling and clean, almost as though no one had ever cooked a meal here. These were hardly the original units installed when the building was new but why have expensive replacements fitted if you didn't intend to use them? I assumed the properties were rented so there was no point in adding to the flat's value.

'It's like a professional chef's kitchen,' I commented.

Patrick had cautiously opened the door. 'Perhaps she likes her food.'

'It's almost . . . forensic.'

'That too would figure.'

I shivered.

He went from my sight and there was a nerve-jangling silence. Then I heard a muttered exclamation.

'What?' I said from the kitchen doorway.

'Have a look at this.'

I went into a passageway. The first door on the left appeared to lead into a living room and when I entered the dingy interior I too exclaimed.

'She's removed nearly all the interior walls,' Patrick said.

Some of which, presumably the weight-bearing ones, had been replaced by planks supported by adjustable steel props. The room was still very dusty from this demolition and there were small piles of rubble in corners. The large space created, which was partly partitioned around two thirds of the way down and probably originally four rooms in all, had been turned into a bizarre shooting gallery. There were cardboard targets strung around, most of which were in tatters, some home-made, a few similar to those used on military ranges, the only items not shot to bits an expensive music system just behind the door and speakers high on the wall above our heads. The partition, a piece of wall that had been left standing – all the walls were pockmarked with bullet holes – concealed whatever was down there around the 'corner'.

Patrick was surveying his surroundings. There appeared to be no infrared intruder detectors but as far as trip wires went the room was too gloomy to be able to see any easily. It was then that I noticed that the windows had been painted over with a ghastly brownish-red paint, the colour of dried blood. Some appeared to have been spilt, or smeared, on the wooden floor.

I jumped violently when the cardboard figures suddenly started to move in a jerking nightmarish way but it was only Patrick pulling on a length of string.

'You might mention next time that you're going to set everything going,' I whispered, heart pounding. But I might as well have been talking to myself.

He set off down the room, utilizing the illumination from his little torch to reflect off any trip wires which may or may not be connected to booby-trap devices. There did not appear to be any and he reached the partitioned area.

'Anything interesting?' I asked when he had taken a look around the jagged edge of the wall.

'Oh, yes,' he whispered, stepping back to look at something. I went down there.

'I know exactly what I'm going to do now,' Patrick said quietly when we were standing, side by side, looking at what was on the wall that hitherto had been out of sight.

It was a very large photograph of the pair of us taken on our wedding day – our first wedding that is, Patrick then an army captain. Happy, laughing, carefree: all those things and more. The image had been shot to bits and more of the blood-coloured paint splattered over it.

We were intended to see this.

After taking some photographs with my phone and examining the rest of the flat, we left. The bathroom, dirty, had been left intact together with a very small bedroom that contained a mattress and sleeping bag thrown down on to the floor. Also in the room were a microwave cooker and a plastic carrier bag containing the stinking remains of instant meals and used plastic cutlery. There were no personal effects, nothing that hinted where this woman might be living now, no further clues whatsoever as to her involvement with crime. The general squalor of her living arrangements led me to think that the kitchen had been installed by a previous tenant and the woman had probably hardly ever entered it.

'But the knives . . .' I mused aloud.

'She likes knives – might even fantasize about cutting people up in there,' Patrick responded when we were back outside. He pushed shut the window having inserted the piece of newspaper to keep it in place, then turned to me. 'I hope what we found hasn't upset you too much.'

'She's very dangerous,' I said. I could still see the images, the holes where our eyes had been.

'That mindset has weaknesses.'

It did not seem like any kind of weakness to me.

We seemed to keep running into a wall. On contacting Bath CID Patrick was told by DS Keen that he would find out the latest on Mick the Kick from Bristol CID but had received no word personally that the man had been located. There was no better luck in reporting to Mike Greenway, his second-in-command Andrew Bayley saying that he was 'out of the office for the day'.

'He's gone walkabout,' Patrick said, spooning sugar into his coffee. 'You know what that means, don't you?'

I did. Periodically, and sometimes in response to an out-of-the-blue prompting by ex-colleagues in the Met who thought he might learn something useful, he visited old haunts, spoke to present or one-time informers, loafed in pubs in the part of London that he still regarded as his patch and generally kept his ears to the ground. He had once told us that apart from acquiring knowledge it was how he escaped for a short while from the stress of his job. I also thought it was the way this career policeman recaptured a little of past excitements when he chatted to contacts in much the same fashion that military people attend reunions. Our problem was that for perhaps as much as twenty-four hours he insisted on a communications silence unless there was a real emergency. That meant something along the lines of the start of World War Three.

'I shall have to get his permission before I talk to Mick,' Patrick went on, stirring morosely.

'Which might not be forthcoming.'

'I'll go ahead anyway.'

'Sorry, I really think you need to have him on board.'

This was the hardest part of leaving MI5; he had been his own boss in those days.

I had taken my work laptop into the coffee bar and wrote a concise report of our findings, emailing it to Bayley together with the photographs. There was not a lot more we could do just then and I felt Patrick's discontentment.

'I wonder how accurate Derek Jessop's description of this woman was,' I said.

'I've seen a couple of old mugshots but surprise, surprise she changes her appearance all the time,' Patrick said.

'Criminals often do but she can't do much about her height and build.'

I rang Lynn Outhwaite. The DS was mobile, of sorts, shopping on crutches in Bristol with her boyfriend and in a much better mood than when I had last spoken to her. She told me that on the night when she had seen Murphy in the restaurant the woman had had medium length blonde hair, although following Jessop's description it was probably a wig. Her eyes were brown and she was quite slim but with muscular shoulders 'like an Olympic rower'. She would be around five feet eight inches tall without the very high-heeled shoes she had been wearing.

I asked Lynn if there was anything else she could remember that might be of significance.

'Perhaps not particularly significant but her voice is the one thing I really remember about her,' said Carrick's assistant. 'Husky like a heavy smoker's or a man's. And loud, interrupting people all the time. She acts tough; might be a lesbian. Even if I hadn't had a good idea who she was with I'd have hated her almost on sight. I got the impression she'd do just about anything to get her own way or her hands on money.'

TWELVE

Detective Sergeant Keen still had no updates on Mick the Kick but was able to tell us that Billy Jessop was at last fit to be questioned. Keen was in close touch with the DCI, who would be returning to work the next day, but meanwhile Carrick was happy for Patrick to talk to Jessop, who was still in the city's Royal United Hospital under arrest. Also under guard, it transpired when we were required to show our credentials.

Jessop's wan appearance confirmed that he had been seriously ill and we were only permitted to talk to him for about ten minutes. He lay, propped up on pillows and resembled, frankly, a wraith with spots. Even his untidy lank hair was fair, almost white, and I saw that when he turned to stare at his visitors that his eyes were a very pale blue. He looked absolutely nothing like his brother.

'More cops?' he greeted us with weakly.

Patrick introduced us, as was our practice not giving my name, and drew up two chairs.

'I don't want to talk to you,' said Jessop. 'Sod off.'

'Well, sorry, but we need to talk to you,' Patrick said patiently. 'You see, now that Derek has admitted that not only were the pair of you in Bath taking part in the turf war and gunning for Mick from Bristol and his mob that night, but you also shot and killed a couple of his gang after they were cornered in Abbey Churchyard. That's history and you're both going to be charged with murder but—'

'Is that what the stupid git said?' Billy raged. 'Well, he's lyin'.'

'Look, Billy, everything's gone well beyond the *denying* stage,' he was gently informed. 'My job is to help catch the bastards who conned you into doing the job in the first place. Any help you can give me will help you in turn.'

'I still don't believe ya.'

'Shall I go and fetch Derek so he can tell you the score himself? Incidentally, if he hadn't told us where you were hiding out you'd be nailed down in a long wooden box by now.'

There was a meaningful silence.

Then, 'I've never seen folk like that London mob,' Billy whispered. 'I've bin thinkin' about it, you know,' he said defiantly as though we would imagine him incapable of such an activity. 'I mean, there's rough boys round and about. Micky's got a few screws loose as well but those mobsters from London . . .'

'You'd be putty in the hands of evil lunatics like that,' I said soothingly and was given a disconcerting stare.

'Yes, you're quite right, Mrs Cop. It was exactly like that. We was conned by madmen who didn't care whether we lived or died. They said, like, all we want is for you to be there with us, armed, to scare 'em off with a big show of numbers. Nothin' about runnin' battles. And Derek said it'd be all right and we'd get paid and come straight 'ome again. But those . . .' Staring at the bedcovers he mumbled obscenities and then lapsed into silence again.

'Did you see the boss man in his car?' Patrick asked.

'That twisted poser? Yeah, at the end it was parked down at the bottom of Southgate. That and a coupla others had been driven all through the pedestrian bit.'

'I'm guessing you knew it was his car but you couldn't see who was in it because of the tinted glass.'

'No, 'cos I'd seen 'im stop part of the way down. He got out and shouted at the woman to get in. Just after that was when Derek and me got shot. She came over, grabbed my gun and our wallets – the bitch kicked me in the ribs and laughed – then ran to the car. Give me a bit of rope an' I'd string 'er up right now.'

'Any idea why she didn't get Derek's gun?'

'He was lyin' on it.'

'Did the boss man call her by name?'

'Yes, Joy. That's a real joke, 'er name.'

'What did she call him?'

'Fred, sometimes Brad . . . or darlin'.' Jessop's thin face assumed an expression of disgust. 'I ask ya. The likes of 'im – darlin'.'

'Would you know him again?'

'Piggy eyes an' all, too right. Look . . .'

'Yes?' Patrick encouraged when the other faltered.

'I'm not just tellin' ya this just 'cos of what you said about it 'elpin' me. I think it was that cow what shot us.'

'But you were working for *her*.'

'To get us out the way, like, and get their gun and the money back – we got half before and was promised the rest afterwards. It follers, dunnit? She was somewhere behind us when it happened over near where the two was that we . . .'

'Murdered,' Patrick said when he stopped speaking.

'She said do it! Screamed at us. Then she—'

'Knifed them so their guts fell out.'

Jessop retched, grabbed a corner of the sheet and slammed it over his mouth. For a moment I thought he might vomit. Then, when he could speak, he said, 'Look, the worst thing I'd ever done before that was get in fights at football matches. I didn't even know 'ow to put ammo in the gun but they didn't give us no more so it didn't matter.'

'Does the name Adam Trelonic mean anything to you?'

Slowly, Jessop shook his head.

'How about Brian Law?'

'There *was* a bloke called Brian but I never knew what 'is other name was. God knows what 'appened to 'im. He was there at the start but I never saw 'im again.'

'But he was one of you, one of the men employed by the London mob.'

'Oh, yes. Real stoopid, mind.'

'Thank you. I'll arrange for you to look at some mugshots. Will you make an official statement of everything you've just told us?'

'If you promise you'll get her – and 'im.'

'We're all throwing everything at it. Is there anything you need that I can get you?'

Miserable that he could not smoke, Jessop settled for some chocolate.

'It looks as though Mike Greenway might be right in reckoning that Uncle used to be a man by the name of Fred Gibbons as

Murphy called him Fred as well as Brad,' Patrick remarked when we were outside. 'A hairy yob with tattoos was the description if I remember what he said correctly.'

'And at last we have a connection with Adam Trelonic,' I said.

'It's still not real evidence. All we know is that a man called Brian was there and that was the name Trelonic used for his false identity scam.'

'I know the Jessops are yobs but they were horribly used, weren't they?'

'And if Billy's right about Murphy shooting them . . .'

My mind went back to the photograph of us on her wall: eyeless, holes roughly where our hearts would be.

'I have to say that I thought there might be a problem,' Patrick said crisply. 'Right here, at Bristol CID. No intelligence forthcoming, a mobster ostensibly gone right off the map. So are we talking about incompetence or are you hoping for an Oscar for finding him all by yourselves? Or do you have a really good idea where he is, ditto?'

This was not the way to talk to a Detective Chief Inspector whom you have not previously met, especially when you are nominally only of constable rank and your delivery is embroidered with carefully selected expletives which, obviously, I have omitted. But Patrick's frustration had boiled over.

DCI Ian Cookson stared back across his desk at us with hard dark eyes magnified by the thick lenses of his gold-rimmed glasses. He was an overweight, world-weary and brutal-looking individual with ugly greying stubble, both on top of his head and on his chin, or rather, chins. When he spoke his voice was deep and melodious, albeit unfriendly, with a hint of an east London accent.

'I understand you used to be in the army,' he said.

'That's right.'

'You speak like someone who expects to be obeyed. Not this time.'

'I worked undercover for most of my career. It's personality that keeps you alive.'

'I fail to understand why SOCA wants to arrest Micky Fellows.'

'I don't want to arrest him. He could be the key to smashing all these gangs.'

'It's unlikely. We know he was conned into going into Bath that night by Charlie Gill and a city hoodlum who calls himself Uncle with the idea of—'

'No, that's what the Met call him because he topped his nephew,' Patrick interrupted. 'He's now assumed the name of Brad Northwood but his original name is probably Fred Gibbons. Joy Murphy, who as you're probably aware is his pet psycho, was heard to call him Fred during the shoot-out.'

Unabashed, Cookson wrote down some of these details and then said, 'The point I was going to make is that Micky is *our* problem. Right, he was involved but only because other mobsters wanted him and his gang ancient history. You sort out the Bath end and I'll sort this. We're building a damned good case against him in connection with other unrelated stuff that'll put him away for most of the rest of his life. I'm perfectly content for there to be continuing liaison between us all but otherwise . . . no.'

'I'm not asking for your permission. Just telling you of my intentions.'

'You won't find him without me.'

'Yes, he will,' I said.

'Then I'll have you . . . discouraged,' Cookson said grimly, still addressing Patrick.

'No, you won't,' I said before my other half could really lose it.

'Lady, how do you *really* fit into all this?' the DCI furiously demanded to know.

'As Patrick's just told you, I'm his wife and we work together. We worked together for MI5. Sometimes I have to act as a buffer between him and other . . . colleagues. Like now.'

The hint that he might shortly be involved in a serious train crash seemed to work and after a few thoughtful moments Cookson said to me, 'You're the one who's been sending me emails with updates on investigations carried out by Carrick and his team and also liaising with DI Black, who's on leave, by the way.'

'That's right.'

Cookson frowned into space for a few moments and then said, 'I feel bound to tell you that I appreciated that.'

'You never know when you're going to need a DCI on board,' I said with a smile.

He actually smiled back, or rather one took him unawares. 'The grapevine has it that someone tried to kill the pair of you recently at a military and police firearms establishment. What was all that about?'

'He was an ex-cop by the name of Warren Rouse who was known within Uncle's gang as Red,' I said. 'He was probably under orders after a tip-off that we haven't got to the bottom of yet.'

'And?'

'He penetrated security with a false warrant card. He's dead. I shot him when he cornered me.'

The man's eyes seemed to grow even larger through his spectacles as he gazed at me.

'Where is Micky then?' Patrick said.

'Even if I tell you he'll sniff out a copper. He's damned clever despite being short of a few nuts and bolts.'

'I have no intention of going undercover for this job.'

'Then he won't let you get anywhere near him.'

Patrick just sat there like something evil carved out of a Dartmoor tor.

'He'll take you apart,' Cookson warned, beginning to sound as though he cared. 'The man's a competition-standard kick-boxer.'

'I don't do kick-boxing,' said Patrick dismissively.

'Then you're finished. I refuse to take responsibility if you go any further with this.'

'Where is he?'

'You're a fool! He's at least ten years younger than you are!'

'Where *is* he?'

After briefly hesitating, and probably hoping by now that Patrick would get his head kicked in, Cookson told us.

'The man had a point about my not finding him,' Patrick said when we had successfully solved the riddle of the return journey through the maze of corridors in the Bristol city centre police station and were making our way across the car park.

'Yes, "Right now he's on a yacht in Plymouth Marina for the weekend" wasn't what I was expecting to hear either,' I said. 'Why Plymouth, though, I wonder. There are plenty of places to moor a boat in and around Bristol.'

'Business associates? A girlfriend? Perhaps he just likes the pubs in the Barbican. Whatever the reason, that's one of my home territories.'

Of course, Patrick had once had a flat in North Ope.

Perhaps the DCI had been trying to confuse us for the Plymouth marina, one of several, to which we eventually tracked down the floating gin palace, was more correctly known as Sutton Harbour. This was once the waterfront of the medieval fortified town of Sutton, the narrow streets and alleyways of which are now home to art galleries, boutiques, wine bars, cafés and a hell of a lot of heavy drinking. The whole area is generally known as the Barbican, the title referring to the gatehouse that once guarded the castle, now the site of the Citadel, a seventeenth-century fortress built to protect the coastline from the Dutch. It is still in use by the military today.

Cookson had told us that the boat was called *Fancy Lady* and we were given to understand by the harbour master that it was impossible to miss as it was painted black with oblique gold-coloured stripes. Needless to say this retired master mariner was not at all impressed with the vessel when we spoke to him in his quayside office but he himself conceded that there were plenty more afloat similar to it.

'How are we going to play this?' I enquired when we had spotted what was probably the boat we sought moored to one of the pontoons.

'Sorry, it's going to be one of those situations where we make it up as we go along.'

This had the effect of making me feel that we were somehow naked. In the past, especially during our MI5 years, we had often worked undercover, almost always assuming some kind of role or false identity, something I knew we were very good at.

I could not think of any occasion where our cover had been
blown through any fault of our own.

'Don't look so worried,' Patrick said, putting an arm through
mine. Then uncannily following my own train of thought, 'The
emperor'll just have to find a set of new clothes.'

'But he was starkers!'

He laughed.

It was a fine morning – we had driven down the previous
night – and the harbour area was thronging with both local
people and visitors, which was encouraging as this particular
bunch of gangsters was unlikely to start a war in public. I
suddenly realized that we were indeed playing a part as,
consciously or not, we had dressed like holidaymakers in jeans,
T-shirts and trainers. In bad moments I sometimes wonder if
Patrick always assumes roles, including those of husband and
father, and even I, his wife, do not know the real man.

Across the sparkling sunlit water in the narrow harbour over
by the marine aquarium the loud two-tone warning siren on the
lock gates started up – there is a pedestrian walkway across it
– as a fishing boat approached and we took the opportunity of
people's attention being diverted to slip through the marina
entrance, which is strictly for the use of boat owners. I knew
that Patrick would not want to have to start waving his SOCA
warrant card around until forced to.

Fancy Lady, the name painted in at least three places in large
gold letters, had several empty berths on either side of her as
though the real boating fraternity, represented no doubt by the
nearby Royal Corinthian Yacht Club, simply could not bear to
be alongside something so ghastly. The vessel bobbed gently
in the wake of a passing pleasure boat; the best part of a million
pounds worth of floating bad taste. As we got closer we could
hear loud rock music, a group Matthew assures me call themselves Road Hogs and Black Pudding.

A large blond minder, painfully peeling with sunburn, was
standing on the pontoon trying to look as though he was
watching the seagulls. Patrick, a little way ahead of me, walked
past the boat and then mimed horror, pointing at something in
the water on the far side of it. He beckoned urgently to the
bodyguard who hurried over. There was what appeared to be

an accidental collision between the two and then a fountain-like splash.

'He *can* swim,' Patrick said tersely, having to raise his voice over the racket, giving me a hand up on to the deck. There was no one in what even in a vessel like this had to be called the wheelhouse but the top of the companionway that led below was guarded by another show specimen of manhood who looked extremely surprised to see us.

Patrick gave him a big smile and said, or rather shouted, 'It's his birthday today, isn't it?'

The bodyguard shook his head and bawled back, 'No idea. Who are you?'

The man over the side started shouting even louder, causing his colleague to run over to the rail. Seconds later he had joined him in the water.

We descended a short flight of carpeted stairs and found ourselves in a large saloon, brightly lit with eye-aching decor, light reflecting off mirrors and crystal chandeliers. I realized I was standing by the control panel for the music and hit every button until there was silence. The room appeared to be empty but then suddenly a couple of nattily nautically dressed young men appeared, little more than youths, running in our direction with obvious intent to eject us, no questions asked.

'Episode three,' Patrick hissed at them.

They sort of fizzled out; he really can look quite intimidating.

'I just want to talk to the boss,' Patrick told them.

'He doesn't want to talk to you,' said a third man, his voice coming from somewhere at the rear.

For answer the nearest henchman, companion, toyboy, what have you, was unceremoniously clubbed into the nearest over-stuffed satin-covered sofa, baby pink, where he remained, inert. The second started to flee but was reeled in by the back of his jacket, wrung unconscious by those bloody-awful strong fingers and tipped with a loud crunching noise into an oversized leopard-print furry bean bag.

'But you don't do kick-boxing,' said the man who now appeared and who I already knew from mugshots to be Michael Fellows, aka Mick the Kick.

'It's an exhibition sport,' Patrick said with a shrug.

'Cookson asked me not to kill you.'

'I'm delighted that you're on such friendly terms with Bristol CID.'

The man strutted forward. To my slightly trained eye he looked fit and lithe but I was worried about his fashion sense.

'All I want is to discuss with you how we're going to get Uncle in the slammer,' Patrick said. Then, urgently, 'I'm warning you. I have no desire to conduct a conversation with a man with a broken neck.'

Micky laughed and lashed out with a foot and then both fists.

Before joining special services Patrick went off on his own and learned things that he refers to as his survival package. He won't talk about it.

This was why.

As Cookson had said, this man was at least ten years younger than Patrick and although I was worried my instincts told me that the mobster's veneer as far as courage was concerned was thin. My insides were tying themselves in knots but it was important that I look cool, bored even, as there were others present now: two women, both young, everything about them proclaiming 'sex industry', and another man I kept an eye on, my fingers curled around the Smith and Wesson in my pocket.

Anyone who aims kicks at Patrick usually ends up by having that particular foot caught, guided to impossible heights and ending up either flat on their back or airborne. It immediately became apparent that there was no danger of Micky getting really hurt – only his pride, that is. After thumping down on to his own Axminster three times he got in a kick that landed, earning a couple of lightning and sickening smacks around the head that bafflingly got through his guard. Then, having proved to his opponent that kick-boxing was not a lot of use against someone trained in the back streets of God knows where, Patrick got him in a less-than-comfortable headlock.

I shuddered. Like this, exactly like this, with little perceptible effort, I had indeed once seen him break a man's neck, the sound akin to snapping a stick of seaside rock between gloved hands. I still have nightmares about it. If he really lost his temper . . .

'So we talk?' Patrick asked, a little breathlessly.

There was an almost inaudible acquiescence.

A pair of lavishly dripping figures squelched down the stairs but stopped when they saw the gun that was now in my hand. They looked at their employer for guidance but received none; Micky, having been released, busy manoeuvring his head into a more conventional position on his shoulders, panting with rage and lack of air.

'I could get them to shoot you dead!' he yelled when he had found enough oxygen.

'My wife would drop all three of you before you'd even opened your mouth,' his visitor calmly told him.

Best described as short, dark and good-looking in a slightly lopsided way, this having nothing to do with what Patrick had just done to him, Micky had not previously noticed the gun but did now and performed a nervous shimmy. 'No! No! Forget that! The cops'll be right here if there's gunfire.'

'We *are* the cops,' Patrick said. 'Or didn't Cookson bother to tell you that bit?'

'He said someone from the Serious Organized Crime Agency, or something like that, was coming after me, personally. I didn't believe him after he'd laughed. Cookson never laughs.' He glared at the two large puddles on his plum-coloured carpet. 'Oh, get out! You're fired! You're like a couple of bloody *girls*!'

My gaze went across to the two women and the other man who I noticed Patrick had endeavoured not to turn his back on. I had an idea he was armed, and also clever.

'I need a drink,' Micky announced, waving his hands in slightly girly fashion and making a move over towards the side of the room. For some reason his mannerisms suddenly reminded me of Johnny Depp in his role as Captain Jack Sparrow.

'Be careful,' said the clever-looking man with a chuckle. 'That lady is itching to pull the trigger if she thinks you're about to do anything stupid.'

'*I'll* fix you a drink,' Patrick offered. 'And you are?' he queried of the speaker.

'I am the captain of this ship. Call me Enrico.'

'Which part of Italy do you come from?'

'Perugia.'

'I think you own this vessel and rent it out to rich criminals at weekends. And do the driving as it saves it from being heavily pranged on the nearest jetty.'

The man smiled broadly. 'Not just hard men. Anyone with . . . the correct funds.'

Micky glowered at the man and said, 'I'm sure there's something you ought to be greasing right now.'

The Italian did not stop smiling. 'But my crew . . .' he said with phoney regret, gesturing to the contents of the sofa and bean bag.

'I'll send them along when they've recovered. And take those damned women with you.'

'I'm not a parcel, you know!' shrieked one of the girls.

'You're like screwing one!' Micky bawled back.

The three went.

Patrick found the drinks cabinet, fixed a large whisky and handed it over.

'You don't want one?' Micky said, seating himself.

'No, thanks.'

I had already replaced the Smith and Wesson in my pocket and sat down where I could watch everyone. The man in the bean bag had been conscious for at least a minute and would suffer nothing worse than a slightly bruised neck; his friend, too, was stirring. They both thought it best to literally lay low.

'I'd just eaten,' Micky mumbled after taking a big swig of his drink. 'Not a good time to fight.' He saw that no one was remotely impressed with this excuse and yelled, 'Well? What the hell do you *really* want?'

'As I said, Uncle,' Patrick said. 'His head, on a plate, lightly boiled.'

'I've no influence with that bastard.'

'Clearly. How did he trick you into going into Bath that night?'

'Tricked? I wasn't tricked. No one tricks Micky.'

Patrick took a deep breath. 'Why do conversations with crooks always resemble the soundtrack for a thirties gangster movie? I know why. It's because you watch thirties gangster movies. Now listen: it is the twenty-first century and things have moved on. There *is* something called the Serious Organized Crime

Agency and I work for it. I served in special operations in the army before joining MI5 and then SOCA and can assure you that on the one-to-ten scale of crime barons you come in at approximately minus fifty. I'm not interested in you and your shitty little empire – Cookson can mop that up at his leisure when he has enough evidence. I want Uncle. He sent one of his hit men after me. And I'm getting impatient so if you don't tell me everything that's inside that flea-sized brain of yours we can continue where we left off just now.'

The man stared at him and then stuttered, 'C–c–cops aren't allowed to do things like that.'

'My boss is around a hundred miles away,' Patrick said nastily.

I reckoned we had progressed to a soundtrack from an eighties gangster movie.

Micky took another large mouthful of whisky, belched and then said, 'And you'll go away when I've told you what I know?'

'Yes, let's get rid of those two.'

The men took one each, shoving them out and shutting the door.

'OK,' Micky continued when he had been reunited with his drink. 'Charlie Gill and me was chums once. Used to knock around together, play darts and stuff like that.'

'But he originally came down from London.'

'Right. When he was in his late teens, yonks ago. We talked of setting up in business together but he didn't like Bristol. Thought there was more money to be made in Bath, more wealthy punters, better cars to steal. So we went our own ways. Then, recently, I got a message from him.'

'And?'

'He said there was a city geezer wanting to take over his patch as it was getting too hot at home. He'd somehow found out about Charlie and offered him a partnership but Charlie didn't trust him an inch. He'd gone along with him to get as much info as he could about the bloke, who kept bragging about what he'd got, what he'd done, how loaded he was. Would I muster with a few lads to show a bit of muscle with his own boys so he got the message and scarpered? He said he'd pay if I had to take people on.'

'Instead of which . . .'

'Yeah. It was us who was really for the chop.'

'Why Bath? What does this man want with a provincial city?'

Mick shrugged. 'Well, the punters are still loaded, I suppose. Quite a few of the big boys are moving out of town as you cops make life too uncomfortable for them.'

'And you didn't have enough in the way of lads for that night so you recruited a few illegal immigrants.'

'They was desperate for money. Starving. Came in on a lorry hoping to get jobs picking fruit and veg and but couldn't find nothing. A couple of them was killed.'

'Sliced to ribbons by all accounts.'

'It was murder. They was little more than boys.'

'Don't try to pretend that you actually care!' Patrick bellowed, making Micky jump.

'Yes, I do care!' he shouted back. 'They didn't know English, perhaps just a few words, and one of them cried when I got him to understand that I'd give him a hundred quid if he mustered with a few other blokes and did one night's work for me.'

'You armed them, though.'

'Well, I had to, didn't I?'

'Did they know how to fire them?'

'We did try to explain,' Mick muttered after a short silence.

'Gill's dead,' Patrick said.

'I know. He was a bloody fool. After the turf war he rang me and said . . .'

'Go on.'

'He said he hoped I hadn't been hurt and he hadn't known it would be like that, a shoot-out with people killed.'

'Did you believe him?'

'I did at the time. Not now. Then he said that Uncle – that's a bloke called Brad Northwood in case you didn't know – was going to make him his right-hand man plus a share of his London takings. It was an offer too good to pass by.'

'If Gill used to be a chum of yours how come he sold you down the river?'

'You've said it: money. Charlie could never resist the stuff. He didn't have to brag about it to me though, did he?'

'It was certainly Uncle who had him killed. Do you know anything about a woman called Joy Murphy?'

'Only that she's Northwood's minder and will kill anything for a laugh. God, if only I'd known . . .'

'He probably won't give up until he's removed all the opposition from the vicinity of Bath. That'll include you.' In offhand fashion Patrick added, 'Of course, it'll tidy things up wonderfully for us cops.'

'I don't see what I can do about it.'

'There's something you could do.'

'What?'

'Put it about as widely as you can that you've been forced into selling your outfit: your boys, loot, where you keep it and anything else important, to a guy who's returning to this country from where he's served a long prison sentence abroad and wants to find his roots. His great-grandad was a big noise in Bristol and Bath a long time ago and he wants to carry on where the old man left off at an early age, mostly because he was hanged for several murders.'

'And who's this guy going to be?'

'Me.'

'You!'

'I'm pretty convincing as a mobster.'

'I think I believe you. What do I get out of it?'

'Not a lot. Revenge for the humiliation and loss of funds that Uncle caused you that night, perhaps. I can't promise you freedom from prosecution for crimes you've already committed and my boss would never sanction the transfer of a large sum of money. I'll think of something. But you'll have to trust me and ask Captain Enrico to take you on a cruise. Just disappear for a while.'

'And if I refuse?'

'I'll just carry on breaking your neck. Slowly.'

'He might have agreed but then do nothing,' I said later.

'He'll do it,' Patrick replied. 'It involves nothing more than having a few words in people's ears in pubs and some phone calls. He's keeping his head right down at the moment crimewise anyway so it might guarantee that he goes off the map for a bit longer.'

'I'm not too sure of Cookson either. I mean, you'd told him

you had no intention of going to see Micky undercover but you could have changed your mind.'

'I don't think he's bent.'

'No, I wasn't suggesting he is. But if he *did* happen to be getting backhanders from Micky and Micky tells him what you're doing . . .'

'It probably wouldn't matter a lot. I can't believe Cookson has a hotline to Uncle. No, I think he was seriously concerned about my welfare.'

Wishful thinking?

THIRTEEN

James Carrick seemed glad to be back at work but there was something about his eyes that hinted of less sleep than was good for him. Patrick gave him a file containing an account of our activities while he had been away, which he read carefully, occasionally glancing up at the pair of us as though in disbelief and uttering the odd muttered Gaelic expletive.

'Bloody hell,' he said, having finished the last page.

Patrick said, 'I asked Ingrid to leave off the latest development as I want to talk to you before I do anything further with it. I've been to see Mick the Kick and asked him to spread the word that he's been forced into selling his business to another mobster. Me – under another name, obviously.'

'Right,' Carrick said, drawing out the word for just about as long as possible.

'And I'd like to stage some kind of large crime here to make Uncle believe I'm taking over Bath as well,' Patrick carried on blithely.

'Patrick . . .'

'I've said nothing to Greenway yet.'

The Scot wagged a finger at him. 'Through Murphy Uncle knows what you look like.'

'By the time he finds out who he's up against it'll be too late.'

'How the hell did you persuade Micky Fellows to do this?'

'Just promised to kill him there and then if he didn't.'

Carrick looked a bit shocked. 'He might have called your bluff.'

'I wasn't bluffing.'

'Bloody hell,' Carrick said again.

'But I knew he'd agree. He might turn Queen's evidence too – if there's something in it for him.'

Carrick pondered. 'We have plenty of evidence to connect Charlie Gill to the case and now you've spoken to Billy Jessop,

Murphy and Northwood are well in the frame. Billy was shown some mugshots yesterday and has positively identified both of them as the people in the big car driven down the pedestrian precinct that night, the woman having recruited him and his brother in the first place. He'd only seen Northwood once before. There is actually sufficient evidence to arrest these people without any theatricals at this end.'

'Good, I'm happy to abandon that idea, but it never hurts to stir the brew a bit.'

Carrick looked relieved. He indicated the report. 'Shall I get a copy of this sent to Greenway?'

'We emailed it to him last night. He told me that surveillance points to the pair of them still being in London.'

'Even better. The Met can arrest them then.'

I said, 'We also have a tentative link to Adam Trelonic, someone Billy remembered calling himself Brian.'

'But we need to be really careful there, don't we?' Carrick observed. 'His widow's promised to make trouble at Hinton Littlemoor if we keep questioning her and until we have more evidence there's no point in doing so. We must be dead sure of his involvement before we try to make any connections as far as she's concerned.'

'The photograph of us taken on our wedding day that was in Murphy's flat was in all the Bath papers,' I told him. 'Carol Trelonic could easily have accessed it from records and sent it to Murphy.'

'Murphy's pure poison,' the DCI murmured, an unusually emotive remark from such a pragmatic detective.

It shortly emerged that the Metropolitan Police had already put in place plans to arrest Northwood and Murphy and it had been discovered that previous intelligence had been wrong and the latter was living in an attic room that overlooked the road at the front of the Hammersmith property. We set off for London, Michael Greenway having said that we deserved to be 'in at the kill', as he put it. He made a point of adding that he had 'thrown his weight about' to ensure our presence.

It was to be the usual small hours raid, SOCA officially being there as observers, no more, and we would only be permitted to enter the house once arrests had been made. So, two hours after midnight the next day, we duly found ourselves loaded as cargo into the back of an unmarked van, one of several vehicles, and travelling blind as there were no windows in the rear of it, jammed in like battery hens with several heavily armoured members of an unspecified incident unit. I felt that should one of them so much as sneeze I would suffer several cracked ribs.

On arrival in a side street that I overheard someone say was a hundred yards from the target they all piled out, taking with them a battering down doors implement and other nameless devices. Under orders from a terse and also anonymous officer in charge, we stayed put. But after several long minutes the inside of the van, despite the brief opening of the doors, became extremely stuffy and still redolent of far too many brewed-up blokes.

'I didn't bring my sonic screwdriver,' Patrick muttered, having tried the door handle to no avail.

'Well, you can't shoot your way out as it might warn Uncle and co.,' I said, knowing the way his mind works and hoping to nip that idea smartly in the bud.

'Perhaps it's just stuck,' Patrick said when another stifling five minutes had elapsed. 'I'll pull down the handle and we'll both throw ourselves at it.'

This we did and bounced painfully back where we had started from.

'Again!' Patrick said.

Nursing a bruised shoulder I then noticed a ventilator grille in the partition between the cab and the rest of the interior. It was closed. I slid it open with little improvement as the windows in the front were probably all shut as well.

'I think I'd far rather be sacked for buggering up the raid than suffocate,' my working partner announced. Grabbing someone's discarded anorak he pushed his Glock down one sleeve, forming a muffler with that and as well as he was able with the rest of the garment, tucking it into the interior bracing struts of the door. I was waved from the immediate area.

There was a loud boom that would have awakened several cemeteries and one door flew open to smash back against the rear of the vehicle. Observed from the outside moments later it did not look as though it would readily serve its intended purpose again.

'We'll probably have to walk back,' Patrick said absent-mindedly after taking several deep breaths, tucking the weapon back in the shoulder harness.

London seemed to be going about its normal 2.45 a.m. business – that is, not much. Nobody appeared to be leaning out of windows, no one came running and I came to the conclusion that the noise had been fairly well contained by the body of the van and had possibly sounded like a vehicle backfiring. Despite having put my hands over my ears though they were still ringing.

'Which way did they go?' Patrick asked.

'No idea.'

'Do your oracle thing.'

'Look, I'm not some kind of cop detection gizmo,' I snapped.

His teeth gleamed white as he grinned at me in the deep shade beneath a tree. Ye gods, how the man loves this kind of enterprise.

'I think they *might* have gone this way,' I told him, pointing in the direction of the main road, which was around fifty yards away. In truth, I had no idea.

We set off, not really hurrying and, as far as I was concerned, quite content for other people to do the rough stuff. Something did tell me, however, that getting hold of Brad Northwood and his seriously bent harpy was unlikely to be this easy.

'I hope Matthew's not bored,' Patrick murmured. 'I'd hate it if he thought we'd just shovelled him off somewhere out of the way.'

'We'll have to get him a better computer for Christmas. Perhaps Benedict's letting him use his.'

'Lads don't usually want to share things like that.'

In the distance, moments later and from the direction of the main road there were thumps and then a crash like the sound of a front door being smashed in. Then came the staccato cracks of three shots being fired quite close by. We ran.

On the corner before the wider thoroughfare we paused for a careful look at what was going on around to the right, the direction from which the shots had seemed to come. There was the wail of sirens in the distance, closing rapidly, but not necessarily anything to do with what was going on here. Suddenly there was the pounding of feet, approaching on the run.

'Stop!' Patrick bellowed, taking a stand on the pavement. 'Police!'

There was a loud report as a gun was fired. Patrick spun around and I thought for a ghastly moment that he had been hit but it was a feint and as the gunman tore past, almost touching him, he was in a perfect position to strike him on the nape of the neck with the side of his hand. I ran out and collided heavily with someone else, a woman, who uttered a scream, choked off by the crook of Patrick's arm around her throat.

'Do we have handcuffs?' Patrick enquired of me.

'No, just a few cable ties,' I replied.

'Do you always carry cable ties, just in case?'

'Only as of yesterday.'

The man, not unconscious but staying where he was on the pavement, was short and powerfully built with fair hair. His companion, wiry with short dark hair, looked mad enough to spontaneously combust.

They were the wrong people.

Wanted to help with other enquiries, no doubt, but still the wrong people. They had been the inhabitants of Uncle's house that the police had recently been painstakingly monitoring, a couple closely resembling Northwood and Murphy. When this had been finally established back at the house after a full search had been made, which took over two hours while we kicked our heels, the Met gathered them up, expressed disappointment about their van and said they would be sending SOCA the bill. Everyone went away and we never saw any of them again.

In the first light of dawn we walked what seemed to be rather a long way back to our hotel.

'They switched over four days ago,' Michael Greenway told us when we saw him later in the morning after having had a couple of hours' sleep. 'And to be fair the replacements have been going in and out hiding their faces as much as possible with hats and, during the recent rain, umbrellas.'

'All clichés along the lines of the birds having flown will be savagely punished,' Patrick muttered to himself.

'Coffee,' the commander decided after a quick glance at his subordinate. 'Did you have breakfast?' he followed this up with.

We said we had not.

'Croissants then.' Never one to go to the door and shout or expect anyone to come running he went away and asked his PA to fix it.

'They're talking then,' I said when he returned.

'Non-stop apparently and now anxious to distance themselves from any connection with serious crime lords,' Greenway answered.

'But he *was* armed,' Patrick said.

'It was his own weapon. The idiot even bragged about it. Some kind of tinpot Mr Fixit. We know all about him and God knows he's stupid enough to be recruited for the job without knowing who he's really working for – if he's even heard of Northwood. That hasn't been established yet.'

'What about the woman?' I asked.

'Just a hooker he knew – she's a drug addict – who was glad to stay in someone else's house, all paid for, plus a little pocket money for as long as required.'

'Do we know how this man was recruited?'

'Word of mouth – or so he's saying. He's not too stupid to know the best plan is to keep your mouth shut about certain matters.'

'Would you like me to talk to him?' Patrick enquired.

'The Met's still working on him and I don't think anything valuable would come of your having a go as well. Uncle's far too clever to leave a trail of useful information with his bum-wipers.'

'So where the hell *are* they then?'

'I'm rather hoping that you'll find out. You're free to go and take a look around Northwood's place even though I've been given to understand that it's been gone over very thoroughly already.' He gave me one of his big smiles. 'Ingrid, you've been known to find things that other people have missed.'

'He'll have other bolt holes to go to,' Patrick said. 'And

probably won't ever return to Hammersmith to pick up his
stuff except when the Met's gone to their effin' Christmas
party.'

Luckily our coffee arrived just then.

'No pressure then,' I said as we approached the Hammersmith
house.

'You've given everyone very good leads in the past,' Patrick
said, definitely in a jauntier frame of mind. 'But don't worry
about evidence against them, the Met can work on that. All we
want is to find out where they're hiding out now.'

There were the usual strands of incident tape draped between
lamp posts and other street furniture and a torpid with boredom
constable on duty at the door. Patrick flashed his warrant card,
actually his driving licence, at the man and then gave him a
furious and expletive-laden lambasting for letting us through.
No, he really was not still in a mood, just an ex-military man
who loathes lax security and sloppy conduct.

We went in and I walked into the first room I came to. Patrick
knows my methods and left me alone to undertake his own
investigations. The furniture: two large sofas, several chairs, a
bookcase, empty but for a couple of cartons that had once held
computing kit, and another set of shelves loaded with newspapers and magazines, was scruffy and had probably come with
the property. The general impression was one of bareness, of
no personal possessions.

Sliding doors partitioned this room from the one to the rear
of it, once a dining room perhaps but now used as some kind
of further living space with two more sofas, the fabric covers
torn and stained as though a dog had been shut in here and
taken out its frustration on them. The curtains were half-closed
and gave a limited view of an overgrown garden. In my experience serious criminals never garden, they are too busy making
money and other people's lives a misery. I mentioned this
theory to Patrick once and he thought it fanciful. I'm sticking
to it.

The kitchen was filthy, the rubbish bin stinking and over-
flowing, the sink piled high with unwashed mugs and plates.
There was no cutlery and the fridge had next to nothing in it

but for a couple of ready meals, some milk and half a sliced loaf. A utility room off the kitchen contained a washing machine plus a muddle of old shoes and coats, mostly on the floor, all mixed up with more newspapers dated weeks previously and several battered empty cardboard boxes.

I wandered back into the hallway, taking my time, and then slowly went up the stairs. There were three bedrooms, one obviously in recent use and squalid with dirty bedding, discarded clothing – again mostly on the floor, a cheap DIY wardrobe that was falling apart, a chest of drawers, ditto, and several suitcases that the police had obviously emptied out and rammed back the contents any which way. The other two rooms, discounting the bathroom, did not look as though they had been used since the place was let, the beds stripped, a couple of built-in cupboards empty, the only other item an exercise bicycle, broken by the look of it, dumped in one corner.

Patrick called to me from the top of a narrow staircase that led to the top floor. 'This is quite interesting.'

'There's nothing interesting anywhere else,' I said. 'Northwood's moved out.'

'So has Murphy.'

This gallery was not dedicated to shooting but graffiti. I have no eye for such an activity but this looked very, very bad and was executed in what looked like lipstick, marker pens in various colours and something that was probably leftover emulsion paint. The subject matter, which was on practically every wall of the attic room, could be described as a marriage between the highly obscene and Gothic horror.

'She *is* raving mad,' I declared, ducking to avoid a particularly luxuriant festoon of black cobwebs, real, that also resided up here. Perhaps they had made the woman feel more at home.

'There's not one atom of a clue as to where they've gone,' Patrick said, slamming the last drawer on a built-in unit. He went over to a small door in the far wall that must give access to the rest of the roof space.

'Do be careful,' I warned.

'The Met have already gone over everything. They'd have triggered any nasty surprises.'

'But a certain amount of time has elapsed and there has to be a back entrance to this place – has the state of security on the front door been as abysmal as this right from the start?' The door was not locked. Having given me an I-hear-every-word-of-your-jewels-of-wisdom bow Patrick opened it with all due caution, clicked down a light switch just inside and then beckoned me over.

Joists, rafters, bare boards and yet more black cobwebs. Nothing else.

'This is getting a bit serious,' I said.

'I was highly recommended by Colonel Richard Daws, four-teenth Earl of Hartwood, late of MI5, now practically running SOCA but can't even find one second-rate mobster. Perhaps I ought to resign, go home and concentrate on writing letters to *The Times* about the state of the roads.'

We had another abortive look round and then left, the hatred of the cop on the door burning between my shoulder blades as we walked away.

The Met had convinced Greenway that the substitutes at the house knew nothing of value so he pointed us in the direction of an informer who had not been heard from for quite a while but had been known to 'come up with the goods'. We spent an equally useless afternoon and evening trying to trace this man in the east end of London and finally established, although not from official records, that he was dead.

'No, that's it,' Patrick said when we were in our hotel room. He threw off all his clothes and made for the shower.

'It?' I called after him.

'The bastard's not here. Murphy's not here. No one's talking and the snout's dead. The case is dead.'

'He has to be in Bath.'

Stark naked, he turned. 'Is that the oracle talking?'

'You yourself said that this is all going to end in Bath. I think that's where they are.'

'If you're right I might even make love to you as a reward.'

'Actually, if you don't mind I'd rather not wait that long.'

His reaction was instant, quite admirable and probably under a minute later he had taken all my clothes off as well, tipped

me on to the bed, kissed me silly and then brought us together
with even more admirable enthusiasm.

Wanting him like crazy apart, it never hurts to remind your
man that he is brilliant at the really important things in life.

We went to an Italian restaurant just around the corner from
the hotel, Patrick still working on tactics.

'No, never mind about Carrick's sensibilities. It's the only
way to go forward, to carry out my idea of—'

My mobile rang and Patrick lapsed into silence while I
answered it. As I listened to the quiet, intense voice of my
adopted son stating neatly and precisely what he now knew I
felt the hairs on the back of my neck moving as though little
feet were brushing through them. I heard him out and promised
to phone him back.

'That was Matthew?' Patrick queried.

I nodded.

'Has something gone wrong?'

'No. He copied those disks and took them with him just in
case, and he and Benedict have hacked into the computers
of what he's calling the mates of Colin Andrews, the manager of
the Ring o' Bells. They think it's a criminal gang and the boss
is referred to as Uncle.'

Unusually for him, my husband became momentarily
speechless.

'Benedict's phoning his father as well, who's working late
apparently.'

'I think I ought to talk to Matthew.'

This he did, remaining fairly non-committal and promising
to contact him again as soon as he had spoken to the commander.
He warned the boys to say absolutely nothing about what they
had done to anyone else and had only just finished speaking
to him when Greenway called.

'Mike wants us to go to his place when we've eaten – he's
heading home now.'

I desisted in making motherly remarks along the lines of it
being rather late to keep Matthew and Benedict out of bed as
in view of what they appeared to have done they could no
longer be treated as children. Well, not right now.

Greenway had brought someone with him from work, the computer expert who had been given the original disks and who touchingly promised Benedict that he would accord his computer every care and attention if he was permitted to delve into what they had been working on. Software goodies to be downloaded having already been promised by his father, the two disappeared into the study for Benedict to explain the bare bones of it all.

I felt that Matthew was rather in awe of his host, of whom he had probably seen little. His greeting to us had been warm but restrained, as he perhaps thought befitted the occasion.

'Do you know about this Uncle then?' he suddenly asked the room at large, Mike's wife having just brought in coffee and biscuits.

Patrick indicated to Greenway that he should provide any insight forthcoming.

'Oh, he's a seriously wanted London mobster,' replied the commander. 'I can't tell you much more right now, though.'

'He's got a girlfriend called Joy.'

'Has he now?'

'They're moving to Bath. Renting a big house.'

'Really?' Patrick said.

'Well, they've probably moved in already actually as there's some big party thing going to happen. All of Bath's going – you know, the mayor and business people.'

'You've dug all this out?' Greenway asked.

'Oh, yes, tons of emails. No security on their stuff at all. Crazy if you ask me.'

'Any idea why they're doing this?'

Matthew shrugged, innocent of the honour he was being accorded: a top policeman asking for his opinion. 'Well, if he's a crook he might like to be thought of as a proper businessman and want to impress the people in charge. Perhaps he's changed his name.'

'What does he call himself in the emails?' I asked.

'Brad. Some are from Fred but I don't know if that's the same person. It's the same email address. There's a Warren too.' Matthew yawned. 'Does this mean I'm not in trouble any more?'

'No, you're not,' Greenway told him. 'Even if I have to come down and talk to someone personally.'

I said, 'How much of this have you told Katie?'

'Only that we've been hacking. She thought I meant gardening and said how boring. I didn't want her to do any more poking around over at the pub.'

FOURTEEN

'Details are still emerging,' Patrick said to James Carrick. 'But it would appear that some kind of party, a house-warming, is being held at a house in the Avonhill area of the city. I think Matthew got it wrong when he said the mayor and people like that were invited but they may well have asked top crooks. Prospective guests are being told to keep it quiet, not blab it on Facebook. The impression is that Uncle's setting himself up as a property developer, possibly in order to launder further takings.'

Carrick was furious, taking the news as a personal affront. 'What's this bloody man calling himself *now*?'

'Warren de la Frey.'

'And presumably he's had a face transplant.'

'Pass.'

'What does Greenway say about all this?'

'That events appear to have moved to your patch.'

'Good of him.'

'But you can borrow me for a while if you want to.'

Carrick rubbed his hands over his face as though tired. He was. 'I'm not sure whether that makes it better or worse.'

Patrick laughed. He has an infectious laugh and the DCI ended up by chuckling.

'I think we ought to have dinner at the Ring o' Bells tonight, ladies too,' Patrick suggested.

'Isn't that a bit of a risk?'

'No, not if we talk about everything else under the sun and pretend to be a bit sloshed and stupid having been drinking before we arrived. Hopefully we can make Andrews relax and think we've forgiven him about Matthew and that he himself can't possibly be under suspicion. Then you both come over to the rectory where we'll decide what we're going to do about this. By then we might know a bit more.'

'OK, all I have to do is find a babysitter. By the way, Mick the Kick seems to have done as you asked. A snout's insisting that he's retiring from crime having sold out to a bod from abroad who threatened to kill him if he didn't agree. According to him Micky's gone on holiday.'

'Cruising with the Mafia?'

Carrick gave him his full attention.

'It's just a guess: that Captain Enrico – who looked far too clever just to be in charge of a boat – was probably under orders to conduct some kind of investigation into British crime barons to see what the competition consisted of. The saloon was probably bugged too. If so he would have heard every word of our conversation.'

'I hope he doesn't know Uncle.' James frowned.

'I'm not sure we ought to go to the pub,' I said.

'Any particular reason?' Patrick asked.

'I just feel uncomfortable going anywhere near that man.'

'Surely it's a good idea to behave normally.'

'OK, but you might put my reservations in the minutes.'

The inclusion of 'the ladies' was a deliberate ploy on Patrick's part as he could hardly exclude me and Joanna used to be Carrick's sergeant. She was a very good detective and I knew he shared his casework with her.

'I did ask him when he proposed to me, you know,' said Joanna, obviously with this same train of thought when we all met up in the pub and had found a table in a corner. 'Do you want me for my fanny or my brain?'

She had not troubled to lower her voice and I knew her husband had primed her about acting 'a bit sloshed and stupid'. But he still winced and gazed around to see if anyone had overheard. They had, sniggering.

'What would you like to drink, darling?' Patrick asked her, as loudly.

'Oh, a big, big G&T, darling,' she crowed.

Patrick quirked an eyebrow in her direction and received a tiny shake of her head in response. He did not ask me what I wanted and this meant that when he returned with the drinks I got the G&T, the nursing mother just a tonic with ice, no one else present any the wiser. The men were on whisky, modestly I hoped: this was war.

As he sometimes does, and egged on by Joanna, Patrick related a few anecdotes from his service days. He is an entertaining speaker, mostly due to being a good mimic and it was a relief, despite the fact that I had heard the stories before, to forget for a short while our main reason for being here this evening.

I suddenly became aware of someone coming to stand behind me.

'This table's reserved,' said Colin Andrew's voice.

Patrick had probably noticed his approach but only now fastened his gaze on him. 'There was no card on the table,' he pointed out.

'Nevertheless, it's reserved. You'll have to leave.'

'Leave?' Carrick said in astonishment.

'We're booked solid tonight.'

'But there are empty tables over there.'

'They're coming later. I hope you're not going to make trouble.'

'Why on earth should we make trouble?' Joanna protested.

'Well, you've been noisy enough already. And drunk. We don't serve the likes of you.'

Patrick rose to his feet.

'Going to threaten me now then, are you?' Andrews shouted, taking a step backwards.

'I was about to leave,' Patrick told him coldly. 'As requested.'

'I'm glad to hear it. You and your thieving kids have been nothing but trouble since you moved here. Throwing your weight about as the big copper and harassing innocent people.'

'Please calm down,' Carrick said. 'There's no need for this.'

'What do you know about it?' Andrews said furiously. 'And his father's no better. Playing the priest while screwing half the women in the village.'

'That's right!' bawled Carol Trelonic, having appeared behind the bar. 'I can testify to that. Had a go with me. You need to arrest the bugger because I'm going to make a complaint about him. *And* I'm writing to the bishop.'

For some strange reason I have no actual memory of leaving

the building, only of James Carrick practically manhandling Patrick outside and just about succeeding in preventing him going straight back in.

'He's really hoping you'll lose your temper,' I said to Patrick, a hand on each side of his face, gazing into the eyes of someone I was terrified could neither see nor hear me. 'Listen to me, Patrick! Don't!'

He seemed to notice me.

'No one will believe a word of it,' I said. 'They've done themselves more harm than good.'

'Let's go home,' he muttered.

'Come home with me, gorgeous man,' said Joanna, an arm through his, acting tipsy. 'I'll drive and then cook everyone a splendid dinner.'

'Everyone was right,' James Carrick said later when we arrived at their house, no doubt endeavouring to mitigate what had been a minor disaster. 'Andrews felt safe enough to act cocky to the point of stupidity while Ingrid was perfectly correct in her reluctance to eat there. I just hope no damage has been done with regard to your father, Patrick.'

'I rang Elspeth just now and told her what had happened – we had previously warned them – and she said the woman might have already been putting it about as she's been getting odd looks from some people. They're both a bit distressed, obviously.'

I thought the mobsters were one step ahead of us all the way but said nothing just then.

'Right, so how are you going to remove those odious people from what used to be a perfectly lovely village pub?' Joanna asked in challenging fashion.

'By removing their paymasters, even more odious people now in Bath,' her husband replied.

The information was trickling out as Greenway's cyber-boffin hacked deeper and deeper into Uncle's network, most of the users of which did not bother with passwords and those who did unknowingly having them brushed aside in a matter of moments. The words in some kind of 'home-made' code that

Patrick had noticed had been easy to decipher as days and dates. By this time Benedict's computer had been shorn of everything in connection with the criminal investigation and this evidence had been taken to SOCA's HQ for further work to be done. It appeared that GCHQ, the Government Communications Headquarters, was now also involved.

Good food and a little too much wine the previous evening had meant that not a lot of planning had been accomplished. I reckoned this to be a good thing as Patrick had not had an opportunity to brood over what had happened and go on to wind himself up with a view to wrapping Andrews around his own beer pumps on our return.

'When's this house-warming, or whatever, taking place?' I asked Carrick in his office at the Manvers Street nick the following morning.

'This coming Saturday. There have been several requests to keep it quiet. They obviously don't want gatecrashers.'

I decided that it was time to share my worries. 'Look, I really don't want to sound pessimistic but I do think these people are running rings around us right now. They're anticipating our moves: our photo in Murphy's flat, the two people pretending to be her and Northwood at the Hammersmith house, the attack on Patrick and me at the training centre. Now this, a party planned at a rented house here in Bath. Is it genuine? Are they hoping you'll raid the place so they can pick off a few senior officers and throw the CID into temporary chaos? I know it sounds fantastic but anything that Murphy has a hand in can't be regarded as normal.'

'They can't possibly know that someone's broken into their records and computer systems,' Carrick observed.

'Are you sure? There were hardly any passwords. Are they really stupid or actually rather clever and wanted it to happen?'

The men glanced at one another and then Patrick said, 'I agree it's cause for concern and speaking personally I suggest we proceed with all due caution.'

'Likewise,' the DCI said.

'Do we know exactly which property in Avonhill's involved?' I asked.

'Not yet.'

Patrick said, 'As you're well aware there are a hell of a lot of big houses up there.'

'Keen's contacting all the letting and estate agencies right now to see if we can pinpoint the place,' Carrick told him.

'Once you do know the address there's nothing to stop you going straight in there, taking them by surprise and arresting them before any social event takes place.'

'My instincts tell me to sneak someone in there on the night of the bash – easy if they have outside caterers – and find out who exactly is present. We've no idea at present as despite lousy security everywhere else they seem to be using nicknames. All sorts of worms might come out of their holes.'

'And take photographs with a concealed camera?' Patrick asked him.

'I'm sorely tempted. Then raid the place and make arrests later when they're all sozzled.'

'Have you anyone in mind?'

'Keen's keen. None of that mob have seen him and he's worked undercover before. You two are out of the question because, as Ingrid's just mentioned, they've not only hunted out a photo of you but fired shots at it!'

'We needn't go together and wouldn't necessarily look anything like we do in the photo.'

'I daren't risk your lives by asking you to do it. No.'

That could only mean one thing: we were going.

My reservations about DCI Cookson must have kept breaking into Patrick's deep concentration on tactics that evening. He had been sitting motionless in an armchair, head back, thinking, even the tot of whisky on a small table at his side forgotten. Then, all at once, he exploded into movement, startling me and the two kittens which had been asleep on my lap.

'Sorry,' he said absently, over by the window, staring out. 'I have to be really sure about this man, Cookson. Perhaps we ought to pay him a call – now.'

'He probably won't be at work this late.'

'Sometimes it's better to grab people at home.'

'D'you know his address?'

He left the room, flashing me a crazy sort of smile on the

way and saying over his shoulder, 'No, but I'm a cop with access to information like that.'

The utilization of several security codes later elicited the information that Cookson was divorced and lived on his own in a flat in Clifton, Bristol, one of the oldest and most affluent areas of the city. Its Georgian terraces rival those of Bath and we discovered that it was at one of these properties that the DCI lived.

'I had an idea you were planning on bursting through the back door in a forward roll firing stun grenades from the hip,' I said and when I received a man-not-amused stare in return as he prosaically rang the doorbell I realized that I might have spoken a trifle sarcastically.

After a longish pause a grille to one side of the door crackled into life. 'Who is it?' Cookson's voice enquired metallically.

'Gillard,' Patrick replied.

'See me in my office tomorrow, at ten.'

'It'll be expensive if I shoot this lock off as well as the one on your front door.'

'I'll have you for criminal damage.'

'But think of all the paperwork and the explanations to your neighbours *and* to SOCA as to why you forewarned a criminal that one of its operatives was looking him up.'

Audibly, Cookson swore and then, after a shorter pause, the lock clicked open.

He lived on the second floor, the first quick impression of the room we were shown into that of stylish, albeit dated, living. Here was a man either of slightly old-fashioned taste or, having inherited some of the furniture and fittings from his parents, could not be bothered to replace them. Everywhere was meticulously clean and tidy.

'Well?' Cookson said, throwing himself down on to a corner sofa. He had not asked us to be seated but we did.

Patrick said, 'He had two large bouncers at the boat – one on the pontoon, one on deck, and the capitano had arranged that two of his crew act as a further deterrent down below. Micky's kick-boxing is rubbish, by the way – he must have blinded the opposition with his dental veneers. I resent that you interfered.'

'I thought he would seriously injure or kill you if I didn't contact him beforehand.'

'There's more to it than that.'

'OK, as I said at the time I didn't want you interfering. I thought a show of force on his part would frighten you off and keep the pair of you in one piece.'

'So what's your interest then? Do you have a monopoly with this mobster? Or is he just contributing to your cost of living?'

'Frighten' had not been the right choice of word for Cookson to use.

There was an edgy silence, during which they stared at one another. Then Cookson dropped his gaze and chuckled. 'Look, I'm not bent. What did Micky have to say?'

'Not a lot. He doesn't know of any particular reason why Uncle was intent on moving into Bath but it's probably due to what we've already thought: that the Met's making life too hot for them at home. And as we already know it was Charlie Gill who lured him into the city that night – they used to knock around together.'

'The brotherhood's as healthy as ever then,' Cookson muttered. 'I heard a rumour that he's planning to retire, whatever that means. That'll probably coincide with the day I finally get to arrest him.' He gave us both a level look. 'He was directly responsible for the death of one of my best officers and I've been playing a waiting game with him for years. I've got him to think that if he slips me bits of info about the other rats that inhabit his particular hole in the ground I'll leave him alone. But as of yesterday we grabbed his one-time partner in crime who had assumed he was nice and safe in Newcastle with a new identity. He's a right little creep and if he's leaned on in the right way he'll be all too ready to drop Micky boy right in it. We've brought him down here and tomorrow I'm going to skin him alive.'

'How do you contact Mick?' I asked.

'The usual ways: by phone and email. But I know he's not on the boat: the little bugger's disappeared again.'

'May SOCA and Bath CID have the details for their records?'

Against all my expectations he had no objection and wrote them down.

*   *   *

'That puts a different perspective on things,' I said when we were on our way home.

'Yes, I had no idea Mick was implicated in a murder,' Patrick said. He had actually poured his tot back into the bottle before we came out and was driving. 'My fault, I should have checked beforehand.'

'You can't let him get away now.'

'I've no intention of letting him get away. If you remember I did say I couldn't protect him from prosecution for crimes he'd already committed.'

'Only I've had an idea.'

'Is that why you wanted his email address and phone number?'

'Umm.'

'Spit it out then.'

'Arrange for Mick to get an invitation to the party. As you always like to do, make things happen.'

'I like that.'

'It would have to be very carefully engineered so he didn't have the first idea who was going to be there.'

'Will he fall for it, though?'

'If you allow me to compose it. And it might mean changing your plans.'

FIFTEEN

This was not conceit on my part, merely looking at it from a woman's point of view. I have a notion that all the low and cunning, if not downright fiendish, moves in history made by kings, princes and other rulers had a female brain behind them; for example, tell your enemy how much you admire and would like his company at dinner, then have the boiling oil ready.

I obtained from Cookson, again against all the odds – perhaps he felt he owed me a favour after the way I had liaised with him – the name of Mick the Kick's one-time partner in crime who, hopefully, he did not know had been arrested. I even got a little background information on the jobs they had done together. It was one of these, a post office robbery in Hotwells, Bristol, that had resulted in the death of Cookson's sergeant in the days when he had been a DI. There had been a tip-off, the police were nearby and the man had been deliberately mown down by a getaway car. His life support machine had been switched off a fortnight later.

I worked for an hour on two emails until I thought I had the wording right. By this time I had Greenway on board and he gave what I had written to his techno-wizard who could apparently arrange to send them to the Bristol mobster and others using specially created email addresses. One drawback would be if Micky was in contact with his chum already and spotted the discrepancy. He might even phone him and realize the whole thing was a trick. It is worth noting that all the coppers – male, that is – in the know about this thought the ruse was bound to fail. Even I was not very confident.

A large detached house in Beau Brummell Drive, Avonhill, was now under surreptitious, and constant, observation. It was the only property that had been recently let in that area and the letting agents had refused initially to reveal to whom. After Carrick had threatened them with a charge of obstructing the course of justice they had, twenty-four hours later, come up with a name: Warren de la Frey. He then promised to slap a prosecution of aiding and abetting a criminal on them if they breathed one word to the new tenant that the police were making enquiries about him.

There were two days to go to the party.

'You appear to have succeeded, Ingrid,' Michael Greenway said, phoning me the next morning with the latest news from the computer man. 'Mick the Kick's accepted an invitation from his old chum for food and lots to drink at his house-warming party with a chance afterwards to shoot up a clutch of his number one enemy mobsters whose whereabouts have hit the grapevine. Mick has said he can't arrive until around ten. That suits us perfectly as we were planning to go in just after then. If we're right on his heels hopefully we can prevent him from getting killed. But we're having to scale back the Internet surveillance now in case they get suspicious as it can make their machines run a bit slow.'

Sergeant Keen had been withdrawn from the job of under-cover photographer even though outside catering had been booked for the party and it had been arranged that he would replace one of the waiters. This was because it had emerged he had once interviewed Mick the Kick in connection with another case, having once been seconded for a short while to DCI Cookson's team to cover for someone who was ill. Possibly to stay one step ahead of Patrick, Carrick immediately scrapped that part of the plan.

These events were somewhat passing me by as I was at home dealing with a couple of domestic problems in the shape of a colicky baby Mark, and Katie, who had a suspected broken arm after falling off her pony on a ride with friends. We had to go to the hospital for an X-ray.

'Disaster!' Patrick announced before I could tell him about this, not so much arriving that evening as hurling himself into the house. He looked drawn, no doubt worn out from meetings and briefings.

I handed him a tot of his favourite single malt, glad that I had decided on a large steak and kidney pie for dinner.

'Some interfering sod of a superintendent at Avon and

Somerset HQ thinks he ought to handle it,' he went on. 'Doesn't think it ought to be dealt with at DCI level. James is fit to slit him from stem to stern with his *skean-dhu*. But what do we do?'

'Phone Greenway.'

The fine grey eyes focused on me. 'Greenway?'

'A commander's already handling it,' I pointed out. 'He won't like being hijacked.'

Patrick carefully put down the whisky and reached for his mobile. 'Sometimes, Ingrid, you're a bloody genius.'

I have never been quite sure of the protocols that have to be adhered to between SOCA and the regular police forces but on this occasion it would appear that the man from Portishead was blown right out of the water. The next morning Greenway arrived, quietly, by train, booked himself into a city centre hotel and then presented himself, smiling, in Carrick's office at nine thirty, much to the latter's great surprise.

'We'll go and take a look at this house in Avonhill,' Greenway was saying as we entered the room a few minutes later. He raised a hand in greeting. 'How's the sprog's arm?'

'Just badly bruised, thank you,' I replied.

'That's a relief.' He turned to Carrick. 'Where's the place being watched from?'

'By the greatest good fortune a house almost opposite is undergoing complete renovation,' Carrick said. 'The entire building, including the roof, is swathed in that plastic stuff they fix to scaffolding to keep everything dry and protect the workers from the weather. With the permission of the owners and cooperation of the security company keeping an eye on it we have gained entry through the rear. There's a back lane that gives access to garages or parking areas at the ends of the gardens.'

'Are you sure the plastic is completely non-see-through?'

'It isn't quite but we fixed it so the workmen left some stuff, crates of tiles and boxes on the planking in front of the window of the room that's being used to conduct the surveillance from, just leaving a suitably-sized aperture. Luckily the guys are working on the roof right now so our people are in nobody's way.'

'I just hope everyone keeps their mouth shut.'

'I spoke to the builders personally,' the Scot responded darkly.

It was late afternoon as we approached the rear of the three-storeyed terraced Regency house, having come through a padlocked opening in the security fencing using a key provided by the builders. They had finished work early, as they usually did on Fridays, our timing deliberate in order to reduce the risk of anything we said being overheard. The only people within the building would be the two on-duty members of Carrick's team.

'Quite a project,' Greenway commented as we made our way down the neglected garden between sorted piles of rubble, old timbers and rubbish.

'There were dead rats under all the floors, I understand,' Carrick said. 'They had to call in a pest controller to put down poison to take care of the live ones.'

'Plus a load more across the street,' Greenway muttered.

Who were poisoning Bath.

The rear door into an old-fashioned scullery was no longer in situ so presumably had been removed because it was rotten. This was the general state of affairs within, floorboards removed in some of the rooms we passed, the whole place stripped of paint and wallcoverings and we had to tread carefully on the wide staircase, the boards creaking alarmingly under the men's weight. I did not envy the people who changed shifts during the hours of darkness as they would be unable to use much in the way of illumination for fear of it being seen from across the road.

The watchers were in a room on the first floor and they were expecting us. Without a word being said they stepped aside from the window where there were powerful binoculars on a tripod and a camera on another. Greenway, Carrick and Patrick each had a prolonged look but I signalled that I would not. This was purely police work.

We were told that there had been the kind of activity that suggested those opposite were indeed expecting to entertain a significant number of people, someone's guess being in the region of twenty to thirty calculated on the large amount of alcohol they had seen being taken indoors. Northwood's fair hair had disappeared and he was now back to being shaven-headed with one gold stud earring and had taken to wearing gold-rimmed glasses. The thinking of the surveillance people was that, probably unwittingly, he now *exactly* resembled most people's idea of a city mobster. A woman with long red hair who sported large sunglasses whatever the weather and strutted about in tight jeans and leather boots 'almost like a goose-stepping Panzer commander' was probably Murphy in yet another wig. There were other people who came and went, fetched and carried: minders and minions.

The law stood there by the window and you could almost see them licking their lips.

I waited for them to finish their examination, about as useful right then as a stuffed toy mascot. I did not share their mood; everything seemed too easy and listening to their whispered conversation it was apparent that not one of them was factoring in the things that might, and could, go wrong.

Over by the doorway I could hear the weather shielding plastic flapping, the sound coming through where a window on the nearby landing had been taken out. A breeze had sprung up and then, downstairs, a door suddenly slammed.

Greenway swore, quietly, and spun round. Then, distinctly, I heard hurried footsteps somewhere below. Making no sound, I went outside on to the landing. There was nothing but silence punctuated by the quiet creaks of the old house and the now strong draught causing some hanging electric cables to tap against the wall. I became aware of Patrick standing by me.

'What is it?' he breathed.

'I heard footsteps.'

'Perhaps someone came back for something and banged the door.'

'No, I heard footsteps after the door banged.'

'And of course there's no door in place at the back and the front one's bolted. Which means they were inside.'

We stood, listening, but could hear nothing.

'I'd better take a look,' Patrick murmured.

I motioned to Greenway and Carrick that we were going down and followed Patrick as he descended the stairs, inwardly cursing at every creak we made. The light was poor as the sky must have clouded over, the interior already gloomy due to the plastic sheeting in front of the windows.

The thought sort of rammed itself into my brain: one ought to expect a woman like Murphy to investigate a property directly across the road that was a perfect venue for anyone watching *her.*

The doors of the rooms at the front of the house that led off the large tiled floor hallway were all closed bar one which had been taken off its hinges and leaned against the wall. Patrick motioned to me to stay where I was on the stairs, keeping low, drew his gun, had a quick look round in the room and came out again. He then went from sight towards the way we had entered, re-emerging around thirty of my heart-thumps later to bend down and, using his tiny torch, gaze searchingly at the very dirty and dusty floor of the hall. The area by one door held his attention. He went over to it, opened it and, standing well to one side, pushed it hard, causing it to swing wide.

Silence but for the very faint sounds of passing traffic.

He went in at speed, ready to fire but reappeared almost immediately. This was repeated with all the other rooms and he came out of the final one to say, 'There's no one here now. But the first one I went in is where the door banged and you can see where the dust and wood shavings were blown away by the sudden blast of air. The window's open in there and I reckon the door slammed as it was opened so whoever it was could leave. Perhaps they'd seen it moving, ran to try to catch it before it banged and then when it did, bolted back to the window to escape. Those were the footsteps Ingrid heard.'

'This is serious,' Greenway said from the top of the stairs.

'It could have been someone who spotted that the gate in the fence was open,' I pointed out. 'Or a prospective squatter.'

'Do we remove the surveillance?' Greenway asked the DCI as they descended.

'Yes, I'm not happy about unarmed personnel being within a stone's throw of people like that who might know they're here. And while it was useful to have them here I have to think of their safety. And we do only have around twenty-four hours left.'

'I'll watch tonight,' Patrick offered. 'I'm not unarmed and can be a hell of a lot less conspicuous than ordinary coppers.'

Carrick was not the kind of man to be offended when presented with bald facts. He accepted and went back to give those upstairs the relevant orders. Then we quietly left.

We had all arrived in the Range Rover, which had been parked three streets away. Once inside it would be possible to have a proper conversation but before anyone could say anything my phone rang as soon as I switched it on again. I apologized and answered it.

'Mark still not right?' Patrick asked when the call was over.

'No, he's much better,' I told him. 'It was Elspeth. They had a visit from someone at the diocesan office this afternoon. Carol Trelonic – only names weren't mentioned – has put in a complaint about your father. That he sexually assaulted her when he went to the house after her husband was killed. Despite the fact that we warned them he's very shocked and upset. Elspeth's wondering if you're free to give him some moral support.'

'This is deliberate timing on Uncle's part, wondering if I'm involved in the case,' Patrick said quietly.

'I'll go home and be supportive,' I said.

'And I'll talk to him now and try to explain.'

'We'll go for a little walk,' Greenway announced, nodding to Carrick and they got out of the vehicle.

Patrick spoke to John for around ten minutes, telling him as much as possible about the situation as he could and, although John said he understood, I was sure Patrick was aware his own actions fell short of what was expected.

'It changes everything,' he said afterwards.

'Please don't do anything rash,' I begged, alarmed at the expression on his face.

'We didn't move to Hinton Littlemoor in order to get my father's name dragged through the mud by a bunch of murdering shits.'

I think we both had the underlying fear that we would be forced to leave the village to protect them in the future. Which negated the whole purpose of going there in the first place.

SIXTEEN

I drove us back, leaving Patrick free to discuss with the others final plans for the following night, dropping the three of them off at Manvers Street before heading home. He had taken from the car a bag that is kept there permanently containing, among other things, dark clothing and trainers to use for his overnight surveillance. Then he went from my sight, blowing me a kiss.

I called in to see my in-laws to find them in their living room in the middle of a large silence. They both looked up when I entered and Elspeth smiled and waved a little greeting.

'I could have done with some advice from Patrick,' John said.

'He'll be here in the morning,' I replied, actually not quite sure about that.

'He has to put his job first,' Elspeth remarked.

'Yes, I suppose he does.'

'Have you eaten?' I enquired, thinking the man so out of sorts he was not himself. This wasn't John at all.

'John says he's not hungry.' Elspeth sighed.

'You expect me to behave as though nothing's happened?' her husband said crossly.

'Would you like me to cook something for you?' I asked.

'No, but thank you,' John said.

I sat myself down on their sofa. 'As he said, Patrick can't come home because he's watching a house, an undertaking that has a direct bearing on what's happened here today. Pretend I'm him.'

'But you're not, my dear,' John said gently.

'But what would he do right now? Be strong and here for you? I'm strong and here for you. Put the right perspective on what's occurred? I can do that too, first by saying that right now I know he's thinking of putting his job on the line to sort this out and when I left him he was still furious. But he can't be expected to be here bloody well holding your hand *as well*.'

There was a slightly shocked silence.

To John, Elspeth hissed, 'It would have been far better if we'd left the news until he got home – as I wanted to.'

I said, 'You're not the first priest to have allegations made against him by malicious parishioners – and no one knows that more than the bishop.'

'You do sound like Patrick actually,' John said with a rueful smile.

'Thank you, Ingrid,' Elspeth said. She got to her feet. 'Oh, for goodness sake! I'm starving and I'm going to cook the dinner. Do join us if you want to when the children have had their tea – there's plenty for three.'

For obvious reasons there would be an overnight communications silence. In some ways I wanted to be with Patrick but knew I would be a distraction. Early training means that he can virtually sleep on his feet, like a cat that naps with its ears pricked to detect the slightest sound. So I spent a couple of hours with his parents, taking Katie with me, played with Vicky and Justin before they went to bed, peeped at Mark fast asleep in his cot, gave the kittens their last meal of the day and then turned in.

I could not sleep, tossing for hours. *Who* had been in that house? The footsteps had not sounded like those of a child. And it had not been the soft pad of trainers either but proper shoes, or boots. I had an idea that Patrick would have had a proper look around before it got dark to make sure that no unpleasant surprises had been planted and tried to convince myself that someone with his military background would be more than a match for anyone in Northwood's circle of thugs and hangers-on. I failed; Patrick was no longer a young man.

In the end I slept and was haunted by the kind of nightmares that fill you with terror but you cannot really remember in the morning, just leaving a vague feeling of dread.

Before leaving the house the men had been discussing the possibility of making arrangements for two officers from the fire-arms unit to relieve Patrick at eight a.m., who would be replaced in the late afternoon by personnel yet to be decided on. I had a very good idea who those personnel might be. So, night-time horrors banished the next morning after a large mug of tea I answered the phone at seven fifty-five expecting it to be Patrick. 'Something's happened,' said James Carrick tersely. 'I'm afraid he's not there.'

'Not there?' I echoed stupidly.

'Not a sign of him. No evidence of a struggle either. Nothing. The equipment's all exactly as it was too.'

I tried to remain practical. 'What about the padlocked gateway at the rear?'

'All locked up.'

'Did Patrick have a key?'

'Yes, he did. The plan was that he'd let in his replacements at the arranged time.'

'So how did they gain access?'

'Climbed over the fence. Not a problem for fit blokes.'

I could think of nothing intelligent to say.

Anxiously, Carrick asked, 'You would tell me if Patrick had contacted you, wouldn't you?'

'Of course.'

'I'm at home right now but meeting the commander at my office in around half an hour. Do you want to come in?'

I told him I would.

'God, why didn't I expect something like this?' Greenway exclaimed. He turned to me and I could see how exasperated he was. 'What did the man say to you after he rang his father? Sorry, but I really do need to know.'

'That it changed everything. That's all.'

'Which, knowing him, could be a pretty monumental comment. Everything from unleashing open warfare to bubonic plague slipped into their water supply. Ingrid, do you really think he's planning to do something like gun down the lot and to hell with the aftermath?'

'Not *now*,' I replied. 'Some years ago before he became a family man my answer would have been that he might do literally anything. But you do seem to be assuming that Uncle hasn't somehow got hold of him – or that he allowed them to.'

'With regard to the latter, to what end?'

'He's at his best when in a tight corner, good at subversion. If anyone can cause trouble with Uncle's mobsters, he can.'

'But look, this woman Murphy . . . sorry to distress you but she's the sort who would want to roast him slowly over an open fire.'

'She's powerful,' I said. 'He might flirt with her and cause even more trouble.'

'I still don't understand. We're going to arrest the lot of them tomorrow. What's the point of it all?'

'I can't make guesses. But if he thinks he can prevent a shoot-out where police personnel might get killed or injured . . .' I broke off with a shrug.

With a tilt to his chin Carrick said, 'He might not think the plan we have is that good then.'

I shook my head. 'He's still a soldier at heart. Civvy things never are.'

Putting a brave face on everything while wanting to scream with despair was proving almost impossible. While it was obvious that Patrick did not want me to become involved I felt I would go mad if I just had to stand around doing nothing.

'Do we carry on with what we're going to do then, sir?' Carrick wanted to know.

'At present,' Greenway decided. 'There are quite a few hours to go yet. We can always make last-minute decisions.'

'Mind if have a look at the case notes?' I asked.

Carrick passed them over.

My cubbyhole just outside the main office had miraculously not been used as a dumping ground for anything – there was always a chronic shortage of space – so I sat down with the file and found the phone number I wanted. How long was the tenancy on the house in Avonhill?

I soon had my answer: six months, the minimum.

Unless the plan was to keep moving around this did not fit with the picture we had built up of a criminal shifting his scene of operations out of London to somewhere a little quieter where he could start afresh under yet another assumed identity. There was every possibility too that the Avoncliff residence had been the only one available at the time of the required standard. But if it was neither of these things?

I had already tried ringing Patrick's mobile but it was switched off so, still floundering around for ideas, I went back to Carrick's office. 'May I have another look around the surveillance house?'
He and Greenway had been in deep discussion.
'Sure. I'll let them know you're on your way.'
They went on talking.
I had to wait a few minutes for one of the members of the firearms unit to unlock the gate but it was not raining *that* hard. Butch, bog-brush hair and with a deep scar on his cheek he led the way indoors mumbling something about the need to keep quiet.
'I understand everything was absolutely undisturbed when you arrived, with no sign of a struggle,' I said as we carefully made our way up the stairs.
He turned to say in a fierce whisper, 'It's best not to talk at all.'
'Look, this place is a building site for most of the time,' I retorted. 'There's a van at the front with a contractor bashing away working on the exterior stonework. How the hell can those over the road hear a quiet conversation indoors with that going on?'
He did not say any more until we were in the surveillance room where his oppo – butch, floor-mop hair scragged back into a rubber band, no scar – gave me a dismissive look.
'Yes, it was empty,' he said. 'No one here.'
'You went right over the entire place?'
He was really resenting my questioning. Perhaps they felt demeaned by being ordered to do ordinary surveillance work. 'Yes, we did. Every room, upstairs and down. Very carefully.'
'No bodies?'
'No bodies,' he replied heavily.
'What kind of activity has been going on over the road this morning?'
'They all seem to be still in bed with the curtains closed.'
'May I have a quick look?'
They stood aside with ill-concealed impatience.
Not particularly interested in close-ups, more the big picture, I gazed at the house without using the binoculars. Unlike the older, terraced, and listed properties on this side

of the road those opposite were detached with quite big gardens and were of more recent build. The front gardens had mostly been turned into parking areas. As my new friends had said, not a lot was going on over there. The place looked dead. A single car was outside, a small hatchback of some kind, and there was a bag of what might be rubbish dumped in the short driveway.

'Do you know how many cars have been parked over there lately?'

'No. This isn't our job really.'

So that was it. 'Are you sure anyone's actually *there*?'

The pair gazed at me as though I was raving mad.

'We heard footsteps downstairs yesterday,' I went on. 'If they discovered that the police were watching them the whole lot might have gone! Come on, the SOCA man who was on duty overnight has disappeared and you're standing there like a couple of *lumpenkinder*!'

Nothing changed.

'I'll contact the DCI,' I told them, with difficulty repressing an urge to box their ears.

I had to search first, not at all impressed by their assurance of having done so thoroughly and quickly investigated each room on this floor. There were next to no places where someone, dead or alive, might be concealed as any fitted cupboards or wardrobes had been removed, no doubt riddled with woodworm: there was plenty of evidence of it.

The ground floor was larger, having had extensions built on over the years, one of which must have enlarged the kitchen. There were several built-in cupboards, together with a walk-in larder. I approached these with trepidation as not all that long ago I had found a decomposed head in one of the former in another house in the city; the stinking remainder had turned up later in a larder just like this one, situated in a mouldering back scullery. Dear God, even the paint on the door of it was the same colour, a horrible shade of dark green reminiscent of old railway stations. His body wouldn't have started to smell yet though, would it? Shuddering, I opened the door and jumped back, almost screamed, when a dark heavy shape swung towards me. Two old sacks stuffed with what looked like newspapers and magazines thumped on to the floor in a cloud of dust and dead woodlice.

This reminder of the previous horror really brought it home to me that I might be looking for a corpse. Otherwise he would have made contact. I kept asking myself why he had not and kept coming back to the same answer: he had been unable to. And of course his body was not likely to be here at all but over the road, probably hastily buried in the back garden by now, or in the River Avon, or tossed into one of the many disused quarries or down an old mine shaft. The gang had killed him, as Murphy had planned to do, and then fled.

Shakily, I made myself carry on searching and then returned to the first floor where I went up a narrower staircase to the second. All the floorboards had been taken up in these rooms and the joists looked rotten in places so I did not venture into any of them; there was no point as there were no places of concealment.

By the door to a bathroom – the fittings were museum pieces, and the high cast-iron cistern over the toilet was smelly and knitted to the ceiling by thick cobwebs – there was a narrow doorway. Gingerly I opened it to reveal a tiny staircase leading upwards. The loft.

There was no light switch and I had not brought a torch. It immediately became obvious, though, that there was dim daylight above; this, I saw when I had climbed the dozen or so stairs, coming through a small dirty skylight. Light was also coming through small holes and gaps in tarpaulins that had been placed over part of the roof for the weekend where slates or tiles had been removed.

The attic was huge and there was a lot of rubbish that had not been removed: suitcases, trunks, wooden and cardboard boxes. All of these seemed to have been opened and any contents taken out before being cast on one side. I then noticed that the brick party walls between this house and those on either side did not go all the way up to the roof, a feature I vaguely remembered reading about and which was the cause of fires spreading so rapidly in historic terraces during the Blitz. The gap was at least a couple of feet wide at the ridge. A hundred bodies could be hidden up here. All one had to do was roll

them over the top of the wall into the loft of the houses next
door.

This was a job for a scenes of crime team, not me.

I rang Carrick.

'You think they might have left!' he echoed.

'Just a feeling. I could be quite wrong.'

'No sign of Patrick?'

'No, but the attic's vast and there's limited access to those
of the houses on either side.'

'We must establish what's going on over the road before I
send in anyone else.'

I told him I understood that.

Feeling completely helpless I went down to the ground floor.
If the gang had left in a hurry with Patrick following them –
although how could he have achieved that without the use of
the car? – he would have reported the fact, if not immediately
then later. Had they seized him and taken him with them for
Murphy to deal with at leisure? I found that very difficult to
believe as how could they have overpowered him without leaving
any evidence of having done so?

There was nothing to be gained by my staying.

Finally, it was Greenway who made the decision and the
house was raided. They found no one, nothing, the interior
trashed – empty spirit bottles, used drugs syringes and rubbish
everywhere. Bloodstains were found in a bathroom but that was
fairly quickly connected to drug taking rather than violence and
was of a different blood group to Patrick's.

They had had their party.

'Someone must have stayed sober enough to drive!' Greenway
exploded with when the three of us went to the house, the
investigation well under way.

'Although there's some damage it doesn't suggest an actual
struggle, nothing like a fight,' Carrick turned to me to say,
repeating something he had already told me, perhaps in an effort
to reassure. 'And I've just been told there's no disturbed earth
in the garden, which is nearly all down to grass and trees.'

The commander was pacing backwards and forwards in the
only space large enough available to him, the hallway, as most

of the doorways into the rooms were cordoned off, forensic teams working within. 'They've only just moved in and now they've gone. Despite all precautions being taken around the clock the watch was detected. But I simply can't believe they realized their computers were being hacked into.'

'They might have a cyber-boffin too,' I said.

'Whatever's happened it reflects badly on Bath CID,' Carrick observed after taking a deep breath. 'Ultimately the buck stops with me.'

'Not while I'm breathing down your neck it doesn't,' Greenway said with a fierce grin before taking the stairs two at a time as though needing to expend more energy.

'I wish I worked for him all the time,' Carrick said wistfully.

'Gives Patrick hell sometimes.'

He gazed at me sympathetically. 'This must be terrible for you.'

'It's happened before.'

'Under what circumstances has he previously gone off the map and not made contact?'

'When Patrick first joined MI5 you found a phone box or one in a pub to report in,' I told him. 'Or had a concealed radio in your car. More recently he's been unable to make contact because his mobile was taken away or smashed, or he was drugged, or unconscious, or in a situation where he'd be overheard. He might even have forgotten to recharge the battery – he does sometimes. Or he's dead.'

'He's not dead, Ingrid.'

'These filthy bastards are still one step ahead of us though, aren't they? And have been, all along.'

I knew I was going to cry which was awful so left him and went back out through the front door. Fresh air helped a little – the house stank as though someone had thrown up – and I wandered through fine rain around the side of the building and into the large lawned garden at the rear.

'Please call me,' I whispered to the sky, the cool dampness on my face mingling with tears.

I walked for a little while among the trees in an effort to regain my composure and when I returned a truck had arrived to remove and take away for examination the hatchback that had been left parked at the front. I looked at it properly for the first time and then dashed indoors. Carrick and Greenway were upstairs in a room which, for some reason, was not barred to them.

I interrupted them, again. 'That hatchback – it's Carol Trelonic's.'

'You're sure?' the DCI exclaimed.

'Positive. I recognize the registration.'

He rubbed his hands together. 'Progress! I'll get someone to go round to where she lives right away.'

'She won't be there,' Greenway said quietly, as if to himself. 'Along with quite a few others I'm guessing she was loaded into a car, stoned out of her stupid noddle, and taken off God knows where.'

He was quite correct, as far as the first conjecture went anyway. Not only that, the Ring o' Bells was closed, barred and bolted and had been since lunchtime opening the previous day.

SEVENTEEN

Again, I was drawn to that room where Patrick had begun his watch. The two members of the firearms unit had gone, thankfully, so I was on my own and Carrick had given me the key to the padlock on the gateway to secure when I left. Like someone who lingers at a place where someone they love has been killed, I stood there almost trying to communicate with him. Endeavouring to ignore my conviction that he was dead or captured, I tried to think the way he thought. I had known him long enough so I thought it possible.

Events had become personal with his children and now his parents involved. I already knew how dangerous this could become for those who meddled with his family. Just about every man who has laid hands on me during the course of our professional life together has ended up dead. Now, though, his priority would be to arrest Uncle and his gang, not go gunning for them because he was bound by the obvious restrictions of his job and the need to stay out of prison. But he would also seek to sear into their minds for ever that you don't mess with Patrick Gillard.

My gaze lifted to the house over the road. Perhaps my writer's imagination kicked in then as I suddenly saw it in the very early hours of the morning, in darkness, the street lights in the suburbs now switched off between midnight and five a.m. to save money. The door was open, the light streaming out, people staggering about, some laughing and shrieking, others reeling outside to vomit: there had been plenty of evidence of that on the parking area and in the back garden. Others would have collapsed completely, sleeping it off, both inside and out. Those who had drunk less who were still on their feet and behaving comparatively normally would nevertheless have had their thinking processes seriously impaired, never mind being well over the limit as far as driving was concerned. And yet according to Carrick when I had asked him just before I left, four or five cars had been parked there in the days previously, of which Carol Trelonic's was, as might be expected, not one. Last night others had probably been parked in the road.

They had brought their party forward by one day. Why? For the hell of it or did they know the police were on to them? Or had they just been sitting around with nothing to do looking at all that booze stacked up in the house, made the decision and phoned everyone who was nearby? Mick the Kick had missed out for one. I made a mental note to remind James to have a suitable reception waiting for him when he turned up at ten tonight.

When I factored in Patrick's ability to make instant decisions instilled by military training, his impatience to make something *happen* and a burning desire to get Uncle and his cohorts behind bars for a very long time, a picture began to emerge. When he had seen what was taking place and with no time to tell anyone he had gone over there, helped those too drunk to recognize him in the gloom load the others into cars, stoned out of their stupid noddles, and been taken off God knows where. On the journey when there would have been an inevitable stop to allow people to urinate in a lay-by or behind a bush, or vomit, take your pick, I hoped he had reduced the competition a little by shoving a couple of them into a deep ditch, preferably Colin Andrews and Carol Trelonic as they would be the first to recognize him.

Was I fondly creating myths to avoid facing the truth? And more practically, had Carrick arranged for any house-to-house enquiries at the neighbouring properties on both sides of the road in an effort to find out if anyone had seen what had occurred? I thought perhaps not as, for one reason or another, the gang had gone, end of story. If so and he had not there was no reason for my getting angry about it as Patrick has always been a maverick with a reputation for having an almost uncanny knack of being able to look after himself. Greenway and Carrick thought him in no real danger. I myself had said as much, soothing their worries by painting a vivid picture of him emerging triumphant having used subversive methods, flirting with Murphy even. Then I remembered Lynn Outhwaite had said she might be a lesbian.

For several moments I hated myself.

Desperate for clues I minutely searched the room but found nothing.

'Oh, no, I'm afraid I didn't hear a thing,' said the woman. 'My bedroom's at the back and my husband's as deaf as a post when he takes his hearing aid out. You say there was some kind of wild party? Well, it wasn't us who complained about it, but you could try Mrs Masters over the road at The Coppice. She snoops on everyone and complains about everything.'

I thanked her. This was my last call at the dozen or so houses nearby and nobody had witnessed anything that had gone on overnight at the house in question. I had already visited The Coppice and without my being able to get a word in edgeways Mrs-silly-old-bat-Masters had moaned about her neighbours, all of them, low-flying planes, stray dogs and the youths hanging around in the city centre, finishing up by shrieking, 'What are you police going to do about that, hey? And here you are asking about *parties!*'

Slam.

In a state of complete indecision I went home, needing space to think away from the nick. Taking a slight detour around the village I drove slowly past the Ring o' Bells. There was no sign of life other than a couple of ancient worthies standing, baffled, by the main door, obviously wondering why it was not open.

'The pub's closed,' was the first thing Elspeth said to me. 'And yet it seemed to be doing so well.'

This was not just a passing comment as, rare these days, it belongs to the parish and was originally constructed, a much smaller building now incorporated into the present one, as a hostel and meeting place for the masons who built the church.

'Patrick was asking questions about it recently,' she went on, hopefully.

'There are . . . questions,' I said. 'Have you seen Colin Andrews since it closed?'

'No. People are worried that he's gone off with the Christmas Club money.'

'Why should they think that?'

'People have turned against him since he insisted on Matthew

being charged and threw you all out of the pub that night. Ingrid,
I have an idea you know quite a lot about all this. Why are
these people doing this to us?'

'In top notch confidence, because they're crooks.'

'Oh! Thank you, I feel much better now. Is Patrick with you?'

'No, he's still on the job.'

In view of the fact that the weight of at least two police forces
and SOCA were involved in hunting down these mobsters I
thought it best to stay where I was for the present and poach
as much intelligence as I could rather than head off blindly
with no real plan. Not only that, our working rule is that should
one partner be off the map with no obvious leads as to their
whereabouts then the other should sit tight with responsibility
for the children in mind. This was horribly difficult and actually
weighted against me as Patrick would move hell and Birmingham
New Street Station, which amounts to the same thing, to find
me should I be the missing one. But as he always infuriatingly
says, 'You're a *mother*.'

Mother then checked over and loaded her Smith and Wesson
and generally kept her powder dry, all the while agonizing about
what might be happening to him.

Looking for something in my bag I came across the piece
of paper with Mick the Kick's email address and phone number
on it that I had forgotten to destroy after making a note of it
somewhere more secure. I screwed it up and then, slowly, an
idea forming, smoothed it out again. It was an outrageous idea
and I sat thinking about it for a full ten minutes, torn first one
way and then the other. Yes, or no?

I rang the number, not for one moment expecting him to
answer. But he did, in an eager fashion that suggested he had
been waiting for a call from someone else.

'It's Ingrid,' I said. 'You know, we came to see you on the
boat in Plymouth.'

'I know who you are, darlin',' he replied warily. 'Who gave
you this number?'

'Cookson, he fancies me.'

There was a dirty chuckle.

'My husband's disappeared and has probably been taken off

by Uncle's mob. In exchange for one piece of news that might have saved your life and another that is also to your advantage I want you to tell me all you know about Uncle's, Brad Northwood's, or Warren de la Frey's, as he's calling himself now, hideaways.'

'Darlin', I don't know anythin' about that bastard's—' he began to protest.

'You must do. You have to know everything in this game to survive. This man was hoping to take over Bath – Charlie Gill told you that and said the man had bragged to him about how successful he was. What else did he tell you to gain your confidence, to make you believe him so you'd walk into a trap?'

'What's this piece of news that *might* have saved my life? Why *might*?'

'Circumstances have changed. I'll explain if you tell me what I want to know.'

'I already knew he had a place in Hammersmith before Charlie told me.'

'Even the police knew about that. He and Murphy have gone.'

'And before that, when he wasn't in the slammer, he lived somewhere in East Ham. He was Fred Gibbons then – that's his real name.'

'I know all about that too. Come on, I said hideaways, not houses.'

'Look, sorry darlin', that's all I know.'

After leaving a long pause I said, 'OK, have a nice time at the party tonight.'

I instantly got the impression that the person on the other end of the phone had frozen solid.

'As you've probably realized, Patrick's a maverick cop,' I went on. 'He hears things from gold-plated, unofficial sources not usually available to the police.' I was almost wishing Matthew could overhear this conversation after the work he had done.

'It was another trap?' Mick's voice had come out as a sort of squeak.

'Too right. The invitation came from Uncle, not your one-time partner.'

'The bugger's still watching me then.'

'Looks like it.'

There was a long silence and I asked him if he was still there.

'Yes. God . . . I'm gutted. That's not good.'

'Hideaways,' I prompted.

'And then you'll tell me the other bit?'

'I will. But if you don't give me all you know I'll make sure Patrick finishes breaking your neck when I do find him.' This was the longest of shots but . . .

'No, no, no,' he keened. 'Uncle'll do it first.'

'Look, he won't know it was you who told me! Come on!'

'There's an old farm,' Mick mumbled, after another silence. 'A big house as well, all a bit ruined and he's got this plan to turn it into a sort of hotel-cum-conference centre and wedding venue, really posh, and attract all kind of punters with masses of loot. You know, footballers and their latest tarts, TV celebs, posers, that kind of bod.'

'Where is this place?'

'Charlie just said it was in the countryside.'

'A farm's bound to be in the countryside!' I raved at him.

'Near the downs.'

'North Downs? South Downs? *What*?'

'Honest—'

'You don't know what the word *means*!' I bawled at him.

'You'll really tell me something worthwhile? It's not just a come-on?'

'I promise.'

'It's near . . . Horsham . . . er, yeah, that's it, Horsham, in Sussex. That's all I know, hon— Really.'

'OK. For some reason they had the party last night. If you'd gone tonight the police would have been waiting to arrest you.'

After saying, 'Jeez. Thanks. You're a real star,' he rang off.

I wondered whether I ought to write my resignation letter to SOCA there and then but decided to confess to Michael Greenway personally instead.

I learned from James Carrick that as the commander was not involved with the ongoing search and investigation at the Avonhill house he had returned to his hotel where, a little later, I phoned him from the reception. He said he had been just

about to contact me and would be straight down. This did stretch
to fifteen minutes but as his hair was still damp when he arrived
I could easily excuse a quick shower.

'I've done the unforgivable,' I said.

He glanced at his watch. 'The sun's well over the yardarm
so a drink is called for.' He then chivvied me into the nearby
bar where he bought me a G&T.

'What?' he asked, having taken a sip from his tot of whisky.

'Given information to a criminal that will save him from
being arrested.'

'What, that little Bristol shit? But it's only a matter of time
before Cookson gets him, isn't it?'

'I hadn't realized Patrick had told you about him.'

'Yes, he did. Did he give you anything in exchange?'

'That Uncle has bought a run-down rural property that he
wants to turn into an upmarket country house hotel and confer-
ence centre, etc., to relieve the rich of their cash.'

'Sounds normal. Where is it?'

'Somewhere in the Sussex Weald near Horsham. He said he
didn't know any more.'

'Did you believe that bit?'

'No.'

Greenway sat back in his armchair and went off into a world
of his own. I knew better than to interrupt. Finally, he said, 'I
don't like it that we haven't heard from Patrick.'

'Nor do I.'

'I can understand that at the ungodly hour of the night when
this happened he would have been reluctant to call out the
cavalry because by the time even a rapid response unit could
have got there the gang would have gone.'

'Or seen the cops in their rear mirrors and scattered,' I added.

'Yes, that too. There's also the nag that, as James said, he
doesn't trust the law to get it right: too many blues and twos
and, again, mob scatters. Would he do that, remain quiet, even
if it meant worrying you half to death, in order to undertake
some or all of the job himself?'

'Yes, he would.'

'So is that conceit, or what?'

'No, he'd be more worried about cops bursting in there and

getting mown down in a shoot-out. These are the people, don't forget, who committed mass murder in Bath.'

'We must find this place, though – but initially without involving Sussex Police.' The commander fixed me with intent gaze. 'When the pair of you were with MI5 did you have any procedures that were put into place when something like this happened?'

'There were three of us then,' I told him. 'Terry Meadows was with us. Having ensured that all was safe at home he and I would have conducted a preliminary recce and possibly gone on from there.'

'You and I could conduct a recce.'

'No, you'd be breaking all your own rules. And you're too valuable. Think of the row if you were shot again – it caused a real stink last time that you'd gone off without proper backup and risked your life on what was regarded as a routine raid.'

'I know who I caught it from too,' he murmured. Despite the injury he had enjoyed himself immensely. 'OK, change of plan. I'll contact Sussex Police with a top priority request for information about run-down rural properties being redeveloped by anyone they regard as dodgy. For all we know they've been watching the place for weeks.'

But Sussex Police had nothing much to report and could only point us to an empty warehouse on an industrial estate in Portslade on the coast being used by drug dealers that they were hoping to arrest shortly, and a barn to the north of Brighton being lived in by travellers thought responsible for local burglaries. This information took three hours to come through, by which time I was at home, my anxiety level now sky high.

'Would this Meadows guy be prepared to give a hand again?' Greenway had gone on to ask.

I had said I would think about it before asking him.

Terry has a wife, who is our previous nanny Dawn, and a young family of his own now. He also has a thriving security business and does not live anywhere near Sussex. After such a long time, several years, he could hardly be expected to have the same loyalty to his one-time boss as he had then, especially taking into account that for quite a lot of the time Patrick had not been all that good to him.

I rang his number, spoke to Dawn and learned that Terry was in the States on business.

Another sleepless night went by like a century. I had already informed Greenway of the outcome of my phone call and he had assured me that extra personnel were being brought in to trace the gang's whereabouts. He intended to contact Sussex Police again first thing in the morning and would go right to the top. He had told me to try not to worry.

Somehow, I got through Sunday. I could do nothing away from home until I'd taken Katie to the opticians on Monday morning as she needed glasses. Grandma simply would not do in this case as one of the boys in her class had told her that 'they screw things into your eyes', a cruel trick that Elspeth was rather impatient about, telling Katie that she should realize he was only teasing. Unfortunately, or not, Katie appears to have her aunt's imagination and I could fully sympathize.

The post had been delivered when we returned and there was a thick A5 envelope waiting for me. Always wary – someone once sent me an explosive device hidden in a bunch of flowers – when I do not recognize handwriting, in this case ugly printing in red ballpoint, I thought about donning a pair of thick gardening gloves and then ripped it open anyway. Inside, roughly done up in rolled up newspaper, was a lock of hair. It was almost certainly human, wavy and black in colour with a sprinkling of grey. There was blood on it where it had been wrenched out wholesale that was smeared on to the wrappings.

If it had been intended that I should scream or faint they had failed for what I actually did was take it in both hands and hold it close; then, the tears ready, I kissed the mauled strands. All at once, in one searing moment, I could understand Patrick's rare bouts of frightening and almost uncontrollable temper.

My movements jerky, I found a clean tissue and wrapped the lock of hair in it. This was not a time to send things off to a forensic laboratory. The sheet of newspaper when smoothed out proved to be the front page of an edition of *The Steyning Advertiser.* It looked to be a very local publication. Reasonably familiar with Sussex as I used to have an aunt who lived there, I knew Steyning to be a village, although no longer the tiny rural idyll it used to be, situated at the northern foot of the

South Downs inland from Worthing. The place is not all that far from Horsham. I asked myself if anyone of Uncle's ilk would buy a paper intended for the residents of a small community when residing near a prosperous market town some twenty miles up the road. Then I noticed that it was a free newspaper and leapt for the phone. Half a minute later I had discovered that the paper was delivered by what were described to me as paid volunteers in the village itself, distributed to filling stations, garden centres, stores and post offices for people to help themselves, the remainder being put through letter boxes in the more outlying areas by helpful neighbours.

I always keep a packed travel bag in the Range Rover for emergency use and, ruthlessly trying to push what had just happened right to the back of my mind, it was just a case of finding money plus a few other useful bits and pieces, putting the Smith and Wesson into its shoulder harness and buckling it on under my jacket, which is showerproof, made in Wisconsin, has an amazing number of pockets and is intended for use by the hunting and shooting fraternity. It even has a zipped 'secret' inner compartment for ammunition. I did not reckon it to be a time for handbags either.

John and Elspeth were having lunch. I knew Elspeth was worried about me as she had found out, probably from the children, that I had eaten hardly anything for two days. I told them I was off to Sussex and hoped to be back very soon.

'You're going to look for him?' she said.

I touched my jacket where the lock of hair lay beneath in a pocket and found myself unable to reply.

'God speed, Ingrid,' she whispered.

EIGHTEEN

I had decided to give Michael Greenway the latest information when I was well on the road to prevent him from clamping down on what I was doing with a big no. This I duly did in the Southampton area but could only leave a message as his phone was switched off, which probably meant that he was in a meeting. He had not contacted me an hour later so I pulled into a lay-by near Midhurst and rang him again, with the same result.

I called Matthew. I was slightly embarrassed about the length of time he was staying with the Greenways but had been assured that as the boys got on so well it was proving to be an immense help as Benedict, Greenway's son by his previous marriage, could be 'difficult' when he was bored.

'Hi, Mum!' said the hatching computer genius.

'Is the commander at home?' I asked when we had had a short chat about what he had been doing.

'No, I think he's still at work. He works very late some days. Is Dad there?'

'No, he's working too.'

'Only I wanted to tell him something. I tried to call him but his phone's off.'

'You can tell me if you like – then I can give him the message when I see him or he calls me.'

'Oh, all right. I rang Grandma and she told me that the pub's all shut up and people are worried that man might have gone off with the Christmas Club money. When Benny and I were messing around with the files we found out that he – Mr Andrews, has shares – Benny told me what those are – in what must be a business in Sussex. It sounds like some sort of hotel thing. So that's where he might have gone. We gave all the info to Gerry – you know, the computer guy from SOCA – but it didn't sound very important at the time and is probably just buried in all the other stuff.'

'Do you have a name for this place?' I asked, hardly believing my luck.

'I *think* it's – hang on, I'll call Benny . . .'

I then heard him yelling loudly enough to fetch the pictures off the walls, followed by yells back.

'Yeah, that's right. It's Lock House.'

I thanked him from the bottom of my heart, adding that they should give the information to the commander if they saw him soon; otherwise I would.

Realizing that I had taken the tiny package with the lock of Patrick's hair out of my pocket – I had rewrapped it in a lacy handkerchief and was clutching it tightly, I replaced it and furiously scrubbed away the few tears. Lock House, concentrate on that.

It was well into the afternoon by now so I pressed on, not stopping again until I was on the outskirts of Steyning. There were roadworks, a large redevelopment of a corner pub, one-way streets: the place was manic and I had no choice but to find a car park. I then began calling on estate agents.

No one had heard of Lock House; it was not in Steyning or the surrounding area.

Finally, when I had exhausted them all – and it was amazing how many there were – the shops were closing and I was famished with hunger. I went back to the car park, put some more money in the machine and headed for The White Hart Hotel. Here, I ordered tea and fruitcake and, on the off-chance, repeated my request for information. Neither the receptionist nor the waitress had heard of the place. When I came to pay another employee of the establishment, a quite elderly woman, crossed the room carrying cleaning materials.

'Hey, Hilda, you've lived here for ever,' called the waitress. 'This lady's looking for a Lock House. Have you heard of it?'

The woman slowly shook her head. 'Changed its name, p'raps?' she offered.

I said, 'It was described to me as a big place, a large house and farm, all very run down. Someone's recently bought it to do up as a hotel or something similar.'

'That sounds like the Keys Estate,' she said dubiously. 'Yes! Someone must have got the name wrong.'

'Do you know where it is?'

'Everyone knows the Keys Estate. It's off the Sompting Road and where the Woodley family lived for hundreds of years. The last Lord Woodley lost all his money in some foreign venture and hanged himself in the stable, leaving his poor wife with a terrible financial mess to sort out. That was at least sixty years ago and although the house has been rented out the farm's going to rack and ruin. Such a shame.' She lowered her voice. 'They say some London businessman's bought it now but by all accounts he's got some dodgy-looking friends.'

'That's only gossip, Hilda,' admonished the waitress.

'No doubt, but they sent the vicar away with a flea in his ear when he called round.'

'A lot of people are heathens these days.'

'True enough,' said Hilda sadly and went on her way after acknowledging my thanks with a lift of her hand.

I took a room – the hotel boasted a car park at the rear – as on no account was I openly driving up to the place. It seemed too much of a coincidence not to be the right place. Perhaps it had been referred to as that deliberately by those in the know in order to keep the real location secret from those who were not.

I felt I was being too slow and cautious but sternly told myself that Ingrid Langley did not muster complete with flame-throwing tanks James Bond-style. My only goal was to find Patrick; others could apprehend the mobsters. He and I have discussed the possibility of situations like this; we have written scenarios like this and worked out solutions and the watchword is always catlike caution.

I had a shower and then, against all the odds, a nap. My cursed writer's imagination was constantly presenting me with one ghastly scenario after another, Patrick being subjected to all kinds of unspeakable violence. They would all be out of their heads on drink or drugs: hell on earth. And all the old nightmares: a body thrown out somewhere, on to an old manure heap, down a well, or buried in a shallow grave. It took me minutes to recover from the thought that the lock of hair was the only thing I would possess of him, for ever.

*   *   *

At last the daylight began to fade. I had already dressed in a dark blue short-sleeved top and matching trousers and had a hood in one of the pockets of my all-important jacket should I need to be really invisible. My hazy recollections of the area were that the Sompting Road was a sometimes steep and narrow route with passing places that crossed the South Downs. Due to the gradients of the terrain any estate would have to be quite close to the village even taking into account that there might be, and probably were, higher pastures.

A little later I went out, using the rear door into the car park so as not to have to walk through the reception area as a noisy group of people had overflowed from a side room where there was some kind of function taking place. One never knew who might be present. It was a perfect summer evening, still warm, no wind and, as I knew already, no moon. As I walked south, the geography of the place was coming back to me. Still in the village I came to the crossroads where if I turned right I would pass the little cottage where my aunt had once lived. My father's sister, she had been very much like him, outwardly conforming and quiet but when you got to know her you discovered her wacky nature and outrageous sense of humour. She had taken one look at Patrick, my intended at the time, and told me that I would either end up famous or in jail. I have managed to become mildly famous by my own efforts but as to the rest of her prophesy time would tell. It might begin to come true tonight.

The road began to climb and soon I came to a fork, a narrower road off to the left. I took it, even though it would not go right past where I was aiming for. I did not want to use the front entrance, did I? The hedges were quite high, which was very useful to me, the verges thick with wild flowers, the white ones almost luminous in the twilight, something I would have enjoyed in different circumstances and which now 'lit' my way.

My powers of concentration are good – they have to be if you write novels in a fairly crowded household – but I was finding it more and more difficult to focus. My whole being wanted to rush into this place, wildly shooting at anyone who tried to stop me. Usually I have Patrick's steadying influence to keep me on track as he had been practically pickled in self-control during special forces training.

'He trained *me*,' I said out loud. 'God, woman, you've done enough of this kind of thing with him. The only thing I don't have is a map.'

But I did not need a map; the whole of a shallow valley was opening out before me as the ground fell away and, through a field gateway, I found myself gazing into a fold in the downs towards an almost secret place: a largish house and farm buildings just visible in the fast-fading daylight. I immediately stepped into the lee of the hedge so I could peep through the outer vegetation without being seen. Was anyone keeping watch on the surrounding countryside? Somehow I doubted it.

As I stood there, a light came on in the house, and then another. Realizing I should be planning my route while I could see I risked going to the gate again and leaning over it. The field was large and adjoined several others, all down to pasture with a clump of trees in the top end of the farthest one visible. All presumably were accessible from the lane and I carried on along it, walking more quickly now.

I reckoned that, once there, if I stayed behind the right-hand hedge of the farthest field I would, initially, be less likely to be seen from the house and could then cut across and head for the cover of the trees, which looked to be only a matter of a hundred yards from the house. But I needed to get off this road before I was mown down by a car; a driver would be unable to see me in my dark clothing.

Then a car did come along and I flung myself aside into the hedge. It roared past, the driver oblivious. I tore myself free from a long strand of bramble with difficulty and carried on, jogging now. It was still possible to see my way and being the middle of summer I knew it would be quite a while before it became really dark. I had no intention of blundering around in the pitch black.

After going what seemed to be quite a long way, the lane curving gently to the right before me, I arrived at another gateway. One quick look told me that I was only at the next field to the first one and had much farther to go than I had originally thought. I set off again, running now, wishing I had worked at getting myself back to full fitness after having Mark.

But when you're a consultant for SOCA do you really have to run a four-minute mile? Apparently, yes.

Blowing like a horse, I reached the next field and saw that I only needed to get to the one following. There were more lights on in the house now but I did not pause to look further. Another car approached, from behind me, and I found a thorn-free niche this time.

Finally, I reached the field and, realizing that I could keep the clump of trees between me and the house for a long way, set off and, having got my breath back, ran again. I had to hold my arms tightly to my sides as the contents of my capacious pockets tended to jingle around. Then I remembered that I had not told Michael Greenway the correct name of the house. It was too late now.

The trees, unmistakably beeches even in this light, had been planted in what appeared to be an almost perfect circle. I headed for their cover gratefully, now feeling horribly exposed in the open pasture, like an ant on a carpet. At last the dark, cool greenery sheltered me and I stood for several minutes in the cathedral-like calm trying to formulate some kind of plan, failing utterly. There was an open space in the centre of the trees and I walked into it and looked up, the first stars twinkling palely above. I'm not really a religious person but right then I did pray for us.

Cautiously approaching the far side of the ring I paused behind a massive trunk and looked at the house. Slightly uphill and almost sideways to me now it appeared as just a jumbled series of rectangles and there seemed to be a boundary hedge, which was logical. I decided to make for the dark outbuildings over to my left.

The upward slope and the hedge, which appeared to be high and straggly, meant that it would be unlikely anyone indoors could see me and there did not appear to be many windows on this side of the house anyway. With this in mind I made for the corner of the field where I hoped to be able to get over or through it. Even better, there was another gateway which I guessed would have originally provided direct access for cattle into the original farmyard.

The whole place was on a much bigger scale than I had imagined and the word 'estate' suddenly made sense. Standing quite still at one side of the gateway, almost right in the hedge, I could see that the yard was huge and cluttered up with derelict machinery of various kinds. The cowsheds and a large barn I thought were brick-built – my mentor had told me that too much intelligence is never a bad thing and in the event of them being wood I could burn them down – the bare roof beams of some of them silhouetted against the sky like the broken ribs of some large animal carcass. The barn appeared to still be in possession of its roof but there was an ominous sag in it.

I pretended I was Patrick and sensed the air, slowly breathing in the evening breeze as it flowed through the gateway. I could smell damp, rotting wood, another earthy scent, perhaps a very old manure pile and . . . a fusty, sweaty smell. Then a strong scent of cigarette smoke. Someone was standing outside smoking.

Why? Were these mobsters so health conscious and house-proud that they did not want anyone smoking indoors? It seemed just about impossible so one must assume that whoever it was was outside for a purpose. And where was he or she? As if to answer my question there was the suspicion of a movement near the barn and then a telltale tiny red glow as the smoker inhaled. This was very useful to me and, judging by the rate at which it was being smoked, the glow moving jerkily, this person was extremely nervous. Then, easy to make out and hear, a figure half-ran towards the house, tripping over something and almost falling in their haste. Half a minute later, when I was on the point of moving, I heard shouting in the distance. I stayed right where I was and, after roughly the same period of time had elapsed, someone reappeared – I had an idea the same someone, only with a bottle this time. I also had an idea he had something in his other hand. He became invisible to me again.

As quietly as possible, I climbed over the gate. There was deep shadow here by the hedge, which had a ditch-like depression at its base, and as I paused again to listen I sensed, rather than saw, that there was something in it, almost at my feet. For some reason all the little hairs on the back of my neck prickled and I first nudged whatever it was with a foot and then made myself bend down to touch it. My first impressions had been correct: it was a body.

Forced to crouch there, my ears roaring as I nearly fainted, I nevertheless ran my hands over that part of the corpse that I could reach. The shoes were trainers; Patrick had been wearing trainers. The cloth of the trousers was denim; Patrick had been wearing a pair of black jeans. There was a leather belt of some kind; Patrick had been wearing a leather belt. By this time I could hardly go on but ended up on my knees by the body, examining the rest. The shirt was impossible to identify but Patrick had been wearing a black shirt, no tie. No tie here. A couple of days of beard stubble – that tallied too. But this man had been quite bald on top.

I almost vomited then. Had she pulled all his hair out? But no, the pate was smooth, normal skin, albeit cold and clammy. I had a sudden thought and felt down the chest, which the body was half lying on, encountering a hefty beer gut. And fool, fool, my husband has an artificial foot – why hadn't I examined that first?

My left hand was sticky; this man had been stabbed to death in the chest somewhere. I had no choice but to wipe it off on his shirt. I then somehow knew that this was not the only body here; there was another dark humped shape a little farther away. Having carefully surveyed my surroundings and listened for a full two minutes – there was still a lot of shouting going on somewhere, probably in the house – I crawled to it, going straight to the right leg this time. It was a real one and I got a lot more blood on myself because this man had had his throat cut.

In a quandary now I eased my cramped legs but did not stand up. Did I just use my mobile to phone the police? Then I froze as someone came into view against the last tiny remaining glimmer of the sunset. The same man? Another? This one had a bottle too, belched and then took a quick gulp from it. He appeared to be watching the barn, not removing his gaze from it. My eyes were really accustomed to the near darkness now and for the first time I noticed the stairs on the side of the barn that gave access to the loft area. Someone was halfway down them, slowly, silently, a frame at a time.

For a moment I thought I had imagined this as then I could

see the figure no longer. On the corner of the barn was a large barrel, no doubt used as a water butt, and it seemed to me that this might be a little wider than before. But when you strain your eyes to see at night it can sometimes appear that even the darkness dances. I transferred my gaze back to the man with the bottle who now, I thought with a twinge of alarm, was facing me. He placed the bottle on the ground and reached into a pocket. It was the last thing he did.

Something he had been holding in his other hand fell to the ground with a heavy thud and then he was lowered to join it. There was what appeared to be a quick examination for any signs of life and a frisking of the body before it was hoisted up in a fireman's lift and brought over to where I crouched in the shadows, concealed by the hedge. The burden rolled into the ditch with the others. Breathing hard from exertion the killer began to walk away.

'It's me,' I whispered.

There was a muffled exclamation and he came back. A hand was extended and I was helped out.

'Bloody wonderful woman – do you have any water purification tablets with you?' Patrick asked hoarsely.

I told him I did and for a moment he clung to me and I was sure he was close to tears.

Slowly, up in the loft in the barn in darkness, a small amount at a time, I fed him purified water from the rain barrel. Although dehydrated he had not dared to drink it as it stank to high heaven and had existed on just a little rain that had dripped through the roof of the barn. I was fairly sure the smell was only as a result of the leaves in it rotting as ours at home smells like this too sometimes before it is cleared out. I had a couple of high energy chocolate bars with me too and some Kendal mint cake.

'They'll storm the barn again soon,' Patrick said after a little while, speaking very quietly, recovering. 'And, sadly, this door's off.'

I had asked no questions yet but with his little torch – he complained about the waste of the batteries – located the bloody place on his head where the lock of hair had been pulled out.

'Someone'll hear the shooting though, surely.'

'No, they don't use guns; they daren't as there's another house around a quarter of a mile away and any firing would probably be heard in the town. So far I've managed to kick most of them back down the stairs and their nerve goes. They took my phone and Glock but didn't find the knife so I taught them to be more careful in future by killing two of them with it. She got me by the hair but I pulled free and made for here. They've left me to stew and weaken, sending in a couple of blokes at a time to wear me down. Cat and mouse.'

'She sent the bits of hair to me.'

'You can put them in a locket.' He chuckled, kissed me and then went over to the door where he was keeping watch every half minute or so.

'But what's all this *about*?' I said, or rather squeaked. 'Why not just go off and call Greenway?'

'There'd be a massacre of cops. You wouldn't believe the weaponry they've got in there, sub-machine guns, everything, together with explosives for bank jobs and safes. No, this is far better for a while. Nearly all of them – and there's around thirty blokes in there – are either alcoholics or drug addicts. It's the hold Uncle and Murphy have over them. She's a junkie too, in case you hadn't guessed already. What you must realize is that most of these people are out of their heads. Mass murder's nothing to them. They'd shoot up the whole of Steyning for a laugh if they'd killed a lot of police and then run for it, just like they did in Bath.'

'So your reasoning is?'

Patrick checked the yard again. 'They know I'm up here and dare not move to leave as they also know I'm on to them. So the thinking is it's far easier to finish me off without making a noise, but I'm dealing, one way or another, with everyone they send out to keep an eye on me. They're all armed but can't see me as there's no electricity in the farm buildings. And if you drink like a fish and/or take drugs it ruins all your faculties over time. Any more choc?'

I rummaged in my pockets and found a Mars bar. 'And then what?'

'They'll crack in the end and start firing.'

'We can fire first. I've got the Smith and Wesson.'

'Yes, if we have to. But I'd rather terrorize the bastards and shorten the odds a bit first. Make Uncle sweat for a bit. With a bit of luck they'll end up by losing it completely and killing one another.'

'Is Carol Trelonic in there?'

'No, I got rid of her on the way here – shoved her in a bush when the car stopped for her to throw up. No one noticed. She was just expendable baggage anyway.'

'And Colin Andrews?'

'He's here. Bleated to me that they'd kidnapped him for ransom and if I helped him he'd drop the charges against Matthew. I managed to throw a punch at him on the way out.'

'How did they get hold of you in the first place?'

'This is their bolt hole and I came along for the ride. But I was just a bit too slow getting out of the car when we arrived. She spotted me. How did you find this place?'

'I exchanged a little info with Mick the Kick that resulted in his not going to the party. Matthew came up with the name Lock House from the computer info but it was the Keys Estate.'

'Ah.' Patrick was over by the door again. 'They're coming. I wonder what he's bribed them with this time? Three, no four. They don't look very keen.'

This was the other Patrick talking, of course, the ex-special services soldier. I dared not try to talk him out of what he was doing, for in my heart I knew it was the right thing. I was sure that this was as I had predicted, to protect his family for ever from the attentions of gangs, to etch into the underworld's mind that Patrick Gillard was not to be messed with. Not only that, he could imagine the sub-machine blazing from an upper window of the house – out of our sight – mowing down the police before they could get into position even if warnings had been given. Who knew what other weapons were indoors: high powered rifles with night sights, stolen hand grenades . . .

'What can I do?' I asked.

'Stay where you are and if one gets past me do your best.'

I still had the torch and used it quickly to get my bearings and to look for a piece of wood or something similar that I could use as a weapon. It was just as well I did for there were

low beams at one end of the loft, which was bigger than I had
thought, on which one could comprehensively brain oneself. I
also found some old implements: a wooden hay rake that was
more woodworm holes than wood, a rusting axe that was too
heavy for me to lift, several billhooks – too horrible – a jumble
of small tools and that was all. Desperately, I went down to the
far end and there, in a festoon of black cobwebs, spotted several
newish pickaxe handles. Thus armed with the chosen weapon
of the thug I trotted back, switching off the torch.

'Fire if you have to – just don't hit me,' Patrick muttered
over his shoulder.

'It's almost impossible to see.'

'That's good for us because they've been in a house with
lights on. Hello, here's number one.'

I saw him duck and something heavy like a brick landed
practically at my feet. I groped for it, found that it was, grabbed
it, ran over to the door, leaned on Patrick to make him stay low
and lobbed it in the general direction of the foot of the stairs.
There was a yell and a general tumbling noise, like sacks of
boulders going downwards.

There was a female scream of anger from below. 'Louts!
Idiots! He's unarmed but for a knife, weak with hunger and
half-dead from thirst by now! Go in there and *get* him! You're
just as much cowards as the morons who ran away.'

Two raced up the stairs with a view to hurling themselves
through the door, hit what amounted to a brick wall, were
grabbed, had their heads crashed together, one then kicked
backwards so that he went straight through the handrail of the
stairs to fall into the void beyond, the other savagely slammed
into the door frame a few times before following the first.

There was another shout from below. 'Go and get a car! Use
the lights to see by. Get a *move* on!'

I heard thumps behind me and remembered that barns have
trapdoors to enable fodder to be thrown down to animals below.
Then there was a loud bang as though one had been flung open
and back. I flicked on the torch for a second to see that a man
was almost right on me, another appearing through the hatch.
Using the pickaxe handle like a spear I ran at him and got him
just below the ribs. He folded over and, guessing my exact

target in the gloom, I whacked him on the head. He went over backwards and, judging by the noise, the other one fell over him.

It was the briefest of respites. They leapt up and came at me again. This time I had reinforcements, my only contribution being to switch on the torch again to locate the aperture in the floor so that Patrick could neatly bulldoze one of them through it, the second jumping down in utter panic.

'There's two of 'em!' one of them yelled when he staggered outside.

'Balls! You're just useless!' another man bawled.

'They're both out there now – Uncle and Murphy,' Patrick said in my ear.

'How long can you keep this up?' I asked.

'Not much longer, honeybunch. I should have noticed that hatch before but at least we can use it as an escape route.' He went over and shut it, having to scrape aside a couple of inches of dirt and semi-rotten hay that had concealed it in order to get it to fit properly. An empty oil drum was placed on top after he had established that I could shift it if necessary.

A vehicle approached slowly, bouncing on the rough ground and was positioned so that the headlights shone directly on the barn.

'I'm not sure how this helps them,' Patrick whispered.

A voice high with terror screamed, 'They didn't run, Brad, they're here, three of 'em under the hedge! Bleedin' dead! You cow, Murphy! You knew this man was a psycho, didn't you, and you're just getting your kicks while he finishes us off one by one.'

'Shut up, it's his turn,' I distinctly heard Murphy say.

NINETEEN

'Shall I phone?' I said.

'Not yet,' was the terse reply.

The sudden illumination had revealed a tiny and filthy window overlooking the yard. Standing well to one side of it I scrubbed some of the dirt and cobwebs off with the sleeve of an ancient jacket hanging on a nearby nail and risked a look out. The view was a narrow one but even so I could see at least a dozen people in the headlights of the car. They were clustered around the couple, although at a respectful or nervous distance, and appeared to be receiving orders. This went on for another couple of minutes, during which I relayed to Patrick in a whisper what was happening, the men and, I thought, one other woman going off in twos and threes.

Silence fell.

Patrick stirred restlessly. 'I don't like this.'

He had promised to make Uncle sweat and it seemed they hoped to do the same to him. Perhaps he was, I thought inconsequentially; he did not normally smell like this. Then my skin crawled and I stretched to touch his shoulder lightly as one might play a few notes on a piano as he stood motionless in the light breeze coming through the doorway. He immediately came to my side.

'We're not alone,' I breathed.

He did not react, returned to his original position and another heavy silence followed. Then, at first very quietly, a dog began growling. Patrick can mimic all kinds of things and Elspeth still tells the tale of how when he was quite young he frightened off a man who was hanging around near the family car when John was away by doing just this through the letterbox.

The growl travelled, but in the shadows away from what light there was shining through the doorway and, weakly, through the window. I had an idea he was bent low, at dog height, the picture perfect in my imagination: fangs bared, hackles up.

Down the barn the growl went. Fear was churning through me: some of these maniacs would probably be able to kill a dog with their bare hands without a second thought.

I then jumped out of my skin when there was a sudden shriek and someone came running. A very tall, seemingly scarecrow figure came thundering down the loft but was halted horribly when he went full tilt into one of the lower beams, going down as though poleaxed.

'Torch,' Patrick said.

By its tiny light he moved away the oil drum, lifted the trapdoor, heaved the unconscious man through the hole through which he must have come with the others and then put everything back in place.

'I'm done,' he mumbled. 'Is there any more water?'

There was just a mouthful or so and although I had more purification tablets I could not go down to fetch water without being spotted. After he had drunk it Patrick checked that no one else had come up through the hatch with the other two. It was while he was right down the other end of the loft, as I kept watch out of the window, that there was a pounding of feet on the stairs and three men rushed in.

Somehow, we fought them off and to my shame my efforts seemed to consist of no more than pecking around, as it were, on the edges of the conflict where I could be sure of not hitting Patrick. Finally, one of them fled and Patrick grabbed my weapon, using it to batter down the other two. One of them had had a knife, leaving him bleeding from a slashed left arm, the only consolation two unconscious, or dead, men – I did not care which by now – on the floor.

'Do I phone now?' I asked, very quietly, mostly because one of them had caught me with a fist on the side of my head.

'No, not yet.'

I made no comment, binding up his arm with a silk scarf I had in my pocket.

'Are you still there?' called a woman's voice from down in the yard, Murphy almost certainly.

'I'm still here,' Patrick replied, going nowhere near the door – right now he did not have the strength to.

'You only have your knife, don't you?'

'You know that.'

They were trying to force open the trapdoor from below again so I went and stood on it with the oil drum.

Footsteps approached: she was mounting the stairs. If I stayed quite still she might not spot me here in the shadows. I saw that Patrick was holding his knife, having not resorted to use it in the hand-to-hand fighting, and had seated himself on one of several large chunks of wood. In the next moment Murphy appeared framed in the doorway.

Someone shouted at her not to be a fool.

'Still getting your kicks?' Patrick said softly. He was in full view of her, in the light.

'You have to get them where you can,' the woman drawled with the merest hint of an Irish accent, raising the gun she was carrying.

'You and your filthy brood are under arrest. If you resist arrest . . .' He left the rest unsaid.

Predictably, Murphy laughed. 'Perhaps I'll just trim you off a little at the edges first, make you a bit kinda frilly.' She laughed again and I detected a hysterical note to it.

Patrick released the blade of his knife, that horrible slicing click.

'Sadly, no match against a bullet,' she sighed and I was sure I saw her finger tense on the trigger.

'I could always throw it.'

'That's really kinky,' she said in mock admiration and then uttered a shriek as his arm swiftly moved. Then she fired, wildly, and I heard the bullet thunk into the roof somewhere.

'I thought you liked knives,' Patrick said, still speaking very quietly, seemingly addressing the blade before him. 'The ones in your kitchen . . .'

'They weren't mine. The previous tenant left them behind. Just things for cooking. I don't cook. Yes, I like knives, but—'

'But not when in the hands of other people?' Patrick interrupted softly. 'You're an exception as the Brits don't usually like them at all. This one's Italian. They're very serious about things like this in Italy. The man who made it for me promised I'd be able to slit someone from throat to belly with it.' He held it up for her to see. 'But it *is* a throwing knife and if I got you from here it might go right through.'

Perhaps her hand was aching, perhaps not, for she lowered the gun a little.

'What the hell are you doing up there?' another man shouted. 'Just kill the bastard and be done with it.'

There were sudden crashes and bangs as tiles began to be wrenched off one corner of the roof behind me and thrown down to the ground. By the sound of it several people were tearing them off and almost immediately I could see quite a large rectangle of light shining through. I decided that enough talking had been done and put a shot into that general area, hearing a yell of fright, a scrabbling noise and then a thud as someone jumped off the roof. There was another shot and I dived to the floor.

Peeping around the oil drum through the swirling cloud of dust I had created I could see neither Patrick nor Murphy so crawled towards the doorway, aware that the roof tiles were still being torn off. Brad Northwood, or whoever, was shouting at them to get on with it.

In view of this I risked raising my voice. 'Patrick, are you all right? Patrick!'

An arm appeared from somewhere to the rear of the log pile and waved weakly. I crawled over there. Patrick looked to be jammed in a small space on the floor between the wood stack and the eaves of the roof.

'Are you hit?' I asked, heaving away at the stack, actually heavy sections of a tree branch, while trying to watch the door. Above the sound of the tiles crashing down I thought I could hear vehicles.

'I don't think so. Just . . . too weak to get out.'

Frantically, I searched through my pockets and came up with a battered half-bar of Kendal mint cake, thrusting it at him while I hauled away the wood surrounding him with the other hand, sending it bowling across the floor. The vehicles I had heard were arriving, their headlights beaming around and then coming to a stop, revealing, for a moment, that my husband's face was as white as chalk under the dirt and that his left arm resembled an uncooked joint of meat, scarf and all.

The sound of gunfire burst out, galvanizing Patrick to free

himself from the last of the logs. Then, a shot having smashed through the tiny window, showering us with glass, he grabbed me and hauled me back into the space with him.

'What on earth's going on?' I said.

'Well, it isn't the cops, that's for sure. They wouldn't behave like this and have the wrong kind of hardware.'

'Shall I phone now?'

'Being as you're on top and I can't move . . .'

I wriggled around to find my mobile and managed to dial our emergency number. In the yard below a gun battle was raging, men shouting, footsteps pounding. I was praying that we had been forgotten about.

'Did you throw the knife?' I asked.

'No, just chucked myself over here when you fired the first shot. God knows where she went.'

It was not the kind of phone number that went directly to Greenway and all I could do was report that we needed urgent assistance, giving the location as best as I was able. The operator seemed to think I should know the postcode and I am afraid I swore at her.

Car doors slammed and an engine revved, the vehicle then smashing into something as it skidded around but it still roared away into the distance.

After this there was silence and for a long time, during which the pair on the floor crept towards the door and disappeared, neither of us moved or spoke.

'It wasn't me! I wasn't even *there*!' a man suddenly bawled somewhere down below.

'Prove it!' yelled someone else. 'And it had better be good or you're as dead as cold mutton!'

'I was in the slammer!'

'I know that voice,' Patrick said.

'Which one?' I asked.

'The second one. Let me out of here.'

This was not easy and I had to give him a helping hand.

'Please don't go out there,' I begged as he headed a little unsteadily for the doorway. But he did and stood at the top of the stairs, lit as if by a searchlight. I braced myself to hear shots but nothing happened.

'Micky, old chum, do we have you to thank for this?' he called.

'It's the cop who breaks necks!' cried Mick the Kick. 'Do you mean by that that you have your excellent woman with you?' His voice came closer. 'She gave me the nod, you know, told me Carrick was going to pick me up if I turned up in Bath the other night.'

I went to stand looking over Patrick's shoulder.

'You *are* here!' the man chortled and I realized that he was nowhere near sober.

Patrick said, 'And if you don't sod off pronto you'll get arrested right now. Have you disarmed Uncle's lot?'

'Or shot them,' said the man with a hiccuping laugh. 'No, actually most of them threw their weapons down and we've banged them up in a garage. We might just chuck in some petrol and make a bonfire of them. But Northwood and the woman got away. I'll find them.'

'You won't. The police will do that.'

'You're not in charge here.'

'Yes, I am.'

I cannot really explain why this mobster, after a heavy silence, accepted this and can only put it down to the fact that lieutenant colonels have always expected to be obeyed, so generally are. Standing there, bleeding and swaying a little on his feet, Patrick still possessed that presence that drew a kind of grudging respect.

'I meant what I said,' Patrick went on quietly. 'We've phoned in. It's only a matter of a few minutes before armed cops arrive. All I can do is to give you a head start. If you're caught I can do no more and when Cookson finally catches up with you I can't do anything for you then either. And I must warn you that if you now attempt an armed stand-off I shall personally blow your bloody head off.'

They all got into a huddle and after not a little muttering had taken place they got into their cars and drove away. I shall always remember the ironic little salute their leader gave Patrick as he went.

I fixed some purified water for him and we stayed where we were, sitting on the top step, he too weary to do anything about the garaged gang members although there were heavy bangs and thumps in the distance as they tried to break out. Soon, we heard sirens and together made our way towards the house, Patrick going indoors to look for his Glock before the police grabbed it as Exhibit Z. Amazingly, he found it, together with a packet of biscuits and a pint of milk, not reckoning them to be particularly important forensic evidence. Anyway, by the time the law arrived we had wolfed them down.

This was not the first time I had booked into a hotel only to arrive the next morning with a dishevelled and unwashed man, introducing him to a bemused young woman behind the reception desk as my husband, when in fact there was every indication that I had picked him up in a hostel for the destitute. But Patrick gave the alarmed girl a smile and told her the truth: that he was a policeman who had been working behind the scenes on the local murder case and had cut his arm. We were told that the village, where it apparently makes banner headlines if someone falls off a bus, was even at this early hour rocking with the news.

Formalities with Sussex Police – after all he had killed five men – had taken almost three hours. The bodies in the house had been found to be armed with handguns, plus a knife, all the fingers of both hands wearing heavy rings to inflict maximum injury. Those outside, in the ditch near the barn, were a slightly different matter. They too had been armed, with handguns, two of which he had thrown over the hedge, keeping one in case he had needed it. But Patrick had been able to provide the DCI in charge with all the background information to the case which would probably save them a lot of work. There would of course have to be a full investigation by the complaints department, especially with regard to the bodies in the ditch as, strictly speaking, he had not killed these men in self-defence. But for now he was free to go. We had been given a lift back to the hotel and I had then driven him to Worthing Hospital as his arm needed a few stitches, the paramedics in one of the ambulances called for the wounded having provided a temporary dressing. With the journey time this took almost another three hours.

Casualties suffering from gunshot wounds among the gang members had been extremely light considering the amount of shooting that had taken place, with only one man seriously wounded and two slightly. Fifteen were found in the garage, including Colin Andrews, some in the kind of state that suggested they had tried to storm a barn and failed dismally. Another three were subsequently found wandering, completely lost, in the countryside by the Mounted Branch; a fourth made it back to Steyning where he tried to break into a cottage only to be beaten off by an old lady with her walking stick. He was arrested shortly afterwards. The rest – Patrick had initially counted around thirty – remained unaccounted for.

But that was all for the future.

When we were back in my room at the hotel I reported all this to Commander Greenway and persuaded him that no, we could not drive back straight away to London to report personally and that Patrick needed several hours rest as he had lost blood.

'You should rest as well,' Patrick pointed out, having overheard the conversation.

I voiced my worries. 'You humiliated that woman – in her eyes, that is. It'll be eating into her – like acid.'

He became very serious. He takes my remarks concerning the female mindset very seriously indeed.

'You knifed those two henchmen right in front of her eyes. I should imagine no one's done anything like that before. Then she chickened out of shooting you because she was terrified you'd get her first.'

'That *was* the general idea.'

'She's raving mad, Patrick. Remember what we found in her flat?'

'You reckon she'll come looking for me?'

'Yes, I do. She might talk him into it too – unfinished business.'

'We're assuming that neither of them was injured.'

'It's safer to assume that they weren't.' I had a truly horrible thought. 'It's possible they'll go to Hinton Littlemore rather than risk coming back here.'

Patrick shot to his feet. 'We must go!'

I drove and we did the journey without stopping. I was glad that after leaving a message on James Carrick's mobile Patrick slept for most of the way, waking only as we ghosted down the village high street at just before seven forty-five. All seemed very peaceful: a few early commuters setting off, a paper boy on his round. Following Patrick's suggestion I parked by the church and we walked across the churchyard and through the gate into our own garden. A man armed with a Heckler and Koch stepped out from behind a hedge.

'Gillard,' Patrick said quietly.

'No problems here, sir,' the man responded. 'There are three of us watching the place.'

'Try to stay out of sight of those indoors – but I will warn them.'

'I suggest a pause for thought before we go in,' I said as we approached our back entrance.

Patrick stepped aside so that we stood beneath the stone archway that is situated between the garden and the paved yard, smaller now the conservatory has been built.

'Where are they?' I said. 'I mean, here we have what is probably a very physically unfit bloke with a woman who probably fanatically works out in a gym. He'll be a drag on her and the pair of them could have been drinking. If they drove here without having a rest he, at least, will be knackered.'

'If they're in Hinton Littlemore at all.'

'Yes, quite. But it might be . . . profitable to assume that they are. So, as I said, where are they?'

'They wouldn't want whichever car they're using to be visible from the road.'

'That's right.'

'The pub? They could have got the keys from Colin Andrews. And as we already know it does have two lock-up garages plus a yard where vehicles can't really be seen unless you go right in there.'

'And there'll be food of some kind and drink left behind, plus somewhere to get a couple of hours' sleep.'

'Here's hoping that if they're there they've hit the bottle again,' Patrick muttered, setting off back the way we had come. He waved to the man to whom we had just spoken, saying, 'Forgotten something in the car.'

Stolidly – I knew he was still feeling weak – Patrick headed for the old gate in the far side of the churchyard boundary wall that we had used on the night we had entered the Ring o' Bells not so long ago. At least it was broad daylight this time, our surreptitious journey no more than what would normally be a pleasant walk in the English countryside using ancient byways. With the pair of us hyper-alert it actually felt more like a commando exercise.

Like the previous time, we said nothing. There was nothing to say.

On the climb out of the railway cutting Patrick sat down suddenly and put his head between his knees.

'I'm too old for this kind of thing now,' he murmured.

'No, you lost more blood than anyone realized,' I told him, actually feeling a bit dizzy myself from lack of food and sleep.

'Any more Kendal mint cake?'

'Sorry, no.'

'Who knows, there might be a packet of crisps in the pub.'

After a couple of minutes we carried on and were soon walking down the lane that ran past the rear of the pub. I had to keep looking round, convinced I could hear footsteps behind us. But no one was there. Perhaps I was hallucinating.

The building came into sight, the gates closed as we had expected. This was actually to our advantage as it screened us from the eyes of anyone looking out of a downstairs window and those on the upper floor were obscured by the lower branches of the oak tree in the small customers' car park. And if we succeeded in getting right up close to the gates, which were quite high, no one indoors would be able to see us either.

'I happen to know,' Patrick said quietly, 'that there's a hole in the left-hand gate where a knot in the wood has fallen out.'

'To look through, you mean.'

'Umm. Matthew told me.'

'In case you needed to spy on the place one day, presumably.'

'Well, as we've discovered, the pair of them have been snooping around here for weeks, if not months.'

By a slightly roundabout route we reached the gates, feigned interest in the overhanging tree as a car drove by, and then Patrick looked through the hole, having to bend down slightly.

'No cars,' he reported in a whisper. 'But it could be in one of the lock-ups.' He straightened, adding, 'If they are here I shall endeavour to arrest them. I'm reluctant to call for backup in case they aren't and there will be no time between finding out for sure and . . .' He shrugged.

'We do have three members of a tactical firearms unit just across the road,' I reminded him.

'They're for family protection. No, and we can't creep about out here any longer. I shall break in through the door into the public bar that's nearest the car park.'

'It might be bolted.'

'It might be bolted. So I might have to get in through the effin' drains.'

The tone in which this latter remark had been uttered made the oracle realize that her pronouncements were no longer required. But all kinds of reservations were streaming through my mind. They might see us and while Patrick was getting in the side door, they would escape through those at the front or rear, probably the latter as that was where their car was most likely to be. There might be others with them who had been posted around the village, watching out for our return.

I mentally strangled the oracle and followed Patrick to the side of the building. The car park was surrounded by a low wall and we were now in full view of the village green and cottages that fronted the lane along one side of it. I stood so as to block from view Patrick's efforts with his skeleton keys, which live practically permanently in one pocket or another of his jackets.

'It's already unlocked,' he said under his breath, slipping in. 'Stay outside.'

I never do, though.

Giving him plenty of room, I went in. A clock ticked, a fridge or freezer motor cut in, thin bars of light with motes of dust floating in them shone through gaps in the not-quite-closed curtains. The air smelt of stale beer, dirty lavatories and, as at the barn, cigarette smoke. I gazed around carefully. The bar possessed several mirrors, possibly with an original view of making the room look larger, some of them in corners, thus giving angled reflections. I silently directed Patrick's attention

to what I could see in one of them: a woman smoking somewhere in an adjoining passageway. She had not seen us.
Murphy.

Patrick, who is extremely familiar with the layout of the
building, walked silently to where he knew she was and, just
around the corner from her, sprang the blade of his knife.
She shrieked and then again when, with the speed of a striking
snake, she was grabbed and hauled in to face us. Holding the
knife in his other hand as he needed his right to keep hold of
her Patrick made a leisurely movement with it in the air right
under her nose: an obscene thrust, with overtones of disembowelling and worse, that actually made me feel sick. It had the
same kind of effect on Murphy. She fainted.

Having had her virtually tossed in my direction, and hearing
heavy footsteps on the nearby stairs, I wrenched open the nearest
curtains and grabbed both sets of cord tie-backs. With them,
and having rolled the woman over on to her front – we did not
want her to vomit and choke to death before she could be sent
to prison, did we? – I tied her hands and then both feet tightly
together, linking both parcels for good measure.

There came a sound from the passageway, as if a side of
beef were colliding with a dresser loaded with pots and pans.
Then there was a crashing descent and silence but for what
sounded like a saucepan lid going round and round on the
quarry-tiled floor until it shivered into stillness. After a short
pause came a dragging noise before the sound of a door being
slammed. Then a click as a key turned in a lock.

Patrick came, or rather staggered, into view, licking the
knuckles of his right hand. 'You should never hit drunks –
normally. Oh, good, you've got her.' He sat down, got up again
and, leaning over the bar, took a couple of packets of crisps
from a display card, throwing me one.

I shall never forget what happened next. With his gaze now
somewhere behind me he fumbled in his jeans pocket, found a
pound coin among some loose change and placed it on the counter.
Then he smiled, again at something over my shoulder. I turned.

'You've caught the crooks!' Katie cried, jumping up and
down, clapping her hands.

TWENTY

I had not imagined the footsteps behind me, Katie following us from home having spotted us from her bedroom window. Careful questioning on my part later revealed that she had not witnessed the X-rated pas de deux with the knife as she had been hiding behind an oak settle at the time. One thing was sure though, her final involvement with the case had rather overshadowed her brother's efforts and, before I could stop her, she was on the phone to him yelling the news the moment we reached the rectory. I immediately rang Greenway before he got the news from Benedict first.

Katie and I had left Patrick peacefully eating more crisps while waiting for Carrick, with suitable backup, to arrive. I gather that the DCI arrested and took possession of his prisoners, a brief statement from Patrick and then, with typical consideration, arranged for him to be driven the five hundred yards or so home.

'I can't take any of the credit for this,' Carrick said with just a trace of resentment.

'Of course you can,' Patrick declared robustly. 'You've just apprehended Carol Trelonic.'

'You mean I knocked at her door and when she finally answered I arrested her, don't you?' the DCI said sourly.

'Yes, thereby saving the local rector's reputation. I understand quite a crowd had gathered to watch her go and there were a few boos and hisses.'

I said, 'I suppose she's acting all innocence.'

'Of course. Saying she only worked at the pub, never had anything to do with Andrews other than that, and that you're making a victim of a poor recently widowed woman out of sheer spite, etc., etc. What she doesn't know is that Andrews is selling her down the river as we speak.'

'*Really?*' I exclaimed.

'According to him she ran the money laundering and moving on stolen goods side of things, as far as the pub went anyway. She also paid your cleaning woman to sniff out any interesting bits of info which must have been how they knew you'd be going for weapons training. I shall need her name and address from you. Andrews is pretty stupid and I reckon they only used him because he'd had experience in running a public house before and no previous criminal convictions.'

'Which would have been checked when he applied for the tenancy,' Patrick commented. 'What about her husband?'

'Like a lot of the others, just a hired oaf.'

There was a reflective silence while we all, I think, remembered how people like him had been used like disposable commodities. And died.

'And Murphy?' Carrick prompted quietly.

'She fainted,' Patrick said.

'I know. That's what she said too.'

'Sometimes, and I have to add, very reluctantly, you have to out-Herod Herod,' Patrick went on when he realized some elaboration was required. 'She ordered a couple of her yobs to help her kill me slowly and messily, and they didn't know I had my knife. I don't think she realized people could be killed so quickly and neatly. It frightened her because, as Ingrid said, no one had ever done anything like that in front of her before. It was one of the weaknesses of her particular mindset and when she thought I was about to do the same to her . . .'

The DCI had, of course, read all the reports forwarded to him by Sussex Police. Soberly, he said, 'Plus three more outside.'

'I can't really claim self-defence as far as they were concerned. But they were being sent into the barn two, three or four at a time to try to get me so, ultimately, it was.'

'I think I'd have run like hell,' Carrick admitted.

'I nearly did. I'm not proud of what I did. In fact—' Here Patrick broke off for a few moments and cleared his throat. 'But I'm hoping it might have saved a few innocent lives.' Then, changing the subject with obvious relief, he went on, 'And now the whole village is waiting with barely concealed impatience for a new landlord to be taken on. The place belongs to the parish, you see.'

'You could always apply,' Carrick said with a grin.

'I've actually given it some thought.'

The two of us stared at him in total disbelief.

'Only very temporarily, you understand,' Patrick said hurriedly. 'Until there is a more permanent arrangement.'

'I understand it's thought Andrews went off with everyone's Christmas Club money.'

'Oh, if he has I reckon it'll be repaid. An anonymous benefactor will come forward.'

Which he did.

This conversation took place before the usual hundreds of hours of police work was undertaken: checking and rechecking reports, taking statements and liaising with the several police forces and departments involved before cases could be brought to court. It took months as so many suspects were involved and the man referred to as Uncle had spread his criminal empire so widely. Patrick and I both helped with this work and eventually it was satisfying to see these people, Northwood and Murphy included, whom the judge described as 'callous gutter racketeers who liked to think of themselves as criminal masterminds' get life imprisonment.

On a personal and family level Matthew did not have to appear before the Youth Offending Team. Commander Greenway was as good as his word and wrote to them saying that the youth in question had a slightly misplaced enthusiasm for investigating and solving what he perceived to be crimes. The boy had since been staying with him personally and while he had received instruction on the inadvisability of such behaviour in future his knowledge of IT and computer literacy had made a huge contribution to police work in apprehending serious criminals.

A couple of months later when we had just returned from a much-needed three-week holiday touring Italy, Patrick had to attend an inquiry by the Independent Police Complaints Commission where, as expected, his actions and judgement were questioned, especially in connection with the three men he had killed in the farmyard. It was known by this time that one of them had been the subject of a European Arrest Warrant, wanted in Germany in connection with the triple murders of his ex-partner and her two children. The other two had been Londoners on the Met's Most Wanted list, one of whom Patrick had recognized from SOCA's crime records. Obviously, this latest intelligence did not make what he had done 'all right'.

At this point Commander Greenway had stepped in to ask what alternative actions his employee could have taken. He had had no mobile phone, no backup and his only other option had been to flee and try to get help. By the time that arrived the criminals may well have gone. Or, discovering that he was no longer there as they were repeatedly attacking the barn where he was 'holed up', they might have stayed to arrange a deadly ambush for the arriving police personnel. But, despite being seriously dehydrated, Gillard had remained where he was. Greenway had gone on to remind everyone that these were the mobsters who had masterminded the multiple shootings in Bath. He had then become a bit heated, demanding to know that as the operative in question had been engaged specifically because of his special forces training for situations exactly like this, was there now a change of mind and would those in the commission rather mainstream cops put their lives on the line instead and that he, Greenway, hired people who bolted at the first sign of trouble?

There were still unanswered questions, one of which had been put to Patrick. Why had he not fired one of the handguns he had taken from the men in the yard to attract attention? There was another house not far away.

Keeping remarkably patient he had answered, 'So this guy, if there was a guy, in the next house might have said to himself, "Sounds as though a poacher's potting game with a pistol." He might have got into his car and driven down the road to tell his neighbour what was going on, by which time a gunfight would most likely have started. He may well have been killed in crossfire. I probably would have been dead by then too as I'd have run out of ammo. Look, the whole object of what I did was to try to save innocent lives. I agree that things were getting a bit desperate by the time my working partner located where I was.'

'You were hoping to arrest them?'

'There was plenty of booze in the house. They'd all have drunk themselves to a standstill eventually.'

'But then this criminal, Michael Fellows, known as Mick the Kick, from Bristol, arrived.'

'Fortunately for me he decided to stage a surprise raid – in revenge after what had happened in Bath.'

'He's dead, I understand,' the questioner had said.

'He is. Last week, when DCI Cookson of Bristol CID had accumulated the evidence he needed to arrest him in connection with the death of his one-time sergeant, he raided the house where a snout had said Fellows was hiding. His decomposing body was found in the hallway. Forensic tests indicated that he had been dead for around a fortnight and had suffered a heart attack, toppled over the banisters on the stairs and broken his neck.'

Which I thought was an ironic fate in the circumstances.

'You then went on to arrest the serious criminal whose various aliases everyone here is aware of by now, together with Joy Murphy.'

'Detective Chief Inspector Carrick officially arrested them. As you know, they were in the pub at Hinton Littlemore, probably because they hoped to finish their business with me later. I just thumped Uncle, locked him in the office and scared Murphy so she fainted.'

'You scared her,' the man had repeated woodenly.

'That's right.'

'Would you care to explain how you did that?'

He had not explained, merely taken out his knife and, looking him right in the eye, sprung the blade.

They had given up then – it was over.